ASCEND

Hosting Gods

Book Three

Lena Mae Hill

Table of Contents

Chapter One

Gwen

I woke cocooned in the warmth of Zeke's strong arms. For a minute, I let myself revel in the coziness of his embrace. His heart beat steadily against my cheek, the rise and fall of his chest comforting and safe and predictable. Everything about the moment was the exact opposite of the way I'd woken the day before. I wished I could do it all over. That I could make the whole day into a dream I was now waking from, from the moment I'd woken alone on the forest floor to the night before, when Xander had punched Finn in the face for trying to jump off the cliff.

Xander refused to hear Finn out, but I understood why Finn had done what he had. Not the suicide part, but I'd fallen for Joaquin's trickery before, too. And considering that Finn had known and trusted Joaquin as a friend for most of his life, it was no surprise that when Finn was feeling guilty and conflicted, he'd been an easy victim for Joaquin.

But I knew Xander now, too. I knew him better than anyone. I knew why he'd hit Finn. It was more than anger that Finn had threatened to jump off that bluff. It was anger that he was just like Finn. He'd never admit it, but I could see it in a way only an outsider could. Finn and Xander might not share the exact same moral code, but they both lived by it, and though Xander might not show it in the same way Finn did, he was just as sensitive. He wouldn't have been standing on that bluff, but if he'd had his bike, he probably would have been doing something just as dangerous.

A loud gasping sound yanked me from my thoughts. I turned to see Finn bolting upright, his eyes glassy and confused.

I pushed myself up on my elbows. "Finn? What's wrong?"

"We need to cross the bridge," he said. "Now."

"Okay," I said, keeping my voice measured and calm, like I did when Mom freaked out. "Let's just wake the others."

My own nerves were on edge by the time everyone was awake. The canyon echoed with the clamor of voices shouting and jeering. Now that Bifrost was so weak, the noise was louder than ever.

"It's the giants," Alvan said. "They gather every day, waiting for the bridge to go out. Once it does, they will cross the river and swarm into Midgard."

"But if they can't cross the bridge, and they can't get across the river of fire, how can they get to Midgard?" I asked.

"They can cross the river," Valdan said. "But they can't enter the cave while Bifrost is in front of it. When Bifrost goes out, they will have access to the cave."

"And what? There's a key to Midgard in there somewhere?"

"There's an entrance to Midgard," Alvan corrected.

"Wait a minute," Peyton said, planting a hand on her hip. "Are you telling me we could have just climbed on through into Boston any time we wanted?"

"It is Heimdall's wish that we complete our task," Valdan answered.

My heart burned with the urge to run down there and leap through into our world. To see my mother. But it was too late now. We had to cross Bifrost now before it disappeared forever.

"Why didn't you tell us?" I asked, clenching my fists to stop my urge to smack the giant elf in the nuts for keeping this from us.

"You did not ask," Alvan said. "And Heimdall does not want you to go."

"But we could have?" Finn asked, narrowing his eyes. "Even against his wishes?"

"You can act on your own," Valdan said. "But why would you deny your god?"

The bridge slowly unrolled into the sky, the flame barely visible. The water was thin and almost still, and the air wasn't shimmering as it had been when we first saw Bifrost. In fact, I couldn't see the air currents at all. There was no time to go home and see our parents—not if we wanted to save them.

"There's no time for what-ifs," I said. "We'll cross the pathetic remnants of the bridge first and then go home. I don't care what Heimdall says. I need to make sure my mom's okay."

"We will," Zeke said, giving my shoulder a squeeze.

"Let's just hope it's not too late for the bridge, too," Peyton muttered, pulling on a pair of tattered leather boots she'd picked up in the elven world.

"What do you mean?" I asked, as we started toward the bridge's flickering remains.

"What if it goes out when we're on it?" she asked. We all stopped at the edge of the bluff and eyed it warily.

"We don't really have a choice, do we?" Xander said. "We can try, or we can stand around for another day talking about it, and then it will definitely go out."

"How do we get on?" I asked, turning to the elves.

They exchanged glances and shrugged. "We don't cross the bridge. We wade through the fire."

"Yes, we know," I said. "In fact, if you were crossing the bridge like the gods are supposed to, it might not have fallen into disrepair."

"We cannot cross as Thor," Alvan said. "Heimdall must cross first and blow the golden horn. Only then can the other gods cross."

"Now that we have all of Heimdall here, we are honored to cross at last," Valdan said, his massive chest swelling with bravado.

"I'll escort Finn," Xander said, glaring at his brother. Finn glared back, one eye swollen shut, the area around it red and shiny. Apparently, the punch hadn't cleared the air between them.

"How does this work, though?" I asked, as we climbed into the goat-drawn chariot.

"We'll just try to climb on," Alvan said, as if he climbed a rainbow through the sky every day.

"I'm having a hard time wrapping my head around this," I admitted. "I mean, I'm pretty small, but I kinda need something more substantial than flame to walk on."

"We're going to literally walk on water," Eliot said.

"You already think you walk on water," Peyton countered.

"You're all thinking like humans," Valdan said. "You must think like gods. For a god, walking on water, air, or fire, it is nothing. It is as simple as walking through a river of fire or killing a giant with a hammer small enough for an elf to wield."

"Think like gods," I said as the goats dropped us off at the bottom of the canyon. "Got it."

The giants on the far side of the lava river roared and clamored to get nearer when we landed. One of them stepped onto the surface of the lava. It hadn't burst into flame today, but remained as it was at night, like a black tile floor with seams of glowing orange between.

"Shit," Zeke said. "I hope he doesn't make it across."

"Let's get on the bridge before they start throwing lava," I said, heading for the cave.

A hideous screeching sound reached my ears and I cringed. My knees almost gave way as a flash of the dragon lunging toward me popped in my memory. When I looked up, it was just a falcon, screaming as it rocketed past us.

"What's that thing's problem?" Smith asked, edging closer to the elves.

We reached the cave and stepped inside, away from the giants and the falcon. The elves turned toward Bifrost, but I reached out a hand to stop them. I wasn't about to cross that bridge without knowing how to get back home. I didn't know what waited on the other side or if we'd even make it back alive. Only two people knew about this doorway, and that wasn't enough.

"We don't have to go through," I said. "Just show us where it is."

"You remember when we rode to Jotunheim in the chariot instead of climbing the world tree?" Alvan said, walking deeper into the cave.

"Quite clearly." I followed him, surveying the damp stone walls for signs of a concealed doorway. I hadn't ventured very deep into the cave before, but it stretched about twenty feet back before tapering off to nothing. It reminded me a little of the cave I'd hidden in with my mother for a month back in our world—with the obvious addition of a wall of water to conceal the entrance.

Alvan stopped near the back of the cave next to the wall and waved his hand back and forth through the air. It didn't disappear into the human world, but a sort of distortion occurred as he waved his arm. "We passed through a doorway. This is another one. You step through, and you're in Midgard."

Midgard. Home. The world of humans, books, coffee, and school. The world of my mother.

"And if we stepped back through from that side, we'd be right here?" Eliot asked, joining us. He cocked his head and studied the patch of mirage-like air. It wasn't unlike the stripe in the rainbow bridge that was made of wind—when it had been visible.

"Yes," Valdan said, stepping up beside Eliot. "There are doorways all over the worlds. Ordinary humans can't see them, but you can, yes?"

"Yes," I said, the longing inside me almost enough to make me pitch forward through that wavering spot in the air. The doorway was right there. I could check on my mom so fast. Everything in me longed to go back there, where things made some kind of sense. Where at least logic and scientific law applied.

But all that was at risk every minute we left the bridge to die. Apparently, it was like some kind of plant, and the gods were the water it needed to thrive. I turned back to the mouth of the cave and the base of Bifrost.

"Think like a god," I muttered as I returned to the bridge.

"You are a god," Alvan said, stepping forward into the gap between the fire and water where the air had once shimmered like a mirage. The flames brightened beside him, and he smiled from behind his long Viking beard. "See? We are all gods. It is not so hard." He turned and began to climb, as if he were walking up an escalator.

"Cool," Zeke said, towing Finn toward Bifrost. Zeke lifted his foot and set it in the water as if he were situating his foot on slippery ice. He began to rise before he'd gotten both feet on. "Way cool!"

"Come, brother," Alvan called from ahead.

Zeke kept hold of Finn's hand. I expected the bridge to wrench them apart or for Finn to be unable to step on. He had resisted for so long, I didn't think he'd ever think of himself as a god. But there he was, climbing higher with each step. If he could do it, the rest of us could.

Valdan herded us closer to the bridge. "I will bring up the rear," he said. "For protection."

"This is crazy," Peyton squeaked.

"Crazy awesome," Eliot said, pushing up his thick glasses. He wet his lips, his eyes glowing with excitement as he watched the others climb. Reaching out, he swiped his hand through the fire, then pulled back, amazement written all over his face. "It doesn't burn."

"Of course not," Valdan said. "You are a god."

"Okay," Eliot said. "I'm going in." He grabbed a handful of fire and swung himself onto the bridge. It swept him up, and he laughed nervously as he looked down at us. My own heart lurched in my chest. It was so easy for them. What if it didn't work for me?

"Ready?" I asked Peyton.

She bit her lip and glanced at me from the corner of her eye. "Where is it taking them?"

"To Asgard," I said, sounding more confident than I felt. Her trepidation made mine fade, and I grabbed her hand and squeezed. "On the count of three?"

"Can I go, too?" Smith asked in his high-pitched, formal accent. Beneath his dark complexion, his face had gone pale.

I held out my hand, and he slid his cold fingers into mine. Xander stood off to one side, and my heart suddenly squeezed. I wished I had three hands, so I could hold onto him, too. Catching my eye, he gave me a nod, his face set in its usual blank expression. At first, it had intimidated me, despite my best efforts to stand up to him, but now I knew that it was just an act. Xander was anything but unfeeling.

Ignoring the flutters in my belly, I took a deep breath and stepped into the water.

Coldness washed over me, soaking my clothes and hair. Water rushed into my nose and mouth. I stumbled back, choking and drenched. Smith fell to his knees beside me, spewing water.

Of course I was the one who couldn't cross the bride. Of course.

"Gwen!"

I looked up to see Peyton rising on the water, reaching back for me. Sucking up my humiliation, I grabbed her hand. She hauled me up, and I thrashed in the water. I could feel my feet lifting off the ground, and panic shot through me as I relived the moment at our parents' wedding where I'd been washed away by a freak, god-induced wave. I wrenched my hand free of Peyton's and dropped to the ground, barely keeping my feet under me as I staggered away from Bifrost spitting water.

"Having a little trouble, are we?" Xander asked, smirking at me.

Anger boiled up in me, replacing the frustration and embarrassment. "Why haven't you stepped on if you're so sure of yourself?"

"Didn't want to miss the show," he said with a shrug. He stepped into the fire and immediately began to swim through it, rising like smoke through the flames.

Xander thought he was a god. Of course he did. Xander had probably always thought he was a god, before he even knew he was literally part of one. Just like Zeke, like Peyton and Eliot, Xander had no shortage of confidence. They all believed in themselves. Apparently, even Finn did. But me? Nope, I was left standing on the ground with a dwarf and an elf who was only there out of pity.

"Buck up, little girl," Xander called from above. "Your magical rainbow ride is waiting."

"Go ahead and laugh," I called back. "It won't be so funny when the bridge goes out when you're halfway across."

"It won't," Valdan said. "So get on it."

"How?" Smith asked. He and I drew closer together, forming a bedraggled pair as we waited for the elf to instruct us further.

"You're a god," Valdan said. "It's not enough to know it. You must believe it."

"I've accepted it," I said, but even as I said the words, I knew they weren't completely true. Accepting it meant agreeing to it. It meant believing I would never be alone in my body, that I would always be wracked with this insatiable need to be close to the others. It meant I would never have the ordinary experiences I'd always longed for. Even if I went to football games and Starbucks and department stores, I'd never see them as an ordinary girl. Believing I was a god meant I would never get to see things through the eyes of a normal person.

"I don't know if I can believe it," Smith said. "I'm not even a good dwarf. Dwarves are supposed to be craftsmen. Look at my hands." He held out his long-fingered, slender hands. His skin was soft and smooth.

"I like your hands," I said, feeling unaccountably protective. I didn't want anyone insulting my people—not even if they were the ones doing it.

"I don't have a trade," Smith said, his narrow shoulders slumping. "I always wanted to be a singer."

"What do you sing?"

In answer, Smith opened his mouth and let out a high, trilling note. Chills exploded across my skin. After taking a breath, he let out another one, holding it longer than the first. I felt his song as well as heard it, felt the depth below that one long note. I felt what it was like to be alone, to be a constant disappointment, to be looked down upon, always measured and always found lacking. I felt his frustration and the sadness of his isolation. It was like he'd pushed the pain of his life through my eardrums and straight into my heart. His voice rose higher, a vibrato almost painful in its sweetness, before cutting off abruptly.

"Wow," I breathed, wrapping my arms around myself and rubbing my shoulders, trying to smooth away the chills. I couldn't seem to clear my mind of the strange invasion.

"That was a good song," Valdan said.

"I'd say that was definitely infused with some godly magic," I said.

"You really think so?" Smith asked, his face awash with hope.

"I don't know much about music, but what happened when you were singing is definitely not normal," I said. "I could feel your...feelings."

"Yeah," Smith said, his face falling. "That's always been a problem. It wasn't so bad when I was a kid, but the longer I wasn't able to sing as I wanted, the worse it got. Now, no one wants me to sing because it's too depressing."

"Well, maybe they shouldn't try to stop you," I said. "Maybe if they'd encouraged you in your gift, you wouldn't have all those sad feelings about it."

"Yeah," Smith said, squaring his shoulders. "You're right. Maybe it is a gift of the gods."

"It is," I said, taking his hand and squeezing. "I'm sure of it."

"Me, too," Valdan said. "Just as my godly beauty is a gift."

"You definitely weren't blessed with humbleness," I muttered.

"What is your gift?" Smith asked me. "Maybe when we find it, we will be able to cross the bridge."

"You found yours," I said. "You should get on. The more of us who cross, the stronger it gets."

"I can't leave you," Smith said. "There must be something you're good at."

I crossed my arms, burying my fists under them. What was I good at?

Reading maps? Making things awkward in record time? Psychic communication with magical flying goats?

Smith and Valdan both stood there, waiting for me to figure it out. I had to say something. They weren't going until we were all ready.

"I—I'm loyal," I said.

I expected one of them to snort, Xander-like, and make a cutting remark, but instead, Valdan clapped me on the back. I really needed to tell him to dial down the back slapping before I lost a vertebra.

"A fine virtue," he said, his chest swelling with pride, as if he were listing his own virtues. "Doesn't that make you feel godlike?"

I opened my mouth and then closed it. It was true I didn't feel particularly godlike, but I didn't think that was the problem. The problem was more of a mental block, one I had refused to release. But now, it was time to let go of that. To let go of that small human dream to be normal. I wasn't normal. I was a god, and I always would be. In truth, I always had been. I would never go back to my old life. And maybe that was okay. It was time to stop crying over what I would never have, time to stop letting it define me and hold me back.

Frankly, my old life had sucked.

My mother had never taught me to be brave. She'd taught me fear. Fear of ravens, of giants and wolves, of government and satellites, and being tracked down. She had taught me to run, but life had taught me that sometimes I had to fight. Sometimes, I had to be brave, even when I didn't know how. I had climbed a tree for days despite my crippling fear of heights. I'd flown on goats and horses and even a dragon. I was done being afraid. I was done wanting to be normal, or charismatic, or anything I wasn't. I didn't have to be a smooth-talker. I was a fucking god.

I reached out and grabbed Smith's hand in one of mine and Valdan's in the other. "Come on," I said. "We're gods, and our bridge needs saving. It's our time."

Chapter Two

Zeke

I'd never been the anxious type, but now that I had something real to worry about—someone—I'd begun to understand why Eliot was always stressing. Since Gwen's arrival, I couldn't seem to stop obsessing about her, how she was doing, and whether she was okay. But hovering around to protect her twenty-four seven was not the way to get a girl, so I tried to rein it in.

When I started to feel that magnetic pull of hers from the ground behind us, though, I turned back. I picked up my pace as I started down the slope of the bridge toward Xander. I wasn't sure how we were actually climbing the bridge, and I was trying not to think about it. Logic might kill the magic, like it did with Santa Claus. When you stopped believing, he stopped being real. If Bifrost was anything like Santa, we needed all the believing we could get.

"She's fine," Xander said, holding out an arm to bar my way. I could have gone around—even in its weakened state, Bifrost was as wide as a football field. There was plenty of room. But I stopped, anyway.

"Doesn't feel that way to me," I said. I could see the wall of the canyon below, and I itched to go down there. I responded to her distress automatically, like when a ref threw a flag on a play. When the whistle blew, you had to pay attention.

"She needs to figure it out on her own," Xander said as Eliot joined us to wait for our girl. "Don't worry so much."

"Easy for you to say," Eliot muttered.

"I'm with you on that, bro," I said. Hovering a hundred feet in the air, supported by three elements without enough substance to hold a human's weight, it seemed like a pretty good time to worry.

"This only works if all nine of us cross," Eliot reminded Xander. "And then we're supposed to bring the other gods across to strengthen it. Remember?"

"Gwen will get up just like the rest of us," Xander said. "You can't go running to her rescue every time she's having trouble."

"Why not?" I asked, remembering that night I'd heard her scream for us. I'd heard her scream loud and clear, even if I'd heard it with my mind instead of my ears. If we hadn't gone running to her rescue that night, she'd be dead right now.

"Give it a few minutes," Xander said. "We won't always be around to help her. She's strong enough to do it on her own. She just needs to figure out that she is."

Though I would have preferred to sweep in and rescue her, and maybe score a few bonus points with her, I agreed to wait a few minutes before I went to help. Xander had a point. We were all gods. If anything, Gwen was strongest since she was our heart. The sooner she believed it, the better off we'd all be.

We waited, suspended on the air, watching the mouth of the cave far below. The bridge wasn't like something solid but invisible, like we were climbing something we couldn't see. And it wasn't exactly like flying, though we were in the strip of air that made up one third of the bridge. It was more like treading water, except we weren't in water. We were walking on wind so stiff it could hold our weight. As long as my feet kept moving, the air kept me aloft. But if I went still, I began to sink.

Maybe we could build our own wings out of cardboard and duct tape like we had when we were kids, strap them on our backs, and feel like we were flying as we swooped up the bridge. If we had to stay a while, Eliot would totally geek out over that project. I hoped we didn't get stuck here another three months, though. I was ready to see Dad and sleep in my own bed with my nightlight nearby.

Suddenly, Gwen's form appeared on the bridge. I just about forgot to keep walking in place, almost plummeting to my death. But after a hesitation that made my body sink fast enough to send a sickening lurch through my stomach, I recovered myself. Relief washed over me when I saw Gwen, Valdan, and Smith climbing the steep beginning of the bridge, and I let out a whoop of triumph, pumping my fist in the air.

I started singing "Eye of the Tiger," and Peyton joined in, a smile on her face that made me happy all over again. Eliot clapped while Finn hovered behind us, Xander watching over him. Behind them all, Alvan stood grinning from beneath his massive beard. All of them were glowing faintly, as if their skin had been coated with fine gold particles. Oddly enough, it wasn't nearly as intense as it had been the times we'd huddled together in a tight group. Even though we now had all nine members and were crossing Heimdall's bridge, the glow around us was mellower. Maybe we were feeding Bifrost our magical energy to heal it.

We waited on the bridge, watching our last three pieces approach. The crazy Viking elf, the strange new dwarf, and the girl who had stolen our hearts. I realized then that no one had answered her proposal earlier—at least not directly. She'd told us she liked all of us, that she wanted to try to make it work with all of us. I was okay with it, if it made my brothers happy. Still, as she joined us, my relief at seeing her okay made me all kinds of selfish. She looked cute as hell even though her face was red and she was out of breath. In that moment, I didn't care about stepping on toes. I wanted Gwen all to myself. Before my brothers could step in and dazzle her, I wrapped her up in my arms.

"Glad you made it," I said, smiling down at her. I wanted to kiss her so bad I could taste it.

"Me, too," she said, laughing a little.

"I was worried about you."

"Me, too," she repeated.

I wished we were alone, so I could show her how happy I was to have her with us. And then I remembered that it didn't matter. I didn't have to hide the fact that I felt the same way about her that my siblings did. I had the same claim to her heart they did. She liked all of us. She liked me. So I kissed her, right there on the rainbow bridge a hundred feet in the air, surrounded by our family. She wrapped her arms around my neck and kissed me back. No matter what anyone thought of our arrangement, I'd found the only girl I wanted, and as long as she wanted me, I was going to do everything in my power to protect her and love her the way she deserved.

Chapter Three

Gwen

When Zeke pulled away, I felt so dizzy from the kiss I thought I might tumble into the fire. And then I realized something. It wouldn't scar me as the fire giant had, wouldn't burn me up as the river of fire below had. I was safe here—I was invincible. I felt strangely light, as if I might float away, and not just because I was supported by the air currents beneath my feet. I had let something go. The weight of it had lifted and I was free.

"I don't know about you guys, but I'm ready to see that city," Eliot said, nodding toward the shining castle in the distance, as if I hadn't just kissed his brother in front of him. Maybe it really was okay with him. Or maybe I couldn't think clearly because my head was still spinning. I had to get a grip on myself, though. I'd let myself go, let my hormones rule me before, and it had hurt someone I loved, which had hurt everyone else in turn. This time, I would be strong.

"Me, too," I said again, and I forced myself not to wince at the realization I'd repeated that phrase about a million times since joining the others. What did it matter if I was weird? I was every bit the god they were.

"Then let's finish this crossing," Eliot said, his big hand enfolding mine. We started walking, now in the lead.

"It's getting brighter," I said, watching the flames lick higher beside us as we walked.

"Things are changing," Eliot murmured. "Not just the bridge."

My heart throbbed against my ribs. "What do you mean?" I asked, fighting the urge to pull my hand away from his, to pull it inside my sleeve. I wouldn't be a turtle hiding inside my shell any longer.

"We're not glowing as brightly," he said. "Didn't you notice? It seemed like before Smith came, every time we got closer, we turned gold. Now, we're sparkling less than Edward Cullen in Italy."

I nudged him playfully with my elbow. "Wow. Is there a closet fanboy in our presence?"

"I'm just saying. I thought when he arrived, we'd turn to gold statues. But it seems to have had the opposite effect."

I thought a minute and then nodded. "Yeah. It's more like those gold dust particles that float in the rivers in Colorado. We're just sprinkled with it now."

Eliot gave me a curious glance.

I shrugged. "I traveled a lot."

"I know."

"Oh, right. You were tracking me with your superior hacking skills."

He grinned sideways at me. "Something like that."

"Okay, so what is your genius brain coming up with this time? Are we losing power?"

To my surprise, the thought of our god fading made something inside me clench. I'd just accepted I was a god. I didn't want to give it up already.

"What do you think?" Eliot asked. "Do you feel less powerful?"

I opened my mouth to give the automatic, expected response. Girls weren't really supposed to feel powerful, were they? In the romance novels I'd always read, women didn't exercise any power at all over men. But then, I'd already learned that those books didn't exactly correspond to real life. And the truth was, I did feel powerful, whether or not anyone else thought it was appropriate.

"No," I said. "I feel the same."

"Do you?" Eliot asked, cocking his head to one side as he studied me.

"Well, yeah. I think so," I said, uncertainty nibbling at the edges of my newfound confidence. "Don't you?"

"Not exactly," he said.

Before I could press him further, an angry shriek sounded above. A falcon sped toward us, its wings folded in, its body as streamlined as a bullet.

Peyton shrieked and covered her head with both arms. My stomach lurched, but not because of the bird. Sure, it was big and ugly, but what really freaked me out was the view. The canyon must have been a thousand feet below by now, a world of unforgiving stone waiting to accept the impact of our bodies.

Zeke cursed and leapt in front of us, throwing up an arm to block the bird. At the last second, the falcon veered off course and swooped sideways, squawking as it circled above us. I grabbed onto Eliot, squeezing my eyes closed. I tried to remember what Xander had said to me when I'd ridden the dragon. I was not falling. I was not hurt. It was only fear.

"What the hell was that?" Zeke asked.

"That bird's got serious problems," Smith said.

"Where's Gracelyn when you need her?" Peyton wailed.

"We don't need Gracelyn," Alvan grumbled. He'd never gotten over the fact that another elf had saved us from a dragon attack when he couldn't. "I'll grab it from the air and wring its neck."

"I thought you were a vegetarian," I said, eyeing the bird as it wheeled above us.

"I didn't say I would eat it," Alvan said.

The bird shrieked again and dove for us. This time, its talons were extended. They raked across Alvan's forearm when he raised his hand in an attempt to snatch the bird from the air. He missed, and the bird dove at Finn. It flapped and squawked, beating its powerful wings against him as he stumbled backwards.

Zeke struck the bird, which let out a hideous screech that echoed into the cavernous space below the bridge. Xander threw out a hand as if to ward it off, but before he could hit it, the falcon careened off the side of the bridge and down toward the canyon as we all stood there, too stunned to react.

Alvan swore in his elven dialect and examined the blood trickling down his arm.

"Apparently, it doesn't want to die in vain," Zeke said, peering down after the falcon as it circled below Bifrost.

"Are you all right?" Eliot asked me, a frown creasing his forehead.

"Yeah, fine," I said, only then realizing I clutched his arm in a death grip. We had stopped on the bridge, and we hadn't sunk through it. When I looked down, I could still see the valley far below, but I could also see the swirling air currents. The fire making up the next stripe in the rainbow was brighter, burning steadily instead of flickering as if using the last of its energy. The water to our left seemed to be flowing a little stronger as well.

"We're doing it," I said, a sense of wonder filling my body and a rush of chill bumps across my skin. "I think we're fixing the bridge."

"It's a start, anyway," Eliot said. "Heimdall said we had to bring the other gods across if we really wanted it to hold."

"And that starts with getting the hell across and getting off this thing," Peyton said. "Before any more nasty, flesh-eating raptors try to gouge our eyes out."

"It wasn't trying to gouge our eyes out," Eliot said.

"Speak for yourself," Peyton said. "My eyes were definitely in danger."

"I'm with Peyton," Zeke said. "Let's get off this thing. I'm no coward, but I think I've had enough near-death experiences to last me for the rest of my life."

We picked up the pace, which wasn't easy. It was like trying to run through water. We had to take our time plodding across the bridge. I kept a lookout below us, searching for signs of falcons and dragons and anything else that might rise up out of the canyon to attack. We were out in the open, which made us vulnerable, but it also made it impossible for anything to sneak up on us if we stayed vigilant.

As if to prove me wrong, a rushing noise filled my ears and a shadow swept over us. But when I squinted into the sun above, I saw nothing unusual. Columns of fluffy white clouds towered above us in a blue sky pierced by the shining spires of the city of Asgard ahead. It was all so idyllic I almost forgot the falcon, and the shadow that had passed over us.

Suddenly, a figure shot through the band of fire beside us. She spread a pair of huge white wings, and sparks rained down around her.

"Okay, that's it," Peyton cried, yanking at the elven dagger she had in a sheath on her leather pants. "I'm so sick of being attacked. I didn't want to have to do this, but I'm about to go all cheerleader bitch up in here."

The girl shook a few errant sparks from her wings. "Welcome to Asgard, godlings," she said in a posh accent that sounded strange after hearing the guttural accent of the elves. Theirs was vaguely German with a dash of Russian. She sounded more like Darcy's snooty younger sister. She didn't look much older than us, but she was clad in a swirling white dress instead of filthy tatters, and her blonde hair flowed around her shoulders as if defying gravity. Atop her head she wore a golden crown with an intricate gold wing on either side.

"Whoa," Zeke said. "Are you an angel?"

"Of a sort," she said, the corner of her mouth quirking in amusement. "At least, I'm what your world might call an angel."

"You're a Valkyrie," Eliot said, extending a hand. "You decide which slain warriors go to Valhalla, the feast hall of the afterlife, and serve the gods at their feast."

"Yes," she said, draping a white hand over the top of Eliot's proffered one. "Like I said, I am what your people refer to as an angel."

"That's not exactly what angels do," Finn muttered.

Eliot hesitated, a frown of uncharacteristic uncertainty furrowing his brow, before he bent to kiss the back of the Valkyrie's hand. "It's an honor to make your acquaintance."

She turned her attention from Eliot, narrowing her eyes at Finn. "Do your angels not greet a dying man and ferry him up to an afterlife of paradise?"

"To heaven," Finn said, his face reddening as her unwavering stare remained on him.

"Call it what you like," she said. "Heaven or Asgard, angel or cherubim or Valkyrie. It makes no difference to me."

"Okay," Finn said, shrugging. "But it does to me."

"What's the difference?" she asked, her wings folding and unfolding like a butterfly perched on a flower. But there was something terrifying about her, too. Her attitude was more like a predator toying with her prey, waiting for him to make a wrong move so she could pounce.

Finn's face darkened under his tan as he blushed harder. He shrugged again. "An angel doesn't have…"

What didn't they have, though? She had wings, dressed in white, and had the ability to choose who went to the big party palace and who got left to descend to Helheim.

"…an iron crown," Finn finished weakly.

The Valkyrie blinked at him, her powerful body taut beneath her gauzy white gown. Abruptly, she threw her head back and laughed, a high, tinkling sound echoing all the way down into the canyon below and high above to the clouds where Asgard waited.

"Oh, Heimdall," she said, linking her arm through Finn's. "How I have missed you."

"I'm not—" Finn's words were interrupted when the bridge heaved under us. I caught a glimpse of the miles of nothingness below us, and black spots dotted my vision. Xander swore. Peyton grabbed Zeke's arm, as if his strength could somehow save her from plummeting through a bridge made of air and into the abyss.

"Don't deny your godliness now," I hissed. "We barely got on the bridge. If you start doubting now, not even a Valkyrie can save us all."

The bridge steadied after a second, and I nearly collapsed in relief.

"It's true," the Valkyrie said. "I can only save the souls of those most worthy."

"People who died valiantly in battle," Eliot said.

"If your job is to carry off dead people, does that mean you're about to toss one of us off this thing?" Xander asked, scooting between the Valkyrie and the rest of us.

Except Finn. She had Finn in her clutches. I swallowed, eyeing her tall, muscular frame.

Note to self—move working out up my to-do list.

"No, you silly godling," she said, her tinkling laughter ringing out again. She hooked her free arm through Xander's and pulled him to her side. "I'm here to escort you to Asgard."

"Don't you have some souls to harvest?" I muttered, eyeing her grip on two of my boys.

"It's gotten quite dull," she said with a flick of her wings. "Besides, so few die in battle nowadays. I'd much rather hear about your human world as we make our way to Asgard. Would you like me to carry these two?"

"We'd better stay together," I said. "We need to cross as one."

"Of course," she said. "I'm Valerie, and nothing would please me more than to cross Bifrost with Heimdall."

"Yay," Peyton muttered. "Lucky us."

"Valerie the Valkyrie," I said. "Interesting name."

"Not especially," she said, peddling her dainty feet through the air to move along with us. "Anyone can be chosen to be a Valkyrie. People from all different worlds and times are chosen."

"Really?" Eliot asked. "When were you chosen for the honor?"

"A few years ago," she said. "Nineteen twenty…" She paused, looking blank, as if searching for the correct year. A small, nervous titter escaped. "I'm really not sure. Isn't that funny? Nothing ever changes here. It's hard to remember one day from the next."

I exchanged a glance with Peyton. "Sorry to break it to you, but that was like a hundred years ago," Peyton said.

"That can't be," Valerie said, her eyes widening. "It was only a few years ago. I'm sure of it." Doubt flickered across her pretty face, and for the first time, she looked less haughty and more human. A twinge of pity pulled at me. I wondered if she'd expected to go back to her human life at some point, like I had. I tried to imagine how I'd feel if I found out that while three months had passed in this world, a hundred years had passed in Midgard. Pain gripped my chest at the thought, but I pushed it aside. That wouldn't happen to us. It couldn't. I had to make sure my mom was okay.

Conversation died out then, and we swam-walked through the air. Valerie floated ahead, her wings fluttering in agitation every few minutes. Zeke fell into step beside me, linking his fingers with mine. I smiled shyly at him, hoping this and the kiss meant he was okay with my decision not to choose one of them over anyone else. After what seemed like forever, Bifrost began to slope downwards, and the city appeared before us. The bridge dipped into a slight descent before meeting a hillside of lush green grass. On top of the hill stood an enormous, shining palace of white marble, silver, and gold. The roof appeared to be made of some kind of round metal shingles, which caught the rays of the sun and cast them back toward the sky.

"Not to insult the gods or anything, but they seriously need to hire a new architect," Peyton said. "That is the tackiest thing I've ever seen."

"That's Valhalla," Eliot said, pushing up his oversized glasses as he stared at the building with reverence.

"Is that the Norse word for tacky?" Peyton asked.

"No, it's the place where the honorable dead go," Valerie said. "They live and feast there and train for when they can fight at Ragnarok. The roof is made of shields, and the supports from spears of the fallen."

"That's gruesome," I said. "But I think it's kind of beautiful."

"You will find that the gods don't worry about going overboard," Valerie said. "They feel quite free to indulge in their whims."

"That sounds dangerous," Xander said, cutting his eyes at me.

"That is often the case," Valerie said. "They are certainly not free from errors in judgment or regrets."

"So even gods make mistakes?" Zeke asked. "That's lame. I was hoping it meant I was perfect."

"Aww, you already are perfect," I teased, pushing my shoulder against his.

He slid an arm around me and pulled me close, planting a kiss on the top of my head.

"At least he's got someone fooled," Peyton said.

I hesitated at the end of the bridge, and the others did the same. Some small part of me was afraid it would blink out once we stepped off. I swallowed, making a circle in the grass below the rainbow with my toe. On this end, there was no cave to spit out the flame and water and air. It simply sprang up from the earth.

Eliot stepped up to my other side and took my hand.

"On the count of three," Zeke said.

"One," Peyton said.

"Two," Zeke said.

I looked up the hill to where the glimmering tower stood. "Three."

Together, we stepped off the bridge and into the world of the gods.

Chapter Four

Gwen

I marveled at the feeling of safety and rightness sweeping over me when my feet were planted firmly on the ground. My heart stammered in my chest when I thought of Bifrost behind me. Holding my breath, I turned slowly.

"It's still there," Peyton said, covering her heart. "Thank all the gods."

"Can we still say that if we are gods?" Zeke said. "Isn't that like thanking yourself?"

"Thank you, *me,*" Peyton said with a flick of her pink ponytail.

Bifrost loomed in front of us, the arc curving up into the sky. It was brighter than when we'd stepped on. I slumped against Zeke for a second, the tension of the past hour melting out of me. He wrapped his arms around me and rested his chin on top of my head. "It's still there," he said. "And we're all here. We made it."

"Yeah," I said, my words wooden. "We did it. We crossed Bifrost. Our mission is complete. We can go home."

I couldn't quite believe it had been that easy. After months of fighting to get here, we'd done it. To be fair, the other worlds as a whole had been more welcoming to me than my own world, which probably said more about Midgard and humanity than anything else. Besides a big bird, nothing had even bothered us on the bridge. Valerie had actually come to welcome us. So, Finn's visions weren't always right. Sometimes, they were a warning, not a prophecy. We had the power to change the awful future…or at least put it off, in the case of Ragnarok.

Asgard was beautiful, with lush green grass swaying in a gentle breeze and Valhalla, which looked more like a palace than anything, shining atop the hill. From our vantage point at the end of Bifrost, we couldn't see much else.

"We aren't done yet," Eliot said. "We still have to rally the gods to go back across."

"Right," I said, ashamed at the relief rising up in me to accompany the regret. To my surprise, I was filled with curiosity to see the city I'd been trying to reach for so long. I still wanted to go home and see my mom. But I wanted to see more of the world than I'd seen from the passenger seat of her car. I had traveled a lot, like I'd told Eliot, but that didn't mean I'd experienced the places I'd seen.

"You will pay your respects to Odin, the All-Father," Valerie said, as we started across the grass. It was lush and soft beneath our feet, and again I let myself revel in the small joy of having solid ground beneath me. After the dry heat on the other side of Bifrost and the cold of the giant world, even the air felt perfect.

"We're basically in heaven, right?" Peyton said. "I mean, it's a golden city in the sky with fluffy clouds all around. The gods live here, and the souls of deserving people come here when they die. They've got angels, too, even if they're a little different than I'd envisioned."

"You can't go to heaven unless you die," Finn said quietly.

"Or unless you're a god," I said.

"There's only one god."

"If you really believed that, you wouldn't be here," Xander said. "You'd be in that cave on the other side of Bifrost right now."

"We can't go in there, can we?" I asked Valerie, nodding to the palace on the hill. "Since we're still alive?"

"You're gods," she said. "You can go anywhere you please in Asgard. It is my honor to welcome you home. But only the slain live in Valhalla with Odin."

Welcome us home.

The fact that we weren't entirely human knocked into my brain again. Just when I thought I'd gotten used to it, the truth smacked me in the face again. I looked around at my stepsiblings. They weren't just beautiful, wealthy, popular kids. They were gods.

We were gods. We had free access to this entire world because we were gods. We belonged here. All six of us, plus our two elven additions and Smith, who I barely knew, but who had shared his gift of song with me. He'd stayed with me while I figured out that I was a god, too. With all that had happened since I'd met them, I'd barely gotten a chance to know them. But they were part of this, too—

part of us. I just didn't know exactly what part they played yet. I hadn't had time to figure out if I felt the same about them as I did for the Keens, or if I'd only been drawn to them because of our god.

I wanted to find out. I didn't want to rush straight home and never come back. Home was here, too. I was part of this world now. Part of the Nine Worlds, not just Midgard. I could feel the rightness of this world in my bones, in my soul. It was as if all my life a part of me had been missing, and it had fallen into place when I stepped into Asgard.

The realization swept through me, and I was suddenly trembling so hard I thought I'd melt onto the ground. Was this how it felt to belong—not just to people but to a place?

I'd spent so much of my life in limbo. I'd thought I belonged nowhere. But maybe it had all been leading up to this, preparing me for this. I didn't have one home but many. I didn't belong to one place because I belonged everywhere. It was so big—the idea of the Nine Worlds, and that we were truly more than human, that we were parts of something divine.

Before I could freak out, Eliot's strong hand slipped into mine. He gave my fingers a reassuring squeeze, a smile playing on his full lips. I squeezed back, drawing strength from him and the certainty of our status. We were godlings. Only a god could cross Bifrost—only one god. There was no question anymore. We belonged here as much as we belonged together.

As we approached the palace of Valhalla, Valerie led us to one of the doors spaced at regular intervals around the towering walls. The building was at least ten stories high, with thousands of spears, swords, staffs, and even clubs making up the walls. Beyond it, we could see more of

Asgard. It wasn't just a palace on a hill. It was an entire city of splendor with shining buildings and smooth white streets.

Valerie stepped inside Valhalla before we had time to study the city much. After stepping in behind her, I stopped and blinked a few times to take in the interior. Instead of a foyer or hall, we had stepped into something resembling a stadium. Instead of spectator seating, tables were set up in concentric circles all the way to the floor. In the center, a giant throne sat.

"Is that Odin's throne?" Eliot asked.

"This is the feast hall," Valerie said. "Odin will be expecting you. His ravens have informed him of your whereabouts."

Ravens. Of course. My mother had always freaked out about ravens, and now I knew why. She had tried to protect me from this, to keep me from it. I understood, in a way. It was dangerous, and the journey here had been painful. Like any parent, she had wanted to spare me that pain. But in the end, I could not escape my fate. The ravens had been watching over us all along, and now they were here, perched on the back of Odin's tall, wooden throne. They had probably been telling him about us all for years.

"Come along, then," Valerie said in her fancy accent. She gave a lazy wave of her pale hand, gesturing for us to follow as she floated through the rows of tables, her gown flowing around her like clouds.

"Think I could ask Odin if I could be a Valkyrie?" Peyton asked. "She looks so badass."

"If he even comes to meet us," I said. "He's not here now, and who knows if he'll find us worthy of his time. If anything, he'll probably tell us not to mess with his horse again."

"Crap, I forgot about that."

"Something tells me he might not."

"Odin sees all and forgets none," Valerie said.

We arrived at the foot of the throne, which was a giant wooden seat towering over the bare floor. "My king," Valerie said, bowing low to the empty seat and lifting the folds of her skirt elegantly to each side, her wings pressed together behind her back.

"Is anyone seeing a god in that chair?" I muttered from the corner of my mouth. "Or is this an *Emperor's New Clothes* situation?"

Eliot bowed and then cleared his throat. "When will the All-Father be gracing us with his wise presence?"

Right before our eyes, a man appeared in the chair. Odin. I gasped and jerked back, stumbling against Zeke's muscular frame. Odin had a weathered face with an eyepatch over one eye. His white hair hung across his shoulders and mingled with the white beard flowing all the way to his lap.

"Heimdall," the old god said, opening his arms. "And Thor. My sons. How good to see you again."

"So, this isn't weird at all," Peyton said.

"Odin," Eliot said, going down on one knee. "It is an honor to be in your presence."

After some hesitating and awkward shifting, the rest of us bowed, too.

"Let your father have a look at you."

We stood and faced Odin. Suddenly, my heart thumped so loudly I could hear it in my ears. This wasn't just a god— it was *the* god. It was the father of the gods, the king. He could probably squish us like mosquitos if we annoyed him. And it might annoy him that we'd stolen his horse.

"You came across Bifrost," he said, holding up a gnarled, thick finger. A raven landed on it, and he held it close to his chest and stroked it absently, looking us over with his one eye.

"Yes, your…majesty?" Zeke said.

"You may call me Father."

From what little I remembered, my father had been nothing like Heimdall's dad.

"Yes, Father," Zeke said. "Heimdall told us to cross Bifrost to strengthen it."

"Yes," Odin said. "That's very good."

"We are actually here searching for more gods to cross it with us," Eliot said.

Odin moved from stroking his raven to stroking his beard. "Ahhh."

I glanced at the group. Odin's answer wasn't exactly an enthusiastic endorsement of our idea.

"And to pay you a visit, of course," Peyton said. "We haven't seen our dear old dad in… How long has it been?"

"It must be sixteen years since," Odin said, staring over our heads.

"We must have some catching up to do," I offered. "Unless, I don't know, maybe sixteen years isn't really that long for you. Being a god and everything, you must be immortal."

I winced at my awkward rambling, but Odin didn't react.

"Wait, are we immortal?" Zeke asked. "Or is it invincible? I always mix those two up."

"Heimdall will die at Ragnarok like the rest of the gods," Odin said.

"Yeah, but until then...?"

"You've just arrived. Why don't you explore our fine city for the day? Stay in Valhalla tonight. Tomorrow evening, you will join me at my table for a feast."

"Thank you," I said.

"Don't we have to be dead to do that?" Zeke asked, his brow furrowed in concern.

"Don't question our father," Alvan said, steering Zeke away from the foot of the throne.

"Is it safe to wander around Asgard?" I asked Odin.

"This is your home," he said.

That didn't exactly answer my question, but I didn't want to push my luck.

"We'll be okay if we stick together," Eliot said.

"Return this evening," Odin said. "Valerie will have your rooms ready."

That seemed like a pretty clear dismissal, and even though I had a million more questions, I knew not to irritate a god. If the stories I'd read were any indication, they might turn me into a horsefly or murder me for spite. Even if the worlds had changed since those stories were written, the gods were the same beings I'd read about. Their personalities probably hadn't changed all that much.

After we bowed to the All-Father, we hurried after Zeke and Alvan.

"That was super weird," Peyton whispered, as we made our way between rows and rows of tables, climbing higher up the circular stadium floor toward a door. At least there were tons of exits. I made note of some of the doors in case we needed them later.

"The man was old two thousand years ago," Smith said. "He's probably not going to be what any of us would call normal."

"Shhh," I said, glancing back over my shoulder. "What if he can hear us?"

I didn't breathe easily until we stepped out of the darkened hall and into the golden sunshine. Odin's ravens could be anywhere, watching and listening. That's why my mother had been so terrified of them, and even though I knew she'd gone way overboard with the paranoia, I didn't want to take chances by insulting our godly father in his own house.

"So, where to next?" Peyton asked, stretching her arms toward the sun. "That was obviously a big, fat fail."

We had come out on the same side of the hall that we entered through, and now we stood on the grassy hillside with a view of the city spread out on the far side of the palace.

"If this is our home, why would he tell us to go explore the city like tourists?" I asked. "I feel like there's something we're missing here." In truth, I didn't know what to think of Odin. I hadn't even known we were meeting him until we arrived, so I couldn't say I was disappointed. But the meeting had definitely left me wanting. For an all-knowing, all-seeing god, he hadn't given us nearly enough answers. Yet again, we had to figure it out ourselves.

"All I know is, if this is heaven, there should be a Starbucks," Peyton said. "I'm all about exploring the city. I say let's go."

In the distance, I could hear cries and the clang of metal on metal. Were we walking into a trap? I kept glancing around as we circled the outside of Valhalla. When we'd gone halfway around, we were on the side that faced the city. We started off through the meadow, which ended at the bottom of a slight incline. There, a white street stretched from the foot of Valhalla's hill through the city, like a carpet rolled out before us.

"Why would Odin want to hurt us?" Eliot asked. "He's Heimdall's father. Yeah, Joaquin borrowed his horse without asking, and we rode on it, but he's not going to kill us for that."

"Are you sure?" Smith asked, edging toward our powerful elves as we reached the street.

I stepped onto the street, which had a slick surface like marble. It struck me then how silent the city was as it lay before us. No engines purred, no dogs barked. No vehicles rolled by, no people hurried from one towering building to the next or sat outside chatting in the sunshine.

"There's no point in standing around talking about it," Xander said. "Whatever we're missing, we're not going to figure it out standing here."

"Agreed," Eliot said. "Odin didn't give us much, but we have nothing else to go on. We'd better obey him. He didn't mention the horse, but I doubt he'd ignore us refusing a direct order."

"Okay," I said with a shrug. "I'm in. We need to find some gods, so we might as well get started."

"Great," Finn muttered as we started forward. "We have no choice. Again."

"Give it a rest, Finn," Peyton said. "We're all in this together. Stop acting like you're the only one going through this."

"Easy for you to say," he said. "You're always happy."

"So sue me, I see the bright side," she said. "You should try it sometime. It's tons more fun than the intentionally miserable side."

"Leave him alone," I said. "It's not his fault."

He shot me a small smile before yanking his gaze from mine, and a quick pulse of awkwardness clogged my airway. Would I ever be able to look at him again without an intense, almost painful, discomfort bowling over my heart?

"Fine, be miserable," Peyton said. "But I'm in heaven, and I choose to make it into an adventure if I can't do anything else."

This might have been someone's version of heaven, but it wasn't filled with peace-loving cherubs. The Viking gods were nothing to mess around with. They had few qualms about killing people or even each other. As we walked between the looming silver and gold buildings, I couldn't help but feel like we were marching down death row.

"Looks like we lost Valerie," Eliot said after a minute.

"A real tragedy," I said.

"She could have showed us around the city."

"I'm sure that's what you want her for," Peyton said, laughing. "It has nothing to do with the fact that she's a hot female."

Jealousy flared in my chest, but it melted a second later when Eliot's hand closed around mine. "Nothing at all," he said. "I'm spoken for."

I squeezed his hand, basking in the glow of his attention. As weird as the world around us had become, we were still us. I was still a girl who had just been publicly claimed by a cute boy, and I was going to enjoy the shit out of it. Like Peyton said, we were all going through the same things. The difference was in how we experienced them. I chose to experience them with my first and only official boyfriend by my side.

Walking away from Valhalla, we headed down a slight incline to a road paved with white stones. The buildings were shaped like giant spears thrusting into the sky in a rather phallic display. Each one gleamed in the sun, from the white marble to the silver and gold.

"Wow," I said. "That's some major bling."

"I'm starting to get the picture," Peyton said. "Gods are like the kids who dumped the whole tub of glitter on their paper and felt zero shame about it."

"Better than the ones who ate paste," Eliot said. "Now, where are these gods we need?"

The street before us stood empty, except for the rays of sunshine bouncing off the white stones and blinding us. "Where do we even start?" I asked. "Should we just walk down the street yelling for them or go pounding on doors?"

"Sadly, I see no coffee shops," Peyton said, scanning the street.

"Do you guys come here a lot?" I asked the elves. "You're a whole god, so you said you could come here whenever you wanted."

"Not often," Alvan said. "I have been a few times to see Odin."

"We travel between worlds," Valdan said. "We spend most of our time in Alfheim. The elves need us there more than the gods need us here."

"You wouldn't happen to know where these gods are?" I asked.

"We do not often see them," Alvan said, scratching his beard. "It has been some years since we came here. Last time we came, we saw Vali and Vidar, two of Odin's other sons."

"There," Finn said, pointing ahead to a building that looked pretty much like the others. As we drew closer, I examined it. On a few stories, a worn rope hung suspended between the building and the next one. A few ragged pieces of cloth hung from them, wavering in the gentle breeze.

"Are those clotheslines?" Peyton asked. "Because I hate to break it to you, but if they are, the person who lived here hasn't been home for a long time."

Still, we continued to the door. Finn's instincts were a little more than hunches.

Alvan drew a small hammer from his belt, but before I could ask if that puny thing was the mighty hammer of Thor, the door burst open. A pair of men stumbled out, their arms around each other's shoulders, singing at the top of their lungs in a horrible, off-key rendition of "Row Your Boat." They listed to one side, laughing hysterically, and careened into us.

"Watch it," Xander growled, pushing one of them off him. The man's body thudded to the ground, where he lay giggling.

"It's a little early to be getting wasted, but a tavern is always a good place to get information," Peyton said.

"When have you been to a tavern?" I asked.

"I haven't," she said, swishing her pink ponytail as she strode up to the door. "But I've seen lots of movies."

For once, I wasn't the only one lacking real world experience. None of us were old enough to hang out in bars, no matter how good Xander might be at holding his liquor. From the raucous sound that had escaped when the two drunks had opened the door, this was not the kind of bar where people went to have cocktails. It was the kind of place where people went to get hammered before noon.

"Are we sure this is safe?" I asked, scanning the street before and behind us, actually hoping our Valkyrie would appear once more. Apparently, her duties only extended to welcoming newcomers, not acting as a tour guide.

"Of course it's not safe," Peyton said. "Has anything been safe since we left Midgard?"

"Good point," I said.

Xander strode up to the door and pulled it open. We had to blink several times to see into the dark interior. It looked pretty much like any bar I'd seen in a movie—dark and shadowy, people lining the bar and crowded in around the tables. Zeke stepped through the door, and everyone in the bar turned as one to see him silhouetted in the sunlit entrance.

Fear shot through me like ice water. Despite the warmth and beauty of the city, we were outsiders, and the stares only emphasized that further. Odin hadn't assured us we'd be safe. In fact, he hadn't told us much of anything about Asgard. I was getting really, really sick of being in the dark about everything.

I stepped up beside Zeke and slid my hand into his. If they wanted a fight, they were going to have to defeat all nine of us.

But no one moved to attack. They all just sat craning their necks in our direction, as if waiting.

"What's with the staring?" I muttered to Zeke. The Keens might be used to being ogled, but it still made me squirm.

"Maybe they were expecting Drunk and Drunker to come back," he said, his hand tightening around mine. Xander nudged me, and I stepped forward to let him enter behind us. The room was large and round with sconces lining the walls. I spotted at least four exits, which made me feel a little better. Tables sat around the room, most of them overflowing with people drinking from mugs. From the strong smell of alcohol in the air, they were consuming some kind of fermented beverage. A long, wooden bar bisected the room, and at least two dozen men and women sat slumped over it.

They were the only people we'd seen in Asgard, though, so there was no turning back.

"You're a god," a man said as we approached in a huddled group.

"Thor and Heimdall," Alvan said, stepping forward and doing his majestic Hercules pose, like he was waiting to be worshipped.

The man shrank back, suspicion darkening his face. "What are you doing here?"

"This is Asgard, home of the gods, is it not?" Smith asked.

"The gods haven't shown their faces here in more than a decade," a woman further down the bar said.

"It's been longer than that," a man said.

"Nonsense, I've seen gods around since then," another said. "I saw one of Odin's sons just the other day. If you ever got up off that stool and left this place, you'd see them, too."

Suddenly, a heated argument broke out as everyone weighed in on when they'd last seen a god.

"Who are you guys?" Peyton asked. "If you're not gods."

"We're humans who died in glory," someone said.

"And elves," another added.

"Smiths."

"Pirates."

"Vikings."

People went on naming what they were. There were even a few giants in the mix. But none of them were gods, who were actually supposed to be in Asgard.

"No dwarves?" I whispered to Smith. "Are your people immortal?"

"Dwarves go to Helheim," he said, scuffing the toe of his remaining boot on the grimy floor.

I drew back, indignant on his behalf. "Why?"

"It's the arrangement between Hel and the gods. That's just how it happens."

I wanted to ask more, but we had to finish our task before we worried about the souls of dead dwarves. *No distractions.* I made a mental note to keep Smith close, though. And alive.

Eliot turned back to the tavern. "What happened to all the gods?"

Everyone stopped speaking and exchanged looks.

"The gods abandoned us," someone said after a heavy pause.

"No, they went off on missions," someone else said.

"They must have been killed because they never came back."

"Gods don't die," another one said. "Not until Ragnarok."

Another argument broke out, with everyone in the bar weighing in. I was starting to get an idea of how things worked here. It was a place full of gossip, speculation, and theory. The truth might be here somewhere, but it was so tangled with opinions, falsehoods, and half-truths that we might never find it.

After a few more minutes of trying to get answers, we gave up and stepped back outside. The white streets glared so brightly we had to squint into the sunlight after being in the dark bar. The silence of the city seemed magnified after the rowdy noise of the bar. The pieces of Heimdall stood, surveying the street in silence for a long minute. It wasn't just silent. It was empty.

"Looks like we got our answer," I said at last. "The gods aren't in Asgard anymore."

Chapter Five

Gwen

On the way back to Vahalla, none of us spoke much. As we approached Valhalla, distant shouts and clangs grew louder and louder. When we reached the palace, without discussion we made our way around the walls toward the noise. We stepped around the far side of the building and halted. A giant battle raged before us. People of all shapes, sizes, and colors were stabbing and slicing each other with swords. Elves and trolls, giants and humans, and even animals raged with abandon in the muddy, bloody grass. A spear soared through the air, glancing off a shield with a loud clang. An enormous Viking fell to the ground at our feet, his skin filthy and his beard matted. A sword protruded from his belly. He screamed in agony, yanking the weapon free of his flesh. Blood sprayed from the wound.

My stomach turned, and my body began to shake. Smith bent double and puked.

"Where is he?" the Viking yelled. "I will have my revenge!"

"The only thing he's going to have is a trip to the cemetery," Peyton said, her face going green.

"These are the honorable dead," said a lilting, accented voice behind us.

"Oh, goody. Our Valkyrie's back," Peyton muttered.

I turned to Valerie, grateful to have someone whole to look at.

"They battle every day in practice for their final battle at Ragnarok," she said. "Don't worry. They're already dead. They rise again in time for the feast each night."

"You say that like it's a good thing," I said, horror still gripping me as I watched the Viking writhe around on the ground. This seemed more like hell than heaven. I'd rather die than relive this every day for eternity.

"It's good for them," Valerie said, as a roaring grizzly charged our way. "Not for us. If a spear hits you…"

"We're not dead," Eliot finished for her.

She nodded. "You will be."

"I think we've all seen enough," I said. "Can we talk to Odin again?"

"You will see him at dinner tomorrow," Valerie said, traipsing lightly along beside us, her wings spread to block us from the battle until we were out of range of the fighting.

"Odin won't be at dinner tonight?" I asked. "I mean, if we're his son, wouldn't he want us to sit with him?"

"The All-Father doesn't eat," Valerie explained. "He only drinks and listens. He is often busy seeking more knowledge. I don't believe he'll be dining in the great hall this evening."

"Then maybe you could answer some of our questions," I said.

"It would be my pleasure," she said. "I so rarely get to welcome a god home."

"Why's that?" Eliot asked. "Where are they?"

"In other worlds," she said. "Like you."

"We're not the only gods in Midgard?" Peyton asked.

"Certainly not," Valerie said. "You see, they have been waiting for Ragnarok for centuries. Over time, the gods began to believe it would never happen. They grew complacent, as did so many of our honorably slain. You probably ran into some of these poor souls in the city."

"So that's who those drunkies were," Xander said. "Bored dead guys."

"Yes," Valerie said, giving him a disapproving frown. "They have no direction. They refuse to participate in the battles to prepare. When the gods and the souls in Valhalla lost a sense of purpose, so much of our city fell into disrepair. The ravens saw the great wolf Fenrir stirring, and Odin, in his wisdom, knew he must shake the gods from their complacency. He sent them into the Nine Worlds to take up residency in other beings such as yourselves. They were to find help and prevent the battle at the end of the world from happening now."

I swallowed hard, gripping my fingers so I wouldn't come completely unhinged. If we had to gather a bunch of gods before we went home, it might take our whole lives and then some. We might never wear human clothes, or eat human food, or enjoy basic human comforts. I might never see my mom again.

"It's not really the end of the world, though," Eliot said. "Because a few gods will live and start over again, right?"

49

"It's the end of the worlds we know," Valerie said. "The end of all of us."

I shivered, tugging my hands into my sleeves. The end of all of us—gods and humans, elves and dwarves. Everyone died at Ragnarok.

"So, the gods got lazy, and then they went to inhabit a bunch of humans to do the job for them," Xander said. "When are they coming back?"

"Some of them are here," Valerie said. "But most are in another form. They will return when they have completed their task, just as you have."

"Somehow when I heard that we had to fix a bridge, I didn't think it would take quite so much time," Peyton said.

"To the gods, that's probably no time," I said, panic scraping at my insides. "Even fifteen or twenty years is nothing when you've lived thousands."

"We'll get back," Eliot said, sliding an arm around me. Tears threatened when he gave me a sympathetic smile, squeezing me against him. His kindness almost undid me.

"Thank you," I said, taking a deep breath to calm myself.

"Let's get rested tonight, have dinner with Odin tomorrow, and see what we can find out," Zeke said. "Then we'll figure out what to do next."

I nodded, not trusting myself to speak. I'd thought we were so close, that all we had to do was cross Bifrost, and the hardest part would be over. I'd expected Asgard to be full of gods who were all too willing to help us by traipsing across our bridge a few times. Now, it looked like we had to start all over—traveling through the Nine Worlds in search of other gods instead of our own missing pieces.

"Let me show you to your rooms," Valerie said. "Odin has requested that you stay in the rooms reserved for honored guests."

"We are his son, after all," Alvan said, looking as if he'd expected nothing less. He had been here before, after all, even if years had passed since then.

Valerie led us inside the palace and to a staircase on one side that hugged the wall. We climbed up and up. Even though only a railing separated us from the drop, my stomach barely lurched when I looked down. I'd conquered my fear of heights. Mostly. At last, we reached a walkway leading along a mezzanine with doors on one side and a railing on the other. Far below, we could see the tables set up in concentric circles, waiting for their slain warriors to come feast.

Ahead, Valerie opened a door. Peyton let out an ear-piercing shriek. Pain ripped through my chest at the sound of her distress, and I raced forward without thought. Before I reached her, Peyton dashed into the room. I dove past Valerie, blood rushing in my ears. Peyton lay on her back on the bed, moving her arms and legs as if she were making a snow angel on the thick blanket.

"A real bed," she moaned.

"You scared me to death, you jerk," I said, laughing. "After all that's happened, you should know better than to scream for joy."

"Sorry, not sorry," she said with a sigh. "Oh my gods, Gwen, you have to feel this. Come lay down." She patted the bed beside her, and after a second's hesitation, I joined her. As I sank into the thick down comforter, a moan of pleasure escaped me.

"Totally not jealous right now," Zeke said.

I couldn't even open my eyes to respond. The bed cradled every inch of my sore, battered body in its cloudlike embrace. I hadn't realized how much I'd missed having a real bed. Even sleeping in the backseat of a car or on a thin mattress on the cement floor of a storage locker was better than sleeping on the ground, as we'd done lately. And it must have been even harder for the Keens, who were used to living with every comfort money could provide.

Peyton sat straight up, her eyes widening. "Do you think they have a shower?"

"Odin can see all worlds," Valerie said from the doorway. "His ravens bring back knowledge of the comforts from many faraway places."

"Does that include showers?" Peyton asked. "With running water and everything?"

"It did get a little old having to carry buckets of water in Alfheim," Zeke said.

"How about hot water?" Xander asked. "That we don't have to heat in kettles over a fire?"

"There are hot showers," Valerie said, giving them an amused, indulgent smile, as if dealing with silly children. I guess we were acting like it. The simple pleasures meant so much more after going without. Just being on a soft bed was enough for me. I wanted to stay there forever with my new family and the other members of my god surrounding me.

"We can eat meat here, right?" Zeke asked.

"There is wild boar for dinner every night," Valerie confirmed.

"Wait, when you say the gods borrow the best from all worlds, does that include coffee?" Peyton asked.

"What about Wi-Fi?" Eliot asked.

"Motorcycles?" Xander asked.

"Beets?" Smith said.

We all blinked at him like owls. I spoke first. "Are you talking about Beats, like the headphones, or beets like the vegetable?"

"I don't know headphones," he said with a stiff shrug. "They didn't have beets in the giant world. I was there looking for you for months. And dwarves live underground. We eat a lot of root vegetables. Beets are my favorite."

"Wait, you were in Jotunheim for months?" I asked. "Why?"

"The runes predicted I would meet you there," he said. "They're never wrong." Though he'd been dashingly dressed when I'd met him, he was now as disheveled as the rest of us. His ruffled white sleeves were filthy, his frock coat torn, and he'd lost a shoe. But aside from his fashion sense, I didn't know much about him.

"You can read runestones?" I asked, bringing my mind back to the issue at hand. "That means you can tell the future, right?"

"Oh, not me," he said. "Your dwarf came back to Nidavellir and told me."

"Rosa," Finn said, looking alive for the first time in days. "Where is she?"

In all the chaos and drama with Finn, I'd almost forgotten their housekeeper. I was a little ashamed of that, but we'd been busy trying to save the entire Nine Worlds, so I hoped she'd forgive us for leaving her to her own devices.

"She had been banished," Smith said. "I grew up hearing her story. She refused to learn an acceptable trade, and so she was cast out of Nidavellir."

"That seems harsh," I said, remembering Smith's story about not being good with his hands. No wonder he hadn't flat out refused. He'd be kicked out of his entire world if he did.

"Dwarves are proud of their heritage," he said. "Sometimes rightly so, but sometimes, they are simply inflexible. Rosa went to Midgard when she was banished, you see. Though dwarves are strictly conformist, they also do not hold grudges. They lifted her banishment, but no dwarves could get into Midgard to tell her."

"Then how did she get in?" Eliot asked.

"She must have found an entrance. Whatever the case, we all knew about the banished sorceress who disappeared into Midgard never to be seen again."

"Wait," Xander said. "You're saying Rosa is a sorceress?"

"She can read rune stones, can't she?" Smith asked. "Apparently when she met Ratr, she learned her banishment had been lifted long ago. She went home to see her family in Nidavellir."

"I bet that dirty rat told her we were planning to stab her in the back or something," Peyton said.

"I'm sure he did," Smith said with a shudder. "And once he gets you alone, when you have no rational person to help you keep your senses, it's easy to believe whatever he says."

"Rosa has a family?" Finn asked. "She never told us that."

"Yeah, well, there's a lot of things the adults in our lives never told us," Peyton said.

"Maybe she didn't want to talk about it," I said. I wondered if Mom talked to Neil about me, or if it was too painful to remember the daughter who had disappeared into another world.

"When she came home, she was a bit of celebrity," Smith said. "Everyone went to see her, so they could have her ask the runes about their futures. Of course, the runes didn't speak to her about most of them, but I guess I was lucky." He shrugged, eyeing the door to the hallway. If I were him, I'd probably need a break from all this craziness, too. I had to remember he was brand new to being a god. The rest of us had months to come to terms with it. He was doing amazingly well, considering.

"If we're going to dine with the god of all the gods tomorrow, we should probably take tonight to get cleaned up and rested," I said, giving Smith a nod.

He hadn't had time to figure all this out, and he probably thought it would be rude to leave us all. I'd gotten used to the constant buzz of energy that wasn't just the gods, but the Keens themselves. I'd had months to adjust, but it had definitely overwhelmed me at first.

I climbed off Peyton's bed and joined the others who were all clustered around the door, some inside the room and some not. "Do we each have a room?" I asked Valerie.

"I thought a few of you could share," she said. "I've had five of our finest rooms made up with all the comforts of your own home. Would you like more?"

"No, that's wonderful," Eliot said quickly. "Thank you for being so thoughtful."

I bit my tongue, guilt flooding through me. We were being treated wonderfully, and I felt like a selfish bitch for wanting more. On the other hand, I wouldn't have minded a room to be alone for just a few minutes. I might have gotten used to being surrounded by eight other people, but that didn't mean I didn't want just one hour of blessed solitude. I'd spent most of my life alone, and though I was glad I didn't have to be alone anymore, the truth was I sometimes missed what I'd spent most of my life hating.

"We can be roomies," Peyton said, bouncing off the bed and linking her arm through mine. "It'll be like we're off at college sharing a dorm room. Oh, this is so exciting."

"I'll take suicide watch," Xander said.

"You don't have to watch me," Finn said, glaring at his brother.

"Fuck that," Xander said. "I'll stop watching you when you start seeing a shrink."

"We'll share," Alvan said, motioning to Valdan.

"We share everything," Valdan added.

"I bet you do," Valerie said, eyeing them with appreciation.

"I can share with the new guy," Zeke said, smiling at Smith. "If you wanted. I don't want to room with Eliot and leave you out."

"It's okay," Smith said. "Really. I'd hate to take anyone's place."

"No one can take Eliot's place," Zeke said, throwing an arm around Eliot's shoulder. "There couldn't possibly be a bigger pain in the ass in all the Nine Worlds."

"There's one," Eliot countered.

"I think you two should room together," I said. "You obviously have some issues to work out."

"Then it's all settled," Valerie said.

Smith shot me a grateful smile over his shoulder as the group went off down the hall to find their rooms. I closed the door and turned, only to find myself alone with Peyton. The silence hung heavy in the air between us. I hadn't been alone with her since she'd sat in a cold bath and held me while I'd cried after losing my virginity. I didn't know what to say, and for once, she didn't have a snarky comment or a complaint about the lack of coffee. In that moment, she was just Peyton, the girl who missed her mom, her dad, and her girlfriend.

I tugged my hands up into the sleeves of my shirt. "So…"

"So." Peyton examined a hangnail.

"Does anyone else feel like this is too good to be true?" I asked. "Like it must be a trap because nothing goes this right for us?"

"If it's a trap, I don't want to know until after a shower," Peyton said.

"Do you mind if I take a nap?"

"Hell, no," she said. "Girl, I'll be doing the exact same thing as soon as I'm done."

I bit my lip. There was only one bed. "I'm not ready to have sex," I blurted.

Peyton drew back, eyeing me as if she thought I might be about to explode. "Okay…"

"Again," I muttered, my face burning.

"Again?"

I took a breath. "I'm not ready to have sex *again*."

"Okay, where is this coming from?" she asked, sitting cross-legged on the bed. "Was I putting off an 'I'm about to jump your bones' vibe?"

"No, but…I mean, there's only one bed, and we'll be sleeping in it together."

"Yeah," she said, giving a slow nod.

"And I just didn't want you to think…I mean, I do like you. It's just—"

"Um, hello, I'm not ready to hook up, either."

"You're not?"

She laughed and shook her head like she couldn't believe me. "Seriously, Gwen. I'm not some horndog who wants to jump into every girl's panties the moment we meet."

"I know," I said, crossing my arms and wishing I'd kept my mouth shut and gone straight to sleep. "But we kissed, and we like each other."

"And you're not ready. So why would you think I am?"

"I don't know," I said. "I guess because you've done it before?"

"So, you think that because I've had sex I'm automatically turned on and ready to go anytime with anyone?"

I had kind of thought that anyone who had sex wanted to do it again whenever they had the chance. Which was stupid, obviously, because I'd had sex, and I wasn't dying to be alone with anyone so I could get it on.

Peyton shook her head and pulled a pillow into her lap. "Wow."

"I'm sorry," I said, slumping onto the edge of the bed. "I'm an asshole."

Peyton smiled, hugging her pillow. "Yeah, kind of."

"I know. I suck."

"It's cool," she said, hopping off the bed. "We all suck at times. Now that that's out of the way, I'm going to check out this hot water. The cold bath yesterday didn't really do it for me." She headed into the en suite bathroom, and a minute later, she started belting out a Beyoncé song as the shower ran.

I was being ridiculous. We'd slept in the same bed—all eight of us—for three months while I was recovering from a dragon bite. I'd slept on the ground next to her a dozen times. It just felt different when it was a real bed, in our size, in a room with actual privacy. It felt intimate.

We'd kissed once, but she'd been drunk. I didn't know if it really counted. I didn't even know if I wanted it to count. I still didn't know if I liked girls, and maybe I'd never know, but it didn't matter anymore. I liked this girl.

I liked this person. The labels and differences people used in Midgard seemed artificial here. It didn't matter that I wasn't attracted to girls in general, and that Peyton happened to be a girl. That didn't change the fact that I liked Peyton the person, regardless of whether or not she was a certain gender, orientation, sex, or even species. She could have been a scaly green dragon for all I cared. She was cheerful and peppy and chatty. She was tough and badass and fierce. She was all girl, and all Peyton, and I loved her.

Chapter Six

Peyton

I don't think I'd ever realized how magical showers could be until the moment I stepped under the hot, steamy water in Valhalla. I mean, they kept me clean and washed sand off after going to the beach, and I enjoyed a bubble bath as much as the next girl, but they were a whole other level of amazing I'd never appreciated until I'd gone without. I'd been lucky to have a cold shower since leaving Midgard, and the only time I got hot water was when we'd heated it in kettles in Alfheim and carried it to the tub. I'd always taken things like warm running water for granted.

Now as I stood shampooing my bedraggled hair for the third time, I wondered how many times Gwen had gone without in her life. Growing up like she did, our house in Cape Cod had probably felt this luxurious to her. She never really talked about it, though. I'd be embarrassed about it if it were me, too, but I decided I was going to at least let her know I was here if she wanted to talk. I was slowly coming to appreciate how hard her life must have been.

ASCEND

I climbed out of the shower and toweled off, only to realize I didn't have clean clothes. All I had were the leathers I'd picked up in Alfheim after the elves stole most of my clothes, and there was no way I was putting those filthy things back on. They'd probably stand up by themselves. I peeked out into the bedroom and found Gwen curled up on the bed, her body sinking into the feather mattress, the comforter pulled up to her chin.

I tucked the thick towel under my arms and started for the closet, smiling to myself at the sight of Gwen's little face peeking out from under the blanket. I was halfway across the room when I caught sight of my reflection in the ornately carved mirror on one wall. The frame depicted two chariots, one pulling the moon and the other the sun, chasing each other around the circular mirror for all eternity. The glass inside the frame showed my face, a ridiculous, goofy grin plastered all over it, my eyes all moony and faraway.

I stopped and took a breath. Oh, this was bad. "You're totally smitten," I accused myself in a whisper.

My reflection blinked back at me like a lovestruck puppy. Shit. I didn't even know if Gwen liked girls. Sure, she'd kissed me, but had it been just the god drawing us together? She definitely liked boys. I'd seen that firsthand. Or was that just the god, too? Without Heimdall, would any of us like each other, even as friends?

Did it matter?

If we were part Heimdall and part human, did it matter which part of us liked each other? Did one part know better than another what our hearts wanted? Was it more real or less if it was the god pulling us together? After all, it seemed like something ordained by even a minor deity must be pretty pure.

But what if Gwen saw it differently? When I'd kissed her, I'd been drunk. Maybe I'd read her response wrong. I'd based a lot of assumptions on that kiss. Now here I was, throwing caution to the wind and tossing my heart in the hat with all my brothers. I'd never competed with them for a girl—I'd never had to. I didn't generally like the type of girl who went after the Xanders and the Zekes of the world.

For the first time, I liked a girl who liked my brothers—all of my brothers. And maybe the twins and Smith, too. She hadn't really distinguished between the Keens and the rest of Heimdall's pieces when she made her big proclamation. I liked to think we meant more to her than the others, but maybe that was wishful thinking. As odd as it had been, it had felt right in that moment. Only later did I think more about it. None of us had really said much back, aside from telling her it was okay to like us all, and we weren't going to make her decide or judge her.

"I like you, too," I whispered into the mirror, looking at her. My heartbeat thumped in my ears, and I checked the bed to make sure she was sleeping and hadn't heard me. Admitting this was harder than I'd expected. I licked my lips and tried again. My palms were sweating. What if she hadn't meant me, but she'd wanted to spare my feelings?

Hey, guys, I like you all. Oh, except you, Peyton. Your lack of penis is going to pose a problem.

Great. Now, I was starting to sound like a tongue twister.

Peyton Piper picked a pickle of peppered peckers.

ASCEND

I closed my eyes, taking a deep breath. I was losing it.

Get it together, Peyton. You're a cheerleader. Tighten up your pony and find your inner pep or get off the field.

I opened my eyes. That was it, then. I wasn't getting off the field. Until she said I was out, I wasn't giving up. Little Peyton was here to play with the big boys.

Chapter Seven

Gwen

I woke the next morning to find Peyton perched on a stool in front of the mirror, running a comb through her long, pink locks.

"Did I sleep all night?" I asked, pushing up on my elbows. A weird jealousy gripped me, like I'd missed out on tons of fun by sleeping when everyone else had been awake.

Peyton slumped and dropped the hand holding the comb to her knee. "My hair looks like crap."

"No, it doesn't."

"Um, hello, two inches of dishwater blonde roots," she said, holding up a handful of hair. "You're so beautiful."

I snorted. "Hardly. And since when do you care about your looks?"

She gave me a strange look. "Since always? Just because I'm a lesbian, doesn't mean I'm not also a sixteen-year-old girl."

"Sorry," I said. "I've just never seen you being insecure."

"Maybe I should just chop it all off," she said. "Think I could pull off a pixie cut?"

"If that's what you want," I said. "Or they might have hair dye here. You never know."

A knock sounded at the door, and Valerie slipped into the room. She'd lost the crown and changed into a golden, satin gown. "Oh good, I'm just in time to help you dress," she said.

Peyton gestured at the towel tied around her body. "This is about it," she said. "Unless you have something that will clean leather."

"I brought your wardrobe," Valerie said, swinging open a set of double doors. Behind her, an enormous closet stretched back as far as I could see, clothes hanging along each wall.

"Oh my gods," Peyton shrieked, flying off her stool and into the closet.

I winced, covering my ears as she shrieked again from the depths of the closet. This time, I knew she wasn't dying—just killing my eardrums.

"Are these really my clothes?" she yelled.

"Yes," Valerie said with an amused smile. "It's really not complicated to bring them through from Midgard. You can't exactly dine with Odin wearing elven leathers. If I'd had more time, I could have taken your measurements to the tailor, but on such short notice, and with so many of you, this was the best I could do."

"Oh, my ever-loving goddess of all that is good and holy, I think I'm in love with you," Peyton called. "Will you marry me? No offense, Gwen."

"None taken," I said, though I wasn't sure. She hadn't said she liked me back, after all. I couldn't be bitter if she wanted someone else when I'd flat out told her I wanted all of them.

"You can't marry me," Valerie said.

Peyton's head poked out of the closet. "Why not?"

"Why, because I'm a woman," Valerie said in her oh-so-proper London accent, which made her sound truly scandalized.

"And your point is?" Peyton asked.

"Well, it just isn't done."

"Just *wasn't* done," Peyton said. "Times have changed, my lady. You can marry whoever you damn well please nowadays."

"You like women?"

"Yep," Peyton said, popping her lips on the final sound. "Is that a problem?"

"I don't know," Valerie said. "I've never met someone like you."

"You mean a lesbian?" I asked, my temper rising. I climbed out of bed and went to join Peyton at the closet entrance. "Peyton's not some kind of freak. She's just as much a girl as me or you. Probably more. And there's nothing wrong with her liking other girls."

Valerie's eyes moved back and forth between us. "You love each other?"

I folded my hand into Peyton's and squeezed. My heart hammered, and my throat went dry. Somehow, it was easier to look at Valerie than Peyton when I said it. I opened my mouth, but before I could speak, Peyton did.

"Yes," she said quietly.

My heart staggered against my ribcage. Now, it seemed impossible I'd almost said those words for the first time while looking at someone else. I faced Peyton, taking her other hand in mine. "Me, too," I said.

To my surprise, her eyes shone with tears. Without thinking, I leaned forward and pressed my lips to hers.

"This is unusual," Valerie said.

I pulled back, heat rushing to my face. Peyton gave me a quick smile before answering Valerie.

"Probably not as unusual as you think," she said. "Women just kept it hidden in your time."

"I imagine you're right," Valerie said. "It's still a little hard to believe so much time has passed."

"You don't have to hang around if it makes you uncomfortable," I said.

Valerie paused a moment before shaking her head. "No," she said. "I should check on the others, though. If they're as excited about their closets as you are, they won't want to miss them."

She glided through the wall like a ghost and disappeared, leaving Peyton and me alone. I was all too aware of her hand in mine.

"Thanks," she said after a long, awkward pause.

"Don't thank me," I said. "I meant it. I love you, Peyton."

"I love you, too," she whispered. For once, she looked as uncertain and vulnerable as I felt.

"I like kissing you," I blurted.

Peyton laughed softly. "I like kissing you, too. A lot."

We stood there looking at each other for a long moment. Then she stepped forward, sliding her small hand behind my neck. Her lashes curled softly against her cheek as she moved closer, her eyes on my lips. Our lips met, just a gentle touch at first. A delicious tingling sensation swept across my skin, and I shivered with longing. I'd never felt anything as soft in my entire life. I brushed my lips across hers again, marveling at her delicious softness, her warmth, her sweetness. Slowly, I parted her lips with my own, sliding my tongue between her lips to touch the warm wetness within.

A tremor went through her, and her body swooned against mine. Suddenly, my shyness from the day before returned. She was almost definitely not wearing anything under that towel.

I pulled away. "I need to brush my teeth."

"And shower," she said, her breath coming quicker.

We stood there, not speaking for a long moment.

"Valerie was pretty freaked out," I said.

"Yeah, she was."

We both grinned, but there was something shy in it.

"So... I'll just—" I gestured to the bathroom.

"Oh, yeah, totally," Peyton said.

We both burst out laughing, the awkwardness too much for even Peyton. She slung an arm around my neck and kissed my cheek. "I swear I'm not usually such a dumbass," she said. "Now, go get a shower. I'm starving."

She gave my ass a little swat, and I yelped and ducked into the bathroom. I caught my reflection, the smile on my face so giddy and genuine it stopped me in my tracks. I was happy. Somehow, despite all the craziness, I'd found a little bubble of happiness. I'd found home. Not in the Keen's crazy mansion, but in their family.

Chapter Eight

Gwen

After a long day of exploring the city and finding out nothing new, we returned to Valhalla to dress for our dinner with the All-Father. Considering what an honor it was, I was doubly nervous. First, because I was likely to say something stupid and wind up banished or something, and second, because I really wanted to ask him a favor, and I didn't know how he'd react to a request from a human on our second meeting. But I had to know about my mom.

I was surprised to find Valerie back in our room when we returned to the palace. She was searching through the closet for a suitable outfit for us to wear to dinner. "I'd like to hear how the world has changed since I died," she said from deep in the bowels of the closet. "If you wouldn't mind sharing that with me."

"You're not going to freak out about us liking each other?" Peyton asked.

"I can't say I truly understand your world, but who you love has very little to do with that," Valerie said, emerging from the closet with an armload of dresses. "I would like to hear more about it, if you don't mind."

Her haughty attitude had been replaced with one of curiosity and wistfulness, and my heart softened toward her again. Of course, she wouldn't be completely enlightened about modern attitudes. She was willing to learn, though, and she wanted to know about the world she'd left behind. If I couldn't go back to our world, I'd want all the information I could get, too.

"As ridiculous as it sounds, people had to fight long and hard for the right to love whomever they want," Peyton said, hovering in the door to the closet. "I don't suppose it would be super cool to show up to dinner with Papa God wearing yoga pants and Uggs?"

"I don't know what that is," Valerie said. "But considering that women didn't wear trousers when I lived in Midgard, I'm guessing my sense of style is a bit behind the times."

"Are you kidding?" Peyton asked. "Flappers are trending so hard right now."

"A gown would be a wise choice," Valerie said. "Tell me what else has changed. Did women win the right to vote?"

"Women can do everything men can," Peyton said. "They might have to work twice as hard to get there, and three times as hard to keep it once they've gotten it, but basically, we can have it all."

While we dressed, we gave Valerie a crash course in the last century of human history. Since Peyton and I were similar in size, they were able to find something that fit me, too, though we had to alter it by adding a sash and a capelet. When we'd finished, Valerie stood back and surveyed us before giving her approval.

"Odin will be pleased to dine with his son again," she said. "So few gods have come back since leaving this world."

"Does anyone know where they are?" I asked.

"Odin does, of course," Valerie said. "His ravens travel between all worlds."

"Do you think they could bring us news about our parents?" I asked.

"I'm sure they could," Valerie said. "But that's a favor you'll have to ask Odin yourself."

My stomach fluttered at the thought facing him and asking for something that must seem like such a petty human concern. But that wasn't going to stop me from finding out about my mother. For the first time since we'd left Midgard, things seemed to be going our way. Or at least they were within our reach. I could find out about Mom at last. We could figure out where the other gods were. Joaquin was gone, Rosa was safe at home with her family, and we'd crossed Bifrost. Hell, Peyton even had her wardrobe back.

We were so close.

Valerie led us from the room, and I paused at a window in the hall. The scene before me was like a child's fantasy. The sun sank low in the west, rays of red and pink lighting up the gold and silver splendor of the city. Every roof and window reflected the sunset with unapologetic purpose. It might be overdone and gaudy, but there was a strange beauty in that. The gods didn't worry about being too much or going overboard. They went all in, almost boasting about their desire to inspire awe, instead of being coy and pretentious about it.

Though I hadn't realized it, I'd gotten used to their ways over the past few months. Alvan and Valdan were gods through and through. I'd thought their pride was an elf thing, but it was clearly not. It was a god thing. I could only hope one day I'd have that kind of confidence.

A hand grazed my back and I startled, sucking in a breath. Eliot smiled down at me, a dimple sinking into his cheek, his brown eyes lit up behind his glasses. He'd changed his leathers for a slim-cut black suit and bow tie. His face was clean-shaven, his hair neatly trimmed and slicked back with the marks of a comb still evident in it. "Wow," I breathed.

The corner of his mouth quirked up higher. "Yeah?"

"Yeah," I said. "You look…good." I winced at my own words, but when he laughed, I joined him. So, I was still awkward. There were worse things to be.

"You look good, too," Eliot murmured. Zeke joined us wearing a suit obviously tailored for his bulkier frame. It fit him every bit as well as Eliot's, showing off his broad shoulders and tapered waist. The Valkyries had apparently worked their magic on everyone's closet.

"May I escort the lady?" Zeke asked, holding out an elbow.

"I'm one step ahead of you," Eliot said, linking his arm through mine.

"I have two arms," I said, slipping my hand into the crook of Zeke's elbow. I smiled up at him and then Eliot, a wave of shyness following my bold statement. "Is this okay?"

"More than okay," Zeke said, tucking my hand against him and returning my smile with that dizzying grin that always undid me.

"It's perfect," Eliot agreed, giving me a more reserved smile.

A minute later, Xander and Finn each appeared dressed in well-tailored suits like their brothers. My head got all swoony, and I cursed my luck that a playboy god had chosen me as his host. Maybe that's why I lusted so hard after my stepbrothers. Finn's hair was neatly combed back and secured in a low ponytail, showing off his fine bone structure and high cheekbones. His lightly tanned skin looked so soft and flawless, I wanted to run my fingertips along his cheeks like I had before.

I pulled my attention away from him, only to find Xander's eyes blazing with desire as his gaze meandered slowly down my body. Taking advantage of his distraction, I let myself admire him, too. His tailored pants hugged his long, muscular legs, just snug enough to make me gulp when my inspection reached the bulge in his pants. He wore a gunmetal grey shirt buttoned almost to the collar, but he'd left a few undone at the top. I could just make out the outline of his sculpted, muscular chest and abs through the thin fabric which stretched taut across his broad shoulders. He held a jacket slung over his shoulder, hooked on two fingers.

Instead of his usual smirk when he caught me looking, Xander stared openly, his smoldering gaze making my blood sing for his. A chord of longing hummed somewhere deep inside me, and I barely kept myself from moaning aloud. It would be a minor miracle if I could keep my hands off him tonight.

Valdan and Alvan joined us wearing what must be formal wear for elves—linen shirts with laces up the front and soft suede pants, their beards combed and hair tied back. Smith was the last to shuffle out of his room dressed to the nines in a velvet suit and silk shirt with lace cuffs and collar. He looked so lost and uncertain I wished I could hold his hand, too. Instead, I offered him a smile.

"This is new to all of us," I said, as he lingered a few steps away. "Just stay with the group and we'll be fine." I wasn't sure if I was trying to convince him or myself.

We descended the stairs to where the tables were filling with the honorable dead. It was strange to think of them that way since they looked as alive as my siblings and me. Beautiful blonde Valkyries swooped between tables, serving food and drink to the dead.

"I have been assigned the honor of serving at your table tonight," Valerie said, gesturing for us to make our way to the center of the room where Odin sat at the head of the longest table I'd ever seen. It must have stretched across an entire acre of floor. Two beings sat to his right, both of them glowing with an unearthly beauty as they watched us approach.

"These are the only gods left in Asgard," Valerie said as she delivered us to Odin. "So you can see why your homecoming has caused a stir."

"Come and sit at my other side, my sons," Odin said, gesturing to the empty seats to his left. Alvan and Valdan strutted over and took their seats. They blended seamlessly with the others, their glow melding with that of the three gods already seated. Their boldness made me feel better about sitting at a table with the highest of all the gods. We all bowed and gave our greetings, and then Zeke pulled out my chair. I shook my head and slid into the empty seat next to Finn instead, letting Zeke fill the seat on my other side.

"I'm afraid in my human form, I don't know these gods," Eliot said.

"Vidar and Vali," Odin said, gesturing to the other two gods. "Your brothers, of course."

The others started introducing themselves and exchanging pleasantries, but Finn turned to me.

"What are you doing?" he asked quietly, his eyes fixing on mine with such hurt it made my breath stop in my throat.

I swallowed past the ache and hunched my shoulders. "You don't want me to sit next to you?"

"No, I do," he said. "But…"

Suddenly, all I could think about was our bodies tangled together in the woods, his skin burning against mine, his breath mixing with mine as I inhaled. Heat spread across my chest and up my neck, and I tugged at the capelet over my shoulders, wishing it covered more of me—all of me. I wanted to be wrapped inside a sleeping bag, buried so deeply I was hidden from his eyes, from the eyes of all of them.

"I'm sorry," I said. "You're right. This is stupid." Tears burned behind my eyes, and I struggled to push my chair back before he could see them. The leg of my wooden chair caught with his, and I lurched to a stop.

"Gwen." He spoke softly, his warm hand brushing my forearm. "It's okay."

But it wasn't okay. I shook my head, staring down at my lap. A single teardrop landed and soaked into the black fabric, disappearing as if it had never been there at all. No one had to know it had been. No one was looking at me.

No one cared what I had done with Finn, done to Finn, except the two of us.

"I'm sorry," I said again, another tear forcing itself between my lashes. I squeezed my eyes closed and inhaled slowly, hoping he wouldn't hear the shakiness in my breath.

"Me, too," he said, his fingertips brushing my elbow again.

A chill exploded across my skin, racing up my spine and tingling all the way to the crown of my head, now piled high with my long hair. I remembered how warm and reassuring I'd always found Finn's touch, how it could settle me when I was freaking out. All that was gone.

I'd fucked up so bad.

Zeke leaned back, placing his arm along the back of my chair and squeezing my shoulders. "Everything okay?" he asked.

I counted to three and then lifted my head. I would not sit at a table with gods and hang my head in shame. Heimdall had instructed me to bring us all together and I had. *I* had done that. And even though I didn't think it had been worth the price we'd paid when we almost lost Finn because he freaked out over it and ran off with Joaquin, I wasn't going to spend the whole night crying because I'd made yet another stupid decision and sat next to him. I'd wanted to pretend things were okay between us, but of course they weren't. I'd wanted him to act like he always had—like nothing had changed. But everything had changed.

He had changed, but I had, too. I had made mistakes, and I was learning from them. I wasn't that naïve, weak, scared girl who had stumbled onto their porch with my mother in tow. I was a god, and if I had to remind myself of it every five minutes to get through the day, that's what I'd do.

"Everything is fine," I said, taking Zeke's hand hanging over my shoulder. I linked my fingers through his thick, strong ones, taking courage from his grip. He was just as steady as Finn, if not as deep. He was happy and easy and uncomplicated, all the things I needed right now.

"Good," he said. "It's nice to have a real dinner and a real bed to sleep in."

"Yeah," I said, relaxing against him, so grateful for the small talk I could have cried all over again. While he made conversation, I found my tears drying. I was okay. I could get through this.

As promised, Valerie served us wild boar, which was almost as amazing as lobster, though about as far from my first fancy dinner with the Keens as you could get. The hall was deafening with the sound of thousands of people eating and drinking the mugs of ale flowing freely. Fights broke out at several tables, with people flinging roasted root vegetables at each other and someone being stabbed. Apparently, when people died, they stopped worrying about personal safety.

Odin told us a long story about a council of gods that he, Vidar, and Vali wanted to form once more gods returned to Asgard. Vali explained how his and Vidar's hosts had been killed, so they were back in god form. Finally, though, I found an opening and asked the question I'd been waiting to ask all night.

"Can your ravens give us an update on our human parents?" I asked, trying to phrase the question in a way that wouldn't deny Odin was our father god.

"I can send them to check on any human I wish," Odin said, his one eye fixed on me.

"Of course," I said, nodding.

"I haven't had a reason to watch your human mother since you left her side," Odin said. "What is your concern?"

"She's not all that well," I admitted. "I just thought maybe you'd know something."

"Do not despair," Odin said. "For you are close to completing your mission and returning to Midgard for a time." He held up his hand, and two ravens descended to perch on either shoulder.

"These are his main spies," Alvan said. "Huginn and Muninn. They can pass through all Nine Worlds without resistance."

"And they're especially nice to look at," Valdan said.

I gave him a little bit of side-eye for that one. It was one thing for elves to be attracted to humans, quite another to be attracted to birds.

"I will allow them to escort you on your quest to find the other gods," Odin said. "And my two sons here will be of much help. They are the strongest of all gods."

I held my tongue, though I knew not all his sons had fared so well. His perfect son, Baldur, had been killed by a trick of Loki's.

"Are they strong enough to repair the bridge?" Xander asked.

"They will help greatly," Odin said. "They will both survive the end at Ragnarok."

So, they were the gods predestined to live on and rebuild when everyone else died. Lucky them. By the time that happened, I planned to be long dead.

"Do you know how many gods we'll need to make Bifrost strong again?" I asked.

Odin closed his eye and stroked his beard. "Thor, Heimdall, and Vidar and Vali should strengthen it quite a bit. If you can add Freya and Frey to your procession, their strength shall add to the power of the bridge, so that others may pass."

Only two more gods to go. We could totally do this.

"It will be good to have the gods back in Asgard," Odin said. "Of course, I hear about their exploits from my ravens, but a feast with many of them together will bring me great pleasure. Would you like to meet my ravens?"

I glanced around at the others. Were we supposed to talk to birds? Then again, we'd talked to a squirrel, and I already knew Odin talked to the ravens. To humans, he'd look like a crazy man, but we weren't in the human world anymore.

"We'd love to," I said.

The two ravens flapped their wings and rose into the air, then exploded in a burst of feathers and flapping wings. After seeing dragons, giants, and an eight-legged flying horse, nothing should have surprised me, but I still gasped when two women appeared out of thin air. Black, feathered garments covered their bodies, and I had to surmise they were some sort of shapeshifting beings. I remembered all the times my mother had told me ravens were watching us. It was definitely creepier if they were half human.

"Pleased to meet you," Eliot said, standing from the table and offering a hand.

"The pleasure is mine," Huginn said in the raspy voice of a middle-aged, chain-smoking bar wench. "We have kept watch over all the gods since they left our world."

"We can easily locate any of them," Muninn said in a sticky-sweet, baby voice that was about as opposite her companion's as possible. "Although of course it will be harder for you to pass from one world to the next."

Damn it. I should have known it wouldn't be easy.

"Then it is agreed," Odin said. "My ravens will guide your way to the other gods, and you will bring them here for a feast. For now, stay here, eat well, and rest for your journey."

"And our parents?" I asked. "The ones in Midgard?"

"I'll check on them," Valerie said. "I can move through worlds, too."

"Thank you," I said, my throat tightening as I smiled at her. I wanted to say more, to hug her until she couldn't breathe. As annoying as I'd found her at first, she had quickly turned into my favorite person in Asgard. She gave me an indifferent shrug before picking up a pitcher, but I caught a hint of sadness in her smile as she leaned to refill my mug.

Chapter Nine

Gwen

When we left the hall, we were all swaying a bit, but I wasn't nearly as drunk as I'd been at the giant's house. The others were more talkative than usual, but otherwise they didn't seem to be too wasted, either. I found my pulse picking up as Peyton and I stopped at our room. Last time she'd stumbled into bed with me after a bit too much to drink, we'd ended up kissing. Did she think because I'd agreed to share a room that it meant I was ready for more? Was I?

After what had happened with Finn, I didn't know if I'd ever be ready. I'd thought I was doing the right thing. I'd been so sure of myself and I'd been wrong. What if I was wrong again?

I shot Peyton a questioning look, but she didn't notice. She skipped into the room and flung herself face down on the bed. "Oh my god, this really is heaven," she said, her voice muffled by the down comforter. "As the gods are my witnesses, I will never sleep on the ground again."

"Did you just semi-quote *Gone with the Wind?*"

"I might have."

"That's my favorite book."

Peyton rolled over and propped herself on one elbow. "I didn't know that."

"Have you read it?"

"Yeah."

We stared at each other for a long, silent moment.

At last, Peyton cleared her throat. "Why are you looking at me like that?"

"I'm just...it's weird, okay? Sleeping in the same bed. It's kind of freaking me out."

There. I'd said it. I'd told them all I'd be more open about my feelings, and I had to at least try, even if it made her mad. I gripped my capelet together, waiting for her to snap at me.

"That's fair," she said. "What do you want to do? I should probably be all noble and volunteer to sleep on the floor, but nope. I'm not that nice. No way in hell am I wasting the chance to sleep in a real bed."

"I wouldn't want you to," I said. "I just wanted you to know how I feel. I can't help it. I trust you. It's just this is all pretty new for me."

"Me, too," she said. "It's okay if you're freaked out, but you should know I'm not going to try anything. I'm not some gropey perv who can't keep my hands to myself. I'll stay on my side of the bed. Cool?"

"Cool," I said. After we both had time to brush our teeth and change into pajamas, I slid down under the blankets, and Peyton put out the light.

The bed shifted as she lay down, too. "Goodnight."

"Goodnight. And thanks for not being mad at me."

"I'm not going to be mad at you for telling me how you feel, Gwen."

I tried to sleep, but even when I heard Peyton's breathing deepen and her body go heavy on the mattress, I was awake. A week ago, I would have been dying to kiss her, to slide across the bed and attach to her like a barnacle. I didn't think it was just my wariness of having a repeat of the Finn debacle that was stopping me, either. Because let's face it, Peyton was not Finn. She would have handled that situation a hell of a lot better than either of us.

But despite my proximity to Peyton and the rare opportunity to be alone, I felt more like...myself. Like a normal, awkward, human girl. The pull of the god to be near my pieces seemed to have lessened since we reached Asgard. I had expected the relief I felt when it faded, but I hadn't anticipated the fear that came with it.

I found myself tossing and turning with anxiety. What if Heimdall's influence continued to fade? What if my feelings for them had been his doing all along, and I didn't want to be with them at all once he was satisfied with our performance? What if their feelings for me disappeared? What if they'd never been real at all?

I scooted over next to Peyton, craving some human connection, some reassurance. I'd thought she was asleep, but as soon as I touched her, she rolled over toward me.

"Can't sleep either?" she whispered, her breath caressing my cheek.

I slid an arm around her, scooting closer and tangling my legs with hers. "No," I said. "I keep thinking about my mom, like maybe I need to go home and just check on her. There's that hole in the cave..."

"That we're not supposed to go through..."

"But it's right there," I said. "What if I just went through for a minute, just to check. I feel like... I don't know. Maybe there's something wrong."

"I thought Eliot was the psychic," she said, but her voice was teasing.

"I'm sorry," I said. "That's stupid. I'll stay and help fix the bridge. I just hope it doesn't take too long to find Freya and Frey."

"I'm sure it will be really fast now that we have the ravens to help," Peyton said. "Odin said he keeps tabs on all the gods' pieces, so it should be super quick. Like it would have been to find our pieces if Rosa hadn't run off."

"You're right," I said. "I'm freaking out over nothing."

Peyton squeezed me, her bare foot caressing mine. "You are," she said. "And speaking of Rosa, I still can't believe that traitor abandoned us to go on *Celebrity Dwarf Match* or whatever her rune-reading act is called. I'm glad she didn't do that at home. Dad's head would have exploded by now."

"Because she left?" I asked, folding my arm under my head.

"Because he's had to take care of five kids by himself," she said. "And one of them is Xander."

I couldn't help but laugh at that, even as my body grew warmer by the second from the skin-to-skin contact. We were both wearing shorts, and her legs were so smooth against mine, her skin so soft, I thought I'd swoon from the sensation of them moving against mine.

"Do you miss him?" I asked.

"Yeah," she said. "I do. But I'm glad we're all together here. That makes it easier. You?"

"I miss my mom," I said. "A lot."

For a minute, neither of us spoke. Her legs slid against mine, and heat built inside me, filling me with a delicious, dizzying sensation. "Is it weird that I want to kiss you right now even though we're talking about our parents?" I whispered.

"Totally weird," Peyton said, her voice sounding as breathless as mine. I shifted off my arm, scooting forward until our faces were only inches apart. Peyton's thigh slid between mine.

My mouth found hers, as soft and warm and amazing as I remembered. I brushed my lips over hers, squeezing her hip to draw our bodies closer together. I marveled at the softness of her kiss, her body, her touch. Her thigh pressed harder against me, and I gasped into her mouth, pleasure rolling through me.

Something in my mind balked, and I almost pulled back. But we were only kissing. I'd done that before, and I'd do it all night if it meant I could keep feeling her silky skin against mine. We had already established that we weren't ready for more, but that didn't mean we couldn't have this. I wanted this, wanted her, and so, I let myself have it. We kissed for hours, our mouths dancing, our legs dancing, our entire bodies making magic together.

Like she'd once said, we were all under the influence of the god. When we sobered up, we'd have to face what we'd done. It had been easy to blame it on the god, though I'd always known it wasn't just Heimdall drawing me to my stepsiblings. I was wrapped up in all of them, and I didn't want it to end. I didn't want to stop having feelings for them. As complicated as it was, I couldn't imagine my life without them. Just the thought filled me with terror. We'd been through so much together—things no one in our entire world could understand. We were tied together by all we'd experienced. It wasn't possible to break the bonds we'd formed.

That didn't mean our feelings wouldn't change. Maybe Heimdall had infused us with those feelings, so we'd bond enough to find our last pieces. Now that we had, we were just ourselves, the god and the human side together. And for now, I was going to enjoy both sides. I was going to kiss her until my lips swelled, until our bodies lit up like glow sticks; to laugh when we laid on each other's hair; to take pleasure in this moment with no guilt. So, I did.

Chapter Ten

Gwen

For the next week, we spent our days crossing Bifrost to strengthen its waning energy and searching for the horn we were supposed to blow that would allow the other gods to cross with us. The giants below clamored and roared, threw spears that didn't even come close to our bridge, and sent giant falcons winging up to harass us. Odin's sons told us to ignore them. As long as we stayed our course, they couldn't reach us.

In the evenings, we explored the city. At night we returned to Valhalla, where I slept next to Peyton after some talking, cuddling, and kissing. It was nice to have a place to rest for a minute and catch our breath without worrying we'd be eaten by dragons or murdered by giants. I finally had a chance to get to know the others a little more when we weren't in life and death situations.

But by the end of the week, I'd grown impatient. My mother was never far from my mind, and I was ready to go home. So one night, I pressed Valerie for news of her, since she'd told me she would visit Midgard.

"I'm so sorry," she said. "I'll do it tonight. To tell the truth, I was enjoying being with the living again."

"It's okay," I said. "It's been nice to be safe again. But I can't really relax until I know she's safe, too."

"I will find her," Valerie said.

That night, I lay in bed wondering. How much had changed while we were gone? Four months had passed now. So much could change in that time. I tossed and turned, worry eating away at me. I felt a strange pull of homesickness, not for the place that had never really been home, but for my mother, who had always been my home, even in the worst of times.

At last, I swung my legs off the side of the bed. I needed some air, needed to clear my head and let Peyton sleep. I should've been happy to feel relatively safe again, to feel like myself again, but I couldn't seem to settle. I was in the driver's seat of my own body, but something inside me was restless. I couldn't seem to relax and stop worrying. I shouldn't be scared by Heimdall's quieting voice inside me. How could I be scared of losing what had confused my life so much and made a mess of everything?

After grabbing a hoodie from the closet, I tiptoed out of the room and closed the door. Lots of people still feasted in the enormous palace dining hall, as they did all night, but there were plenty of exits I could slip through. I crept down the stairs and stepped out a side door.

No sign of that day's bloody battle remained. Moonlight illuminated the hillside, casting Valhalla's shadow across the dewy grass. I started back toward Bifrost, though I knew it disappeared at sundown every night. When I spotted a figure sitting on the hill, my heart began to pound, but I didn't slow. With each step closer, my feet moved faster, until I was almost running. I hurried up the slope, trying to make out the identity of the silhouetted form.

For one second, I thought my heart would stop altogether. Was this what my disquiet had been trying to tell me? That the danger hadn't passed?

But then he turned, and I saw Eliot's easy smile and soft, warm eyes.

"Couldn't sleep?" he asked.

"You scared me," I said. "I thought you were...someone else."

"Who?" he asked, leaning back on his hands.

"I don't know," I said, folding my legs to sit beside him.

"Finn?" he asked.

"No. He wouldn't be out here alone."

"True," he said. "Xander's not letting him out of his sight."

"That makes sense."

"Why's that?" Eliot asked, cocking his head to one side.

"Because Xander wasn't there when your mom died," I said. "Right?"

Eliot didn't answer for a minute and then he nodded. "For someone who grew up basically without human contact, you're not too bad at figuring people out."

I snorted, and since we were sitting on the hill above a giant canyon, it magnified the humiliating sound by about a hundred.

"So," Eliot said at last. "Who did you think you'd find up here? Xander or Zeke?"

"I knew it was one of you. That's why I came up here. But at the last second, for some reason I thought when you turned around, I'd see... Joaquin."

"Ah," he said, nodding. "Because we never saw the body."

"What?" I asked, drawing back.

"We never saw his body down there in the canyon. He's Loki. We know he's a trickster. And we know he's still alive at Ragnarok."

"But he was in Joaquin's body, which *can* die."

Eliot shrugged. "Maybe it works like that. Maybe not. Think about it. He's a shapeshifter. We've seen a lot of birds in this canyon, don't you think?"

"You think he's still alive?" Fear raced up my spine, and blood rushed in my ears so loud I could hardly hear my own question.

"I think there's a strong possibility."

We sat in silence for a long time, staring out over the distance we'd crossed on a bridge made of air. A falcon had attacked us. Had that been Joaquin? If he could shift into animal form, it would certainly be convenient to turn into a bird when you fell off a cliff. I tried to remember if anyone had looked down right after it happened, if anyone had heard him hit the ground. But we'd been too busy worrying about Xander and Finn. We'd just been glad to be safe from Joaquin. If he was still out there, though, we weren't safe.

For now, though, I didn't have to be afraid. No birds flew at night. No one was around but Eliot, who sat watching the darkened canyon. His knees were pulled up, his elbows resting on them, his chin in his hands. The peaceful silence grew awkward as I began to feel the space between us, the charge in the air that began so faintly I hardly noticed and then grew until I couldn't think of anything else. Was he still thinking about Joaquin and the valley, or could he feel the electricity, too? Was his arm tingling with my warmth? His quiet, steady breathing seemed expectant, as if he were waiting for me to speak. If only I were the girl who always knew what to say, like Peyton.

The danger of Loki's existence seemed far away from this moment, when I was just a girl sitting on a hill with a cute boy, wishing he would talk to me. Eventually, I got tired of waiting. "What are you thinking about?"

"There's only one right answer to that question," Eliot said, shooting me an easy smile.

"What? Why?"

"I'm thinking about you."

"Oh," I said. "Is that the right answer or the truth?"

Eliot's smile grew. "Can't it be both?"

"Can it?" I examined his face, trying to see past the carefully calculated persona. It was like he'd studied people and learned what to do and say, who to be. That was who he was. But there had to be something under all that. What did he act like when he was alone? What went on in his head?

"You don't trust me?" he asked.

"It's not that," I said. "But I feel like I hardly know you. Everyone else has opened up to me, but it's like you talk in riddles."

"You don't like riddles?"

"Regular people are hard enough to figure out."

"People are more than riddles to be solved."

I sighed. "How am I supposed to get to know you if you won't tell me anything?"

Eliot leaned back, propping himself on his palms with his legs sprawled out in front of him. "What do you want to know?"

"Anything," I said, throwing my hands up in frustration. "What are you scared of?"

He answered with an easy grin. "A magician never reveals his secrets."

"Come on," I said, nudging him with my shoulder. "It doesn't have to be your greatest fear or anything. Zeke's afraid of the dark, Peyton's afraid of wild animals, and Finn's scared of snakes. You're not scared of anything."

"I'm sure there's something."

"Like what?"

He grinned. "Can't think of anything just now."

"Then tell me something else," I said.

"You first."

"You already know that one. I'm afraid of heights."

"Okay," he said, licking his lips before smiling again. "Favorite musician?"

"Lorde. Favorite movie?"

"*Death to Smoochie.*"

I choked on a laugh. "What the hell is that?"

"It's a great movie," he said. "What's yours?"

"*Clueless.*"

"And you laughed at mine," he said, shaking his head.

"Hey," I said, fighting not to blush again. "Don't knock my movie. Favorite book?"

"*The Great Gatsby.*"

"How very un-nerdy of you," I said.

"Favorite childhood memory."

I faltered, not sure where to go with that one. My childhood hadn't been full of happy birthdays and merry Christmases. My happy memories were, to be honest, totally weird. But Eliot was waiting, his eyes shining with interest and a smile on his lips. He was having fun. So I gave him something fun, something that wouldn't replace the playfulness on his face with pity.

"Petting a giraffe at a zoo. It licked my hand."

"Favorite food?"

"Hey," I protested. "You can't ask all the questions."

"Sure, I can."

"That's not fair. What's your favorite memory?"

"Meeting you," he said, his voice dropping. His eyes moved from mine to my mouth, and I had to swallow past the thickness in my throat. My heart was suddenly stampeding. I watched the muscles in his shoulder bunch as he leaned closer. "Are you ready for a serious question?"

I bit my lip, my pulse fluttering like a trapped moth. "How serious?"

The intensity in his eyes made my chest throb. "What turns you on?"

"What?" I squeaked, adrenaline rushing inside me.

"What do you like?" He leaned even closer, angling his face into the curve of my shoulder, letting the warmth of his breath caress my neck. A delicious shiver of anticipation raced through me, and my eyes fell closed.

It was easier to be brave when I couldn't see his cool reaction. "You," I whispered.

His hand circled the side of my neck, drawing me against him as his mouth descended to the hollow of my throat. "Do you like this?" he murmured, his lips skimming up to my ear.

My breath came so quickly I could hardly speak. "Yes."

I lifted my hand to his, closing my fingers around his wrist and holding on, holding myself up. Shivers exploded across my skin when his lips brushed the rim of my ear. His pulse thrummed under my thumb, and I felt a surge of relief rise within me. His heart was pounding as hard as mine.

"And this?" he asked, his teeth grazing my earlobe.

I nodded, words deserting me. Eliot's lips pressed gently below my ear, finding the pulse on the side of my throat. A low growl built deep in his chest, the vibration sparking something to life within me. His lips slid down, his teeth grazing over my collarbone. His tongue touched my skin, and he let out a slow, hot breath against me. For a long moment, nothing moved except his tongue tasting my skin.

Everything in me was weak, wanting.

This was different than what I'd felt with Finn—when I'd been so determined, so bold. This time, I felt like I could just melt under him, and he'd take care of everything. He knew how. It would be so easy, would feel so good.

"God, Gwen," he murmured. "You make me dizzy."

Dizzy. That was exactly how I felt. Spinning until I lost all control. My brain knew I didn't want to do this, that it was too risky, but my body didn't. My body said yes, and it had drowned out my brain.

"Wait," I gasped, tightening my fingers around his wrist.

He pulled back, his eyes full of concern. "What's wrong?"

"I'm... scared," I admitted, another bubble of adrenaline bursting inside my chest.

"What are you scared of?"

"You," I said, a breathless laugh escaping my lips.

"Me?" he asked, shaking his head in bewilderment. "Gwen, I would never hurt you. You can push me away every time I come near you, but never, ever be afraid of me. Never be afraid to push me away."

My nerves set in, and I pushed my hands under my arms, so he wouldn't see my fingers tremble. Why did I have to be such a complete wreck in these situations?

"I'm not afraid of that," I muttered, my face hot. "If I thought you were that kind of guy, I wouldn't be sitting here with you."

He reached up and smoothed my hair behind my ear, cocking his head to one side and peering at me through those adorable, ridiculous glasses. "Then what are you afraid of?"

"This," I said, gesturing between us. "This doesn't scare you at all?"

"Not even a little," he said, his hand cradling the back of my neck. He gave me a pained little smile that made my heart squeeze with love for him.

"Aren't you unsure about anything?" I asked.

"Sure," he said, his knuckles sliding along my shoulder, sending tingles spiraling through my body. "But not this. Never this."

I didn't know if that was a good thing. When I stopped being afraid of how much I loved them, maybe it would mean I didn't love them as much. When my heart stopped hammering at his touch, when my breath didn't come faster and my stomach didn't do flips, did that mean we were comfortable, or did it mean we'd gotten as complacent as the gods were about their fate?

Eliot took my hand and squeezed it against his chest. "What if we just kiss?"

"Won't that just make it harder?"

He grinned and scooted closer, sweeping my hair back over my shoulder. "I can control myself," he said, his eyes alive with the challenge. "Can you?"

"I don't know," I admitted, dropping my gaze.

Eliot shifted around, sliding his hand under my hair and cradling the back of my head as he pulled me in for another kiss. "Don't worry," he murmured. "I've got enough self-control for both of us."

It turned out, he was right. As his full lips caressed mine, I lost myself in him. His kiss was gentle, but not tentative like Finn's. Eliot kissed like he knew exactly what he was doing. And what he was doing was making me insane. His soft kisses weren't enough. I needed more, needed passion. I tugged at him, digging my nails in. When that growling sound came from his throat again, it did me in. I opened my lips, pushing into his mouth, pulling him closer. My mind shut off, and there was only my body *wanting*.

"Eliot," I whispered, pulling back and tugging his shirt up. His skin was hot under my hands, and I pushed him back on the ground.

He wrapped his arms around me, pulling me down with him. "Damn, Gwen," he said, sliding his hands under the back of my shirt. "You're so sexy."

"I need you," I gasped. "Now."

"I thought you wanted to wait."

"I can't," I said, the need inside me like something animal and alive, raging and clawing.

"I can take care of that," he said, grinning as he leaned in. "If you'll let me."

"Yes."

His warm lips claimed mine again, and his hands moved over me, finding their way to exactly where I needed them. He slid lower, his mouth moving down my neck, my chest, my belly. His kiss pushed me higher and higher until I was soaring out over the world, one with the stars. But I was not afraid. I was strong, powerful, and more alive than I'd ever been.

Chapter Eleven

Gwen

I didn't know how to act with a guy after a sexual encounter. In my very short list of them, I'd ended up alone every time. But Eliot didn't jump up and run away the second we were done, and he didn't tell me to go to sleep and then sneak off. He rested beside me, propped on his elbow, talking to me and touching me. We kissed until I was dizzy with him all over again. We talked for even longer, asking each other's favorites from the most mundane to the most absurd. We talked about our families, dreams, and memories. I had never talked to someone so long, never opened up so completely. And no one had ever opened up to me that way, shared themselves with me without holding back. The more we talked, the more I wanted to tell him and ask him. It was intoxicating and terrifying, at once completely ordinary and the most amazing experience I'd ever had.

At last, we fell asleep sometime toward dawn. I woke to the roar of Bifrost surging into the sky. I sat up, fully expecting to be alone. But Eliot was still there, his arms wrapped around me, his red lips parted slightly as he slept. In the soft light of morning, he didn't look like the ever-vigilant scientist tech-geek who never stopped studying people and things. He just looked like a boy. All along, I'd been searching for an answer under the surface, but it had been right there for all the world to see. He wasn't putting on some kind of act.

He was a curious, observant person who wanted to know how things worked, what made people the way they were. Maybe it had been hard to see that because we were so similar in that way. But his inquisitiveness wasn't a mask. It was him. He'd been genuine since the moment I met him. He wasn't pretending to be someone he wasn't. He was just Eliot—my Eliot. Open, beautiful, smart, and caring. And he'd stayed with me all night.

Now that the sun was rising, I didn't know what to do. I didn't know if I should wake him or if anyone would miss us inside. Would Peyton freak out if she woke and I was gone? I didn't want anyone to worry, but I also didn't want to do the walk of shame with Eliot, both of us grass stained and sleepy, people laughing and giving us knowing looks. Maybe that's why the others had left me sleeping. It was easier to walk out alone than together. And waking the other person meant facing them right now. If I left Eliot here, I could plan what to say when I saw him again.

But I couldn't do that to Eliot. Not after he'd stayed with me all night, holding me while I slept. Maybe it was easier to walk away, but I knew how it felt to be the person who woke up alone. I knelt and shook his shoulder.

Eliot sat up and adjusted the glasses that had somehow stayed on his face all night. "Hey, girlfriend," he said with a sleepy smile, catching my hand.

"Hey," I said. I chewed at my lip, trying to think of what came next. I should have at least planned that before I woke him.

Eliot hopped to his feet and held out a hand to me. I felt somehow shy as I slipped my hand into his. He pulled me close to his side, and we started across the damp grass toward the palace on the hill.

"Are we good?" Eliot asked.

"I don't know what that means," I admitted.

Eliot smiled and squeezed my hand. "Just making sure you're okay with what we did and where we are as a couple."

A wave of warmth swelled inside me, and I pulled his arm around me. "More than okay."

If things had gone further, I knew I would have regretted it. I wouldn't have blamed him—I was the one who had wanted to. Lucky for me, Eliot had more than respected my wishes. He'd made sure that I did, too.

When we reached the door to the room I shared with Peyton, Eliot took my face between his hands and pulled me in for a long, slow kiss.

"Thanks," I said when he released me. "You're a pretty great boyfriend."

"Glad to hear it," he said. "Feel free to take notes and let me know if I have any areas of improvement."

"I'll do that." Resting my hands on his hipbones, I stood on tiptoes and gave him another quick kiss. "Goodnight."

"Good morning," he said, stepping back but holding onto my hand as if he, too, couldn't bear to let the night end. After giving my hand one last quick squeeze, he stood watching as I slipped into my room. I turned and gave him a little wave through the crack in the door and then pulled it closed behind me. I didn't think it was possible to be any happier.

*

A few hours later, I woke again. My body felt deliciously relaxed and rested, even though I'd gotten less sleep than usual. Eliot's attentions seemed to have done wonders.

"Somebody was out late," Peyton said when she emerged from the bathroom to find me sitting in front of the mirror, wrestling to get a comb through my impossible hair.

Damn it. I'd hoped she had slept through my return.

"I was with Eliot," I said, steeling myself for her response.

"Oh," she said. "Okay."

"Does that bother you?" I asked, watching her in the mirror.

She sat on the edge of the bed, winding her wet hair up into a bun. I appreciated she didn't give me the answer I wanted before she thought it over. But waiting for her answer was agony, nonetheless.

"You know what?" she said. "I don't think it does. Which is kind of a miracle, actually. I'm not usually into all that free love stuff he believes in. People get hurt despite the best of intentions. But in this case…"

"What's special about this case?" I asked, realizing as I waited for her answer again that I was nervous as hell to hear what she had to say. Of all the Keens, Peyton and I talked the most. And after this week, we'd kissed the most, too. Pretty much every night we lay up talking and making out. Now I wondered if she'd taken that to mean I'd chosen her over the others.

Peyton secured her hair before standing. "What's not special about this case? We're sharing a god. Why can't we share a girlfriend?"

I let out a breath in relief. I not only trusted Peyton, I valued her judgment. It meant a lot to me that she was okay with sharing my time. "That's an interesting way to look at it," I said. "And did you just call me your girlfriend?"

"Maybe I did," Peyton said, laughing. "Now, are you going to let me help with that, or are you going to chop it all off? Because you have seriously made zero progress on it since I got out of the shower."

A few minutes later, Peyton had gotten my hair under control. We'd both dressed in our own clothes, though after a week, I was down to my last pair. When we joined the others, Eliot gave me a smile that showed off his dimple, and my heart did a little flip.

Xander gave me a cool look, his hands resting in the pockets of his leather jacket.

"What?" I asked, feeling instantly self-conscious and defensive.

"I didn't say anything."

"Your face said it," I muttered.

"Did it say that we should do something about that hoodie?"

"It said you should do something about your superiority complex."

He smirked. "Using the big words today, are we?"

"Sorry," I said. "I can use the smaller words if you're trying to keep up."

"As cute as this is, I'm starving," Peyton said.

"I wasn't going to interrupt," Smith said, sidling over to Peyton. "But I'd be much obliged if you'd join me in the dining hall."

Forgetting my sparring match with Xander, I gaped at Smith, wondering what else was in his closet. He'd managed to surprise me every day. Today he was wearing plum-colored satin pants with pleats up the sides, a puffy cream shirt, and a vest made of maroon fur.

"Let's go find some food before the dead people eat it all," Zeke said. He held out his arm, and I slid my hand into the crook of his elbow. We might have both been wearing jeans and hoodies, but I felt like a queen as he escorted me down the circular staircase.

"Don't listen to Xander," he said, squeezing my hand against his side. "I think you look cute."

"Thank you," I said. "You, too."

"Maybe we should go find some food in town today," Peyton said. "I mean, these honorable souls seem to eat and everything, so there must be food somewhere. And some of them are from more modern times, so we might even find normal food. I'd kill for a bagel and cream cheese."

Just then, Valerie dropped down from above and settled on her feet, her feathers still ruffled. "Greetings, Midgardians," she said.

"Did you find my mom?" I asked, not bothering with a greeting.

"Yes," Valerie said. "She's alive."

Because of course, that's what a Valkyrie would notice.

"Where is she? Is she okay?" I asked, something gnawing inside me like Ratr's squirrely little teeth nibbling at my nerve endings. Something was wrong. I could feel it. The sense of belonging in this place had lulled us into complacency. We could live comfortably in Asgard, feasting at the table with the father god, free to enjoy the luxuries of our own world without its restrictions. But Midgard was still there, still in danger.

"She's in a room at a place called Cedar Crest," Valerie said.

I caught a look flying between my stepsiblings—raised eyebrows, surprise, sympathy.

"That sounds like a hospital," I said, turning from one of them to another, not sure who would give me the answer I wanted—the impossible answer. "Why does that sound like a hospital?"

"It is a hospital," Eliot said quietly.

Panic burst inside me like a balloon that had been growing bigger and bigger in my chest since the moment I left my mother. I should never have left. I'd always known she couldn't handle this on her own. She couldn't handle *life* on her own.

"Why is she in a hospital?" I asked, grabbing Valerie's shoulders and shaking her, as if that would make the answers fall out faster.

"It's not just a hospital," Peyton said. "It's a really nice place, Gwen. If she's there, she's getting the best care there is."

The terror inside me bloomed into fury. Blood raged in my ears so loudly I couldn't hear myself think. "The kind of care your mom got?" I demanded.

Peyton stepped back, her perfect lips dropping open and her eyes widening. She looked like she'd been slapped, and I wanted to slap her. It wasn't fair. She got everything, and I got…Mom. I hated the unfairness, and I hated her obnoxious obsession with coffee and her whining about her wardrobe when we all had to wear the same things. I hated that she had nothing to worry about but when she'd get her next bagel. She didn't have to worry about Neil while she was gone.

"That was way harsh," Zeke said, dropping my hand and putting an arm around Peyton's shoulders. He'd abandoned me. Of course he had. Zeke would always take Peyton's side. Their family stuck together and had each other's backs. Just like me and Mom. Except I hadn't stuck around. I'd abandoned her. In truth, I wasn't mad at Peyton or any of them. I was mad at myself.

I stared at them, standing there together, forming a solid wall I could never break through. I wasn't part of their family. I never had been. Somewhere along the way, I'd let myself get caught up in their world and forgotten reality. I wasn't a Keen, part of a huge family of privilege and love. I was part of a two-woman team with my mother. I'd known better than to leave her. I'd let Heimdall tell me where to go, how to live. I'd given these people my whole heart, my body, my soul. And they had saved theirs for each other.

"I have to go," I blurted, pushing past them.

"You can't leave until we're done with the bridge," Eliot protested.

"Watch me," I said, hitting the door with my full weight. It flew open, and I flew out, across the grass. What was Heimdall going to do—leave me?

To my surprise, my mind balked at the thought. I'd spent my whole life not knowing I was part god. I hadn't even seen what I could do. But what did it matter, if I couldn't save Mom?

Eliot called after me, but I didn't turn. He was a Keen and I wasn't. I'd trusted Neil with her. I'd trusted him to keep her safe and take care of her while I was gone. And he hadn't. There were no tears as I ran down the hill. My eyes remained dry. This was not a time for tears, no matter how bad the betrayal hurt. This was a time for action, like all the times I'd run with my mom before. I had only one instinct. Survival. Her survival.

Don't let her get arrested. Don't let them take her away. Make it out of here together, before she breaks down completely.

My biggest fear had always been getting separated and losing her. But in the end, I'd walked away from her like it was nothing, with barely more than a promise to return.

"I'm coming back for you, Mom," I muttered, stopping at the end of Bifrost. The rainbow sank into the grass itself. I wasn't sure how to step onto it alone.

"Gwen."

I hesitated, the panic inside me receding. It was Finn's voice, soft and steady, how it had always been. I didn't want to turn around, didn't want to look at him. If I looked at him, I might not be able to leave.

But he'd left me.

Mom had never left me. Never. I'd been the one to leave.

"I'm sorry," I said, and I stepped into Bifrost.

ASCEND

The air caught me up, lifting me on its current like the falcons we'd seen in the canyon. My stomach dropped and my gorge rose. I closed my eyes, trying not to faint. In my memory, I heard Xander's voice telling me to open my eyes, that I wasn't falling. My fear was irrational. This time, I didn't have to have his arms around me to find that courage. I forced myself to open my eyes on my own.

Don't follow me, I prayed. I didn't want them to get hurt. I didn't want them to see me like this. I didn't want them to see my mom like this, to know what my life had really been like. I'd told them as much as I wanted them to know, but some bits of it were too terrible for anyone who hadn't lived that way to understand. I didn't want them to see the grotesque parts, the craziness, and to see me differently because of it.

And yet, I couldn't bear the thought of being away from them. At last, I looked back. The Keens stood at the foot of the bridge, but they didn't follow me. Smith stood off to one side, looking alone and uncertain. Zeke still had his arm around Peyton. Xander's arm was out, holding back Finn and Eliot. My eyes met Xander's stormy blue gaze, and I gasped in pain. I couldn't do this.

I couldn't leave. But I couldn't leave my mother where she was any longer. Mom hated hospitals. Leaving her there was crueler than leaving my stepsiblings here. They would survive. We had crossed the bridge together. That was our task. They'd have to gather the gods on their own.

As I rose through the air, weightless, drawing farther away from them with each moment, my heart strained in their direction. Tears filled my eyes, pain spiraling through me. I curled my hands into fists, tugging my sleeves over them. It was all I had to hold onto now. I couldn't go back.

Not even if it felt like they held a rope tied to my heart, and every inch I ascended, the rope pulled tighter.

A sound tore from my throat, a wordless cry of pain, terror, and anguish. My heart was being dragged out of my chest, arteries ripping as it went, breaking the bars of the cage where I'd held it all my life.

I'd always relied on myself and only myself. Not even my mother could be trusted to provide safety, stability, or basic necessities. With the Keens, I'd gotten to be someone else. Someone who didn't have to be strong all the time, who didn't have to take charge when I didn't want to. Now, I was waking up from that fantastical dream. I had fallen in love in that dream, though, and there was no going back from that. Mom had warned me that would happen, and she'd been right. Reality was calling, and I had to save her again. If the price of that was leaving my heart in another world, then that's what I would pay.

Chapter Twelve

Smith

I had spent a lifetime being looked down upon and criticized, then another year roaming the worlds trying to stay alive and not be eaten by dragons, wolves, machines, zombies, giants, and about a dozen other dwarf-hungry beasts. But in this moment, none of that seemed as hard as watching a piece of my god go flying off into the sunset. Or into the sunrise, as it may be.

"Let her go," Xander said. "It's what she wants."

"She doesn't know what she wants," Zeke said. "She's upset."

"Then let her figure it out," Xander growled, looming over Zeke with his superior meanness factor. Zeke didn't seem the least bit intimidated. I didn't know how. Xander was scarier than Hel herself.

I couldn't tell which of them was the leader, but I knew it wasn't me, so I kept quiet as they continued arguing. As an unskilled child, I'd learned to stay quiet and out of the way, so as not to attract attention. Now, I wanted to shake them and demand how they could even talk about this. Were they not feeling what I was feeling, like my heart was being carried off by a rabid wolf?

I didn't even know Gwen, really, though she seemed kind. I liked that she smiled at me sometimes, as if she knew how I was feeling. But this wasn't about knowing her. It was about knowing she was part of me, and it was wrong to let her leave. I'd spent way too long finding them to let us get ripped apart again. Maybe my lack of deeper feelings was the one thing making me see the situation clearly. Or maybe it was because I was a dwarf. I didn't really know.

"She might not even be able to cross into Midgard," Eliot said. "Heimdall said we had to finish our task first."

"Bifrost looks pretty good to me," Peyton said. "We've been crossing it all week."

I glanced up. Gwen was disappearing into the mirage at the top of the arc. I thought I'd vomit with the anguish of being away from her.

I stepped forward, as if I was being dragged involuntarily in that direction.

"She told me not to follow," Xander said.

"When?" Eliot asked, cocking his head.

Xander hesitated before answering. "Just now."

"How?" Eliot asked.

"I don't know," Xander replied. "But she did."

Eliot appeared to ponder this. I didn't have to hear her to know she didn't want us to follow. And I didn't need permission to disobey her orders, either. I wasn't afraid of making her angry.

I stepped forward, weighing my options. Dwarves worked underground, and I'd spent plenty of time in the mines and caves, watching others forge their crafts in the flames of the earth itself. I had some misgivings about fire, but then, being an earth-dweller, I didn't really like the feeling of flying through the air, either. Despite my un-dwarfish inclination for singing rather than working with my hands, I felt a great comfort at the thought of being surrounded on all sides by sturdy, dependable stone. Why wasn't a stripe of the rainbow made of dirt and rocks?

I decided water was the least intimidating choice, so I scooted in that direction, ignored by the others. I didn't understand what had happened with Gwen, and like usual, no one had bothered to fill me in. But that wouldn't stop me. If I could stay alive this long, one little human girl wasn't going to be the death of me.

I called up a song inside me, but instead of letting it out, I held it in my chest as I'd done so many times before. It swelled like magic inside me, and suddenly, I felt like the god I was. I turned to step into the water when a hand clamped down on the back of my neck.

"Where do you think you're going?" Xander growled.

"Where you aren't," I said, before I could bite my tongue. I was good at staying quiet, not necessarily saying the right thing when spoken to.

Xander's eyes narrowed, and I reevaluated my certainty that humans were less dangerous than giants and wild beasts. "And where is that, Little Man?"

I didn't appreciate having my manhood challenged. Just because I was a dwarf didn't make me less than him, or the elves who hadn't bothered to follow us because it was their time to cross the river of fire below, or even the giants who stood three houses tall.

"I'm going to stop her," I said. "What are you going to do, Big Man?"

"Are you challenging me?" Xander asked, eyes flashing.

"I'm not challenging anyone," I said. "I'm not interested in fighting pointless battles. There's only one person you should be angry at and it's not me."

"What do you know?" Xander asked, pushing me backward. I stumbled, nearly losing my footing and spoiling my clothes with grass stains. He turned and stormed off toward Valhalla.

"You think he really heard Gwen?" Peyton asked.

"Why shouldn't he?" Eliot said. "I've heard her before."

"You have?"

"Haven't we all?" Eliot answered, looking at the others. "The night Joaquin had her."

"Yeah, I guess," Peyton said, a troubled expression on her usually cheerful face. "So, what now? Does that mean we should let her leave like Xander said? If that's what she wants..."

"She's going to get her mom," Eliot said. "Maybe we should just let her go. She'll come back here when she's done. She'll have to. You know Heimdall won't let her just walk away from this. And we won't, either. We need her too much."

"Then let's go get her," Zeke said, stepping forward.

"We also need her to be focused," Eliot said. "Not worrying about her mom, and not held hostage here."

"I guess we'll find out how much free will we really have," Peyton said. "Gwen's defying Heimdall right now."

"That's if she can even get back into Midgard," Finn said.

"Did you try?" Zeke asked. "When you left Jotunheim, did you try to get back home?"

Finn blinked at him for a second, as if he was surprised someone had asked him a question where his input would be valued. I knew what that was like, and I felt a kinship with him I hadn't before.

"No," Finn said at last.

"Want to try now?" I asked.

"Yeah," Finn said. "Yeah, I do."

"All right," Zeke said. "Eliot, you and Peyton go tell Xander where we're going. And if it's safe to start looking for Freya and Frey, stay with the raven guides."

Peyton planted a hand on her hip. "And you're going home?"

Zeke stood tall, his shoulders back, confidence and determination radiating through his stance. "We're going to get our girl."

Chapter Thirteen

Gwen

Part of me expected Heimdall to rise up out of the shimmering air where the door to Midgard waited. Surely, he would stop me from disobeying. Maybe I even wanted him to stop me. The pain in my chest was almost unbearable now.

I felt the others coming while I stood in the cave on the other end of Bifrost. A surge of anger rose up in me. I knew it was irrational. It wasn't their fault I'd fallen in love. It wasn't their fault we were all stuck in this together. It wasn't their fault that although we'd both lost a parent, they had a functional father who gave them all he had while I had…Mom.

Still, I resented their presence. I needed to focus on my mother, and I knew how hard that would be with them nearby. Already, I could feel the pull of them, the urge to turn around and go back. The urge to be whole.

But no. I would not be Heimdall's pawn any longer. If he wanted me to do things for him, he had to let me do things for myself, too. Not even for myself—for my mother.

Sucking in a ragged breath, I pressed my fists to my belly, as if I could fill the hunger for my pieces the way I had staved off real hunger before. I squeezed my eyes closed and pictured a map where all roads led to my mother. A stillness spread through me, and I opened my eyes. I stepped up to the mirage-like doorway.

"You don't want to do that."

The voice was so close I almost jumped out of my skin. I knew the others hadn't descended Bifrost yet, but the voice had come from somewhere in the cave. It wasn't Heimdall's booming, consuming voice, either. It was a raspy, husky voice I'd heard before.

I turned to find Huginn standing in the mouth of the cave, her strange feathered garment fluttering in the breezes coming off Bifrost. My mother had taught me to fear ravens all my life, and even though Huginn was in human form, I shrank back.

"Did you follow me?" I asked.

"We are bound to Odin," she said. "We obey his commands."

"And he commanded you to follow me?"

"He gave you our services on your journey."

I debated whether to tell her I wasn't rushing off to find the gods. Odin had told us to find the gods and bring them back to Asgard, and he'd given us the guidance of his ravens while on our mission. If he found out I took her to find an ordinary human, how mad would he be? A shiver went through me. I wasn't just disobeying Heimdall. I was disobeying the All-Father.

I had no choice, though. I had to get Mom out. And if I wanted to find her, the raven could help. "Why don't I want to go through here, and where do I want to go instead?"

"The worlds exist not on other planets, but on other planes," she said. "Each one intersects the others at many points. And there are many points of entry between them."

"Okay," I said. "Suppose the worlds are layered on top of each other, but they're all on earth. Which means…what? That this opening might be in the middle of traffic or the ocean?"

"It's in a cave, like here," she said. "There are places where the worlds are closer, where the planes intersect, and what you find on each side is similar, though not entirely the same. You can step through. You will not be in danger. But you will not be near your mother, either."

"I'd be in Midgard, though."

"Yes," she said, smoothing her hands over her feathered midriff. "Are you prepared to walk for several months? Or do you have what you need to travel faster, as I do?"

"What do I need?"

She blinked at me, her big eyes resembling an owl's more than a raven's. "You should know what you need to travel in your own world."

"Right." I'd been gone so long, traveled by such fantastical means, that I'd almost forgotten how our world worked. If I stepped through into some cave, I'd probably be in a rural area. I'd walk to a road and then hitchhike. I didn't have money or any form of ID, so I couldn't buy a ticket on a bus or buy a cheap car the way Mom always had. I didn't even know Neil's phone number, though I could probably find him easily enough, if I could get online at a library. But did I really want to ask Neil for help? What if he had me locked up, too?

After all, I would sound every bit as crazy as my mother if I tried to tell anyone where I'd been or what had happened.

Before I could ask more questions, three figures came sliding down the water section of Bifrost. They had huge smiles on their faces as they skidded to a stop and hopped off the bridge to join me. I looked from one of them to another, wondering how they'd chosen who would try to stop me. They must have flipped a coin or something because their choices made no logical sense. Still, I couldn't focus on anything but the smile on Finn's face. It had been so long since I'd seen him smile. It almost took my breath, the beauty of it twisting into an ache in my chest.

Apparently, their experience of Bifrost was a lot more fun than my vomit-inducing fear.

"Okay, Baby Keen," Zeke said, still grinning. "What's the plan?"

"You're not here to stop me?" I asked, narrowing my eyes at them as I edged a step closer to the window between worlds.

"We're not?" Smith asked, giving some serious Zeke side-eye.

"If we can get into Midgard, we'll go with you," Finn said. "We know how important your mom is to you."

"My mother, who your father had thrown in a hospital the moment we left?" I asked. "You're going to help me get her out?"

117

"We don't know why she's there," Finn said, scuffing the toe of his Converse sneaker on the stone floor of the cave.

"I know exactly why she's there," I said, clenching my teeth with irritation.

"You don't know Dad put her there," Zeke said. "Maybe something happened to him. We're all worried here, Gwen."

"There's only one way to find out," I said, turning toward Huginn. "Where's the nearest entrance to Mom?"

"Is that the plan?" Zeke asked. "I'm good at running plays, but you gotta let me know what they are if you want me to do them right."

"I don't have a plan," I admitted.

"Isn't a hospital a place of healing?" Smith asked. "If she's sick or hurt, why do you want to take her out?"

"It's not that kind of hospital," I said, shame sweeping over me. "She needs someone who can take care of her. Apparently, I'm the only one who can."

"It's not our fault," Zeke said, crossing his arms and frowning at me. "We didn't put your mom in a hospital."

"You're blaming us for what our dad did when we weren't there," Finn said, shoving his hands in the pockets of his ripped jeans.

I looked from one of them to the next, and my shoulders slumped. "You're right," I said. "It's not your fault, and I know you're worried, too. No matter who put her there, I just…I hate that I wasn't there to keep her from having to go through that." My breath hitched on the last words. Dammit. I really didn't want to cry right now. I needed to be strong for Mom.

"You don't know how long she's been there," Finn said. "The ravens said they hadn't been keeping tabs on her since you left."

"Yeah, maybe she just got committed," Zeke said.

"Are we breaking her out of a jail?" Smith asked. "I think something is getting lost in translation. Is a hospital not a good place to be?"

"Not if you hate hospitals," I said. "And this isn't the kind that heals a broken bone."

"It's more for a broken mind," Zeke said, tapping his forehead.

"My mom is not broken," I said, heat rising to my cheeks. Smith was looking at me differently already. I could see it in his eyes—the way strangers looked at us when Mom started to slip into one of her visions but hadn't gone completely ballistic yet.

"Shit, sorry," Zeke said. "I didn't mean it like that. I'm a dick. I should have let Peyton come with me. She always shuts me up before I can say stupid shit like that."

"Was your mom broken?" I asked.

"Well…yeah," Zeke said, shrugging his wide shoulders and appearing so uncomfortable it was frankly adorable.

"Aren't we all broken?" Finn said quietly. "Isn't that why we need each other to be whole?"

I stared at him, my heart suddenly throbbing against my ribs. "Do we?" I whispered.

"Of course we do," Zeke said, throwing an arm around each of us. "Now, let's make our plan and get moving."

Huginn, who had stood against the cave wall blending into the shadows in her dark feathers, spoke again. "There is an entrance close to your mother's location, but it's in another world."

"Of course it is," I muttered.

"Which world?" Smith asked. "Because there are a couple I'm not going back to, not even to protect a piece of myself."

Without warning, a gigantic creature smashed through Bifrost's wall of flame. All four of us screamed, and Zeke dove onto us, flattening us to the ground.

"Calm yourselves. We're here to rescue you," said a familiar, heavily accented voice.

Zeke's body was lifted from mine, and Valdan dragged me to my feet, scraped and bruised from the floor. A huge dragon sat crouched on the cave floor, and I could have sworn it looked amused by our reaction. Only Huginn hadn't moved. She stood serenely against the wall of the cave, a raven perched on her shoulder.

"What the hell," I said, turning on Valdan. "You could have warned us."

"We could have," said a leather-clad girl as she hopped off the dragon's back. "But this way, we got to hear your girlish screams." Gracelyn smirked at Zeke, and a dart of jealousy pierced through me. I didn't appreciate her flirting with one of my stepbrothers.

"Not cool," Zeke said, but he dazzled Gracelyn with his mega-watt smile as he said it.

My jealousy ratcheted up a notch.

Get it together, Gwen. This is not the time to worry about who's flirting.

"Now my breeches are dusty," Smith said, swatting at his purple pants. At least I wasn't the only one worrying about something mundane.

"What are you doing here?" I asked the female elf.

"Muninn said you needed a ride," Gracelyn said, tossing her brown hair back. "Your elf here asked nicely, so I offered to help."

I raised an eyebrow at Valdan. "You asked a girl for help? That's so progressive of you."

"She's not a girl," he said. "She's an elven knight-in-training. If I had a dragon fleet at my command, I'd have given you a ride myself. But I was busy taking care of Thor's business when the knights were chosen."

"I'm sorry."

"I am Thor," Valdan said, puffing up into his prideful stance. "There is no greater honor."

I didn't know much about elven politics, but despite Valdan's words, it sounded like I'd hit a sore spot. I couldn't blame him. He'd been doing the whole god thing a lot longer than I had. I was only just beginning to see what I'd miss while away on god business.

"Is your goat-drawn carriage out of commission?" I asked.

"Alvan's using it for god hunting," he said. "He and the rest of our pieces will find Freya and Frey while you take care of your business."

I hadn't expected that. A tug went through me again, filling me with the urge to go back and join them, to go on this new adventure with them. To thank them for letting me do this and for working on our task even when I had to go. As ever, my mother came first.

"Are you coming with us, then?" I asked, hope rising in my chest at the thought of having such a skilled protector with us.

"I would stand out in the human world," Valdan said, sounding disappointed.

"Understatement of the century," I said, my heart sinking. Even if he used his long hair to cover his pointy ears, there was no way he could fit in with humans. Not only was he seven feet tall, he looked like he'd walked straight out of a Viking village.

"Just the four of us, then," Zeke said to Gracelyn. "Do you know where we're going?"

"Following the ravens," Gracelyn said, nodding to where Huginn still stood like a shadow on the wall, Muninn perched on her shoulder.

"I'll fly to a doorway between worlds," Huginn said. "Muninn will lead the other group to Frey."

Muninn spread her wings wide, waved them as if to say farewell, and swooped out of the cave, riding the hot air currents up just as the falcons had done.

"You're not going into Midgard with us?" I asked.

Huginn nodded. "I will escort you. The dragons and elves stay on this side."

"This is my biggest dragon," Gracelyn said. "It can carry four. Can any of you shapeshift?"

"Just the raven," I said.

"Or size-shift?" she asked, examining Zeke's muscular build with a little too much interest.

"No," I said, gritting my teeth.

"Valdan, can you fly one of my fleet?" she asked the other elf.

"I would be honored," Valdan said with a slight bow of his head.

"Good," she said, jerking her chin at me and Finn. "You take those two. I'll take the other two."

"I'll ride with Zeke," I said, slipping my hand into his elbow. No way was I letting her ride off with him after the way she looked at him like a piece of meat.

"Sweet," he said, smiling down at me. "I love dragon riding. It'll be even better with you."

Too late, I caught the flicker of hurt on Finn's face as he turned away.

My heart squeezed so hard I nearly lost my breath. Dammit. I'd let my jealousy flare up and hurt Finn in the process. Not that I wanted to ride with Finn—the awkwardness would have been agony—but I didn't want to reject him either. We'd been carefully avoiding each other as much as possible for the past week. It was too late to take back my words now that Zeke was so excited about riding with me, though. No matter what I did, I would hurt one of them.

Zeke was already settling onto the back of the serpentine dragon, holding out a hand and giving me a beautiful smile full of excitement and hope. I gazed after Finn, who had shuffled out of the cave to where the other dragon sat waiting on the bank of the lava river. Valdan seemed to be convincing Smith to get on the dragon's back. To my surprise, Finn climbed on without hesitation and sat, waiting for the other two.

"You coming?" Zeke asked, his smile disappearing as doubt creased his brow.

"Yeah," I said, and I took his hand and climbed on.

Gracelyn straddled the dragon's neck with the ease of a seasoned rider and spoke a few words in another language to the beast. It lurched forward, and my hands flew out, bracing on the scaly skin of its back.

"I'll hold you," Zeke said. "Don't worry. I know you're scared of heights, but you'll be totally safe in Gracelyn's hands. And I won't let go. I promise."

"Thanks," I said, relaxing back against him and holding onto his arms as the dragon lumbered out of the cave. From the laborious way it walked, it was clearly not designed to be a land animal. Outside, it began to beat its leathery wings. The flapping sound reminded me of the dragon that had attacked us in the world tree—the one that had put me in a coma for three months. Had Mom seen that and freaked out? Was that why she'd been institutionalized?

The dragon waddled down the bank, at first slowly and then faster as it flapped its wings. Finally, it lunged forward, and for one second, I was sure it was going to plunge into the lava river. My fingers clenched around Zeke's arm, and my throat shut so tight I couldn't even scream. And then we were lifting into the air, the animal's muscles straining as it beat its wings furiously.

Zeke whooped, laughter shaking him as he held onto me. At first, I was gripped with the usual fear. After a few seconds, though, my muscles began to relax, shaking as tension was released. I could do this. I could be brave.

"You want to go fast?" Gracelyn called back over her shoulder.

"You know it," Zeke yelled, still laughing.

The fog swallowed us, and I swallowed the urge to scream. I forced myself to relax into Zeke's embrace, to hold to him, and trust him. He'd promised not to let go, and he'd kept his promise.

"Isn't this awesome?" he yelled, giving me a squeeze.

For the first time in my life, I realized I wasn't scared of being high above the ground. Something in Zeke's simple, boyish excitement caught me up, and by some miracle, I found myself grinning. At first, I was smiling at his exuberance, but pretty soon, I found a strange thrill beginning to build inside me. I was riding a freaking dragon. I was *flying*.

For a while, lost in the encompassing fog between worlds, I couldn't see much of anything. I could feel the others nearby, though. When they drew ahead, the particular anguish of being torn apart began to grip me, but it was nothing like when I'd crossed Bifrost alone. The pain of that had been like turning myself inside out. As long as some of them were near, though, it didn't hurt. It felt like something was missing, as if I were always expecting to find them, like a phantom limb I could feel even when it wasn't there.

"Can we talk?" Zeke said after a while.

"Now?" I asked, nodding toward Gracelyn.

She sat up front, manning the dragon, but she was only a few feet away.

"I want to talk to you," Zeke said. "And I can't remember if we've ever been alone. This might be the best chance we get."

Gracelyn showed no indication of having heard us, but I knew she must. At least she was being polite. My heart hammered, though. I didn't know what she'd shared with my pieces in the three months I'd been comatose in the elven world. I only knew she'd been a part of their lives, and she flirted with Zeke. Maybe he didn't want a girlfriend who liked all his brothers. I couldn't blame him for turning me down. I wouldn't want to share him with five other girls.

"Okay," I said, my heartbeat hard and erratic, like someone had reached into my chest and was squeezing it.

"I know everyone thinks I'm an idiot," Zeke said. "I'm not the smart one, and I don't have all the right things to say."

"Oh, Zeke," I said, turning to look up at his face. "I'm not any of those things, either."

"But the rest of them are," he said. "Eliot and Xander, even Peyton."

Now, my chest squeezed for a whole different reason. I twisted around more, so I was sitting sideways on the dragon, and wrapped my arms around Zeke. "I'm not mad at you for what you said about my mom. I say stupid stuff all the time."

"I'm not blind," he said. "I saw you how you were looking at Finn before we took off. I know you wanted to go with him. And I know you shared something with him that you don't share with me. Not that I wouldn't want to share that with you if you wanted to. I totally would."

I squeezed him harder, pressing my cheek to his strong chest. I was glad he couldn't see the blush creeping up my cheeks. "I don't know if I'd say I wanted to ride with him," I said. "I just didn't want to hurt his feelings."

I thought about how completely awkward this would be if I was in Finn's arms instead of Zeke's. He'd be stiff with trying not to touch me, trying not to feel our bodies pressed together. I'd be so aware of it that it would just about hurt, and I'd probably be scared stiff because he wouldn't be holding me and promising not to let go. Where had the Finn I met when I first arrived at the Keen's gone, the one who was sweet and caring, not aloof and ashamed? I knew that boy was still in there somewhere. I just didn't know how to get him back.

"Well, I know it's hard to get alone time with all of us around," Zeke said. "So, I just don't want you to feel like you have to be with me when you're really wanting to be with him. Or any of the others."

With my face against his chest, listening to his beating heart, it was easier to admit my feelings. "What if I really want to be with you?" I whispered.

"Do you really?" he asked, drawing back to peer at my face. My cheeks blazed with heat, but he wouldn't let me bury my face and hide. His sun-streaked hair caught the light, shining golden, and his eyes crinkled at the corners when he smiled.

I nodded, swiveling around, but Zeke took my chin and turned it back toward him. "I really want to be with you, too, Gwen," he said. He took my face between his hands and kissed me. When he pulled away, my heart staggered in my chest, and I thought I might black out from the rush inside me.

"Even after what I said?" I asked. "Even if I want the others, too?"

"Even then," he said. "Your feelings for someone else don't change my feelings for you. I told you I liked you the first night we left Midgard. Maybe I'm not a smooth talker, but when I tell you how I feel, I mean it."

"Me, too," I said, dropping my gaze. I was drowning in him, in the swell of emotion rising inside me and around me like a tidal wave.

"Then stop pulling away," Zeke said, leaning forward and lifting my chin again. "If you want me, then let me have you, too."

The thought of letting go of myself was scarier than the thought of lifting my hands like I was on a rollercoaster as the dragon descended. I'd let myself go once, and it had driven a wedge between me and Finn that might never dissolve. We could barely speak to each other, and when we did, we had to look at something else as if we might die if we directly addressed each other. The pain of it still took my breath. His betrayal and my own mistakes were too much to bear at once. It was easier to dance around one other, pretending the other didn't exist, unless we absolutely had to acknowledge each other. And even then, we could never, ever acknowledge what we'd done.

But Zeke was not Finn. I'd opened up to Peyton in a different way, and that hadn't killed me. I'd trusted Eliot with my heart, and he hadn't crushed it. Those nights we'd spent together in Asgard, we'd shared something maybe even more intimate. I had trusted them both to really know me, and physically to stay within my comfort zone. And they'd done it beautifully.

I closed my eyes and held onto Zeke, and I tried to let go, to trust both myself and him. His lips touched mine, his arms sliding around my body, cradling me against him. His big hands moved down my back, gripping my bottom and drawing me to him. I pressed into him, burying my fingers in his blond hair, hungering for more of him as his mouth moved smoothly against mine. In his hands, I felt small and delicate, but also safe.

Chapter Fourteen

Gwen

A few minutes later, the wind began to rip at the dragon's wings. Coldness wrapped itself around us, wet and clinging. Zeke's arms tightened around me, and his body shuddered against mine. I opened my eyes to find us descending into a world of blinding white snow and stark, unforgiving black stone. A lone raven soared ahead, her body tossed by gusts of vicious wind. A churning black river raged down a chasm between two mountains, and a cluster of bleak iron towers jutted from the mountainside.

"What is this?" I asked, nestling into Zeke's embrace.

"Welcome to Helheim," Gracelyn called over her shoulder. "You're lucky you got warmed up before visiting here."

"Isn't this where dead people go?" I asked, too distracted by the scene below to be embarrassed by her little jab. "The dishonorable ones?"

"We will drop you at the window to Midgard," she said. "Get through as fast as possible. Hel's army does not like company of the living variety. Once you're in Hel, they will do all they can to prevent you from leaving."

"My mother's in a hospital near the entrance to hell?" I asked. "That does not bode well."

"Worry about getting yourself through alive," Gracelyn said. "Then worry about your mother. The Midgard side is as safe as anywhere in Midgard."

"What's that supposed to mean?" Zeke asked. "Our world is totally safe."

Gracelyn snorted. "For you."

The raven shrieked and dove, folding her wings and plummeting toward the rugged landscape below. As we descended, I made out dozens of figures on the mountainside near the towers.

"Is that Hel's army?" I asked.

"Everyone here is in Hel's army," Gracelyn said. "You cannot kill them. They have already died. And yet, they will live forever—or until Ragnarok."

"Zombies," Zeke said.

"I was going to say immortal," I said.

"Yes," Gracelyn said. "Both are good words for what lives here."

"Big difference," I muttered.

"They are dead but not dead," she said.

"So were the people in Asgard," I pointed out. "They didn't seem very zombie-like. Crazy, yes. But they were definitely still people."

"They live freely," Gracelyn said. "They are honored. They eat and sleep well. Here? No. Imagine endless years of this frozen enslavement with no escape by death. It is no wonder they are less pleasant in this world."

I shivered against Zeke, who squeezed me tighter. "Don't worry," he said. "We'll get you through first."

"When they attack, you will run, and we will fight them," Gracelyn said, sliding a long, silver sword from a sheath on her hip. "I brought my fire-breathers. They are adept at fending off attackers."

Ahead, I could see the other dragon now that we'd left the fog. And I could feel a distinct distress signal pulling at my god side. It took me a second to realize it was Smith. I hadn't been around him enough to recognize his signature right away, but I knew it wasn't Finn, and Valdan wasn't afraid of anything.

We'll be okay, I said inside, willing Smith to feel my calm determination. We were so close to getting back to Midgard. Nothing could stop me from seeing my mom now.

"Are you sure about that?"

I startled, glancing around, even though I knew I hadn't heard him with my ears.

"What is it?" Zeke asked, craning to see what I was looking for.

"Nothing," I said. "Did you hear something?"

"Wind and dragon wings," he answered as the other dragon circled back to descend parallel to ours.

A grinding noise cut through the air, as if two enormous metal plates were sliding against each other. It made me cringe and cover my ears as it intensified.

"They are opening the gates," Gracelyn yelled, her dragon plummeting. I tried to scream, but the sound stuck in my throat as I froze with terror. The ground shot toward us at breakneck speed, and my head swam with dizziness.

The dragons landed in a spray of ice crystals. A growling, ravenous sound like a pack of wild dogs fighting over a fresh kill met my ears.

"Run," Gracelyn yelled.

Before I could recover from the shock, Zeke was off the dragon, dragging me with him. A mob of filthy, grey humans streaked toward us. In the second I had to take them in, I saw grey skin, blank eyes, and gaping maws for mouths.

Finn and Smith slid off their dragon at the same moment we did. Zeke wrenched me forward, gripping my arm as we both ran for the spot where a raven hovered in the air, beating her wings frantically. Below her, a shimmering mirage of air signaled the entrance point. This one had a faint, darkish hue, and I could make out the vague outline of trees through it, though there was nothing but barren snow on this side. Snow and corpselike people.

Swallowing a scream, I dashed toward the raven, running like I'd never run before in my life. Finn ran up beside me, keeping pace, with Smith and Zeke right behind us. Just as I reached the door, Finn stopped dead in his tracks. His eyes widened, his body going stiff as a roaring snarl filled the air. A pack of giant, slathering dogs appeared around the side of the iron towers. Their black lips pulled back, revealing teeth the size of my forearm and as sharp as razors. Strings of saliva streamed back as they raced toward us, their eyes mad with hunger and fury.

"Go," I screamed, and I slammed my shoulder into Finn as hard as I could. I dove after him, blind panic stealing every thought in my desperate, brainless scramble to get through. I hit the ground on top of him, and a grunt of pain escaped him as our bodies collided with bruising force. Before I could rise, Smith landed flat on his back on top of me. He knocked the air from my lungs, and the back of his skull hit mine so hard that blackness bloomed in my vision.

The three of us groaned in pain at the same moment, and Smith rolled off me and onto the dry leaves of the forest floor where we'd landed. He grasped the back of his head, sucking in loud breaths through his teeth.

I sat up, rubbing my own temple, which throbbed, as if someone were stabbing a fork into my cranium. Finn rolled away and curled up into the fetal position with his arms around his middle.

My heart slammed against my sternum, every beat filled with anguish and longing.

Zeke. Zeke. Zeke.

I screamed and dove for the entrance.

Heimdall's words echoed in my head.

You will lose one in another world.

Not today, Heimdall. Not today.

I dove back through, the cold hitting me like a slap before I could even take in the scene. A giant dog stood over me, snarling and snapping at Gracelyn's dragon. Zeke lay in the snow, blood pooling around his head. My stomach lurched, and I raced forward, ducking under the dog to get to my missing piece. I dropped to my knees and wrapped both arms around Zeke, heaving to lift him.

He didn't budge. The guy was huge compared to me, and I'd be lucky to drag his deadweight to the door if I had all the time I needed. Now, I had no idea when the dragon would roast us alive, or the dog would turn and snap us in half with its powerful, slobbering jaws.

My heel slipped in the blood on the ice, and I fell to my knees. I scrambled back up, grabbed one of Zeke's legs, and started dragging him. That's when I saw Valdan slashing at the zombie soldiers.

Help me, you big elven Thor! I screamed.

Valdan threw a few punches before turning and running toward the dog. He dropped at the last second, executing a perfect baseball slide under the dog's legs.

"I've got him," Valdan said, picking up Zeke and tossing him over his shoulder. Together, we ran out from under the dog.

The dog chose that moment to turn around.

"Throw him," I screamed.

Valdan was already heaving Zeke through the window by the time the words left me. Before I could move, the dog lunged at us. Valdan threw his arm out in front of me, the force of it sending me flying backwards. The last thing I saw was the dragon rearing back and blasting them with a torrent of flame.

I scrambled up, ready to beat the flames out. But there were no flames. There was no clamoring, rioting mob. There was no slathering dog. Dry leaves crunched underfoot instead of snow and ice. Silent, barren trees stood around us, their limbs looking spindly and brittle after Yggdrasil. The air was balmy and cool instead of painfully icy. Three boys lay on the ground at my feet.

"Valdan," I said, turning back to the shimmering rectangle. Panic clawed at my chest like a terrified, trapped animal trying to break from its cage. Had he just sacrificed himself for us?

"He's not coming," Smith said, standing and brushing himself off. "He's staying there."

"The dragon just fire-blasted him," I said, tears burning my eyes. I felt no cries of pain from him, though, no obliterating anguish as I expected if I ever lost one of them. Did our connection cross worlds, our bond carrying from one world to the next?

"He walks through fire every day by choice," Finn said, pushing himself into a sitting position. "He's going to be okay, Gwen."

I took a few breaths, trying to calm myself. It was true. He'd be fine. He had to. He was one of us, and we needed him. The others needed him to protect them if they were world hopping to look for Frey. They really shouldn't have even gone while the group was split. I'd been thankful they'd want to do that while I was gone, but now that I'd been reminded of the dangers waiting outside Asgard, I cursed my siblings for not waiting for us to return before starting the next part of our mission.

I had insisted on coming here, though, so I had to make this a short trip. The longer we were apart, the more danger I'd put us all in. The sooner we got Mom out of the hospital, the sooner we could return to help the others find Freya and Frey. I needed to focus and do the job I'd come to do.

I crouched over Zeke, feeling his throat for a pulse. I had to let Valdan do as he would. He had planned to stay there. If he'd wanted to leap through the portal like a flaming torch, he could have. But I didn't think he'd run easily. He was probably enjoying the fight, and besides, it wouldn't be very fair to leave Gracelyn there to fight her way out alone. Right now, I had bigger concerns.

"Zeke?" I asked, shaking him gently.

Above, a raven circled and landed on a tree branch.

"Help us," I said, gesturing at the bird.

It swooped down, and a moment later, Huginn appeared. "The hospital is near," she said.

"Is there a real hospital nearby?" I asked, smoothing my hand over Zeke's head. A knot the size of an egg was swelling on the back of his skull. "He hit his head. We need to get him to a doctor fast."

"Cedar Crest has a medical clinic," Finn said. He knelt, shrugging out of his flannel and tying it around Zeke's head to stop the bleeding.

I turned to him, then back to Zeke. "Can we carry him?"

"We'll have to," Smith said. "Unless you know a farmer with a donkey and cart that can get through these trees."

"Um. We don't really use that kind of transportation," I said. "Help me lift?"

Between the four of us, we lifted his body and managed to keep his head supported as we stumbled through the woods. After a minute, I heard a sound was so blessedly familiar it brought tears to my eyes. The sound of an engine approached, and the whir of tires on pavement flew by.

"We're almost to a road," I said, nearly collapsing in relief. We hurried on, scrambling down a small embankment into a huge ditch, then up the other side. Dead grass and gravel crunched and slid underfoot, but at last we made it up to a winding, two-lane road.

"Which way?" I asked Finn. I kept sending mental feelers out, trying to find something inside Zeke. I knew he was alive, but I couldn't feel him the way I had felt where Finn was when we'd lost him—the way I could usually feel where my pieces were. All I felt was a growing urge to put him down and lie down beside him, put my arms around him, and snuggle into his hoodie with him. I was pretty sure that was Heimdall's urging us to heal him. But I knew it took more than three or four of us for a wound this size.

Finn looked both ways, as if an answer might appear in his memory. I'd guessed right when I'd said their mother had been at this hospital, but Finn didn't seem familiar with the road. To be fair, it looked like any two-lane road through any forest in winter—grey pavement, grey sky, barren trees. But I still had to fight the urge to shake an answer out of him. We didn't have time to waste going in the wrong direction. The sound of an approaching engine kept us from standing there avoiding each other's gazes any longer.

"What's that?" Smith asked, whipping around.

"Relax, it's just a car," I said.

It crested a small hill to our left, its headlights on, though it was only afternoon. Smith shrieked and dropped Zeke's leg to jump behind me. The rest of us struggled to keep our grip on Zeke and reposition ourselves, so we wouldn't drop him as Smith started shaking his hands and jumping up and down. "Oh my Helheim, what is that?" he squeaked again.

The car slowed and gave us a wide berth before speeding off.

"What the hell, Smith?" I said. "We could have flagged it down. Zeke needs help now!"

"Was that Midgard's version of a machine?"

"It's a car," I said through gritted teeth. "It's what we use instead of donkeys. And it could have gotten us somewhere."

"We don't know if it would have stopped, even if we'd waved," Finn said.

"You're right," I said, my irritation melting. Somewhere along the way, I'd gotten used to the other worlds. Nothing in the other worlds ignored us or left us alone. Everything we'd met had either helped us or attacked us. Apathy seemed to be a Midgard-specific ailment.

"You mean there was a human inside that thing?" Smith asked.

"Yes," I said, trying to be patient. But with Zeke hurt, my mom in a mental hospital, and the others in danger because we weren't there to help them find Frey, my nerves were worn pretty thin. "And Smith, you probably shouldn't go around calling us *humans* while you're here."

"What else would I call you? I call myself a dwarf."

"How about you call everyone a person?" I suggested. "You and us both."

"Humans are funny," Smith muttered, but he bent to gather Zeke's leg again.

"I'm used to spending my time in Midgard in raven form," Huginn rasped. "I signed up to show you the way, not to carry bodies."

"Then show us," I said. "Where's the hospital?"

I realized that somehow, they'd started looking to me to make decisions. Our leader was down, and the other two weren't Heimdall's boldest, which meant I had to step up.

"North," Huginn said.

I glanced around, getting my bearings, then sighed. "Of course, it's up the hill," I said. "Everyone's going to have to help if we want to get anywhere. Are you in, Huginn? If not, maybe you can go back and make sure Valdan's okay.

Or bring him back to help, I don't care. We need Zeke to be okay."

She looked thoughtful, then shrugged and picked up the pace. "I said I don't spend a lot of time as a human, not that I didn't want to. This could be interesting."

We started up the hill. I wasn't sure how far we'd make it. There was a better chance the cops would pick us up than a driver. Even if Smith didn't freak out the next time he saw a car, we looked pretty suspicious. He looked like he was trying out for the lead role in a movie about Prince, and Huginn wore a dress consisting entirely of black feathers. Not to mention we were carrying a body along the side of the road.

"So, uh, you fly through all Nine Worlds?" I asked Huginn, trying to distract myself. "That sounds pretty fascinating."

"It can be," she said. "It can also be depressing when people are doing horrible things to their worlds. But then there are people doing great things, too."

"Like cars?" I asked, as the sound of another motor grew closer.

"Like what you're doing for your mother," she said.

"Cars," Smith said. "A little too much like the ice weapons in Helheim. I count that among the horrible things."

"You've been to Helheim before?" I said. I'd barely gotten a chance to talk to Smith, but I could feel the god inside him pulling me closer. Itching to be closer. Crap. I'd thought that irresistible urge to be constantly near Heimdall's pieces had calmed, but it seemed to be getting stronger again. When we were all together, I only felt my natural attraction to them. I was learning to distinguish that from the pull of the god to be with its pieces, which was more like an incessant, nagging anxiety.

"I've been to all Nine Worlds," Smith said with a shudder. I didn't know if it was the memory of those worlds or the sight of a pickup truck speeding toward us. A loud, long honk came from the truck as it blew by without slowing. A gust of hot exhaust and dust blasted us in its wake.

"If there are really people inside those things, why aren't they stopping to see what we're doing?" Smith asked. "Are the machines in control, or are the humans?"

"That's a question for another day," Finn said as we crested the hill. Below lay a tiny town of the type my mother would hate, but which I'd always loved. It was really nothing more than a handful of shops, one gas station, and a diner. Beyond that, I could see a few dozen houses dotting the low hills.

"Oh, thank all the gods," I said, my knees nearly buckling with relief. It may not have been a bustling metropolis with a hospital, but it would have a phone. We hurried down the hill, which was longer than it looked. About halfway to the town, a truck came roaring down the hill behind us. It slowed, and I prepared an answer for when they asked about Zeke.

The window rolled down, and a thick, freckled arm appeared, followed by a thick, freckled head. The man wore a camouflage baseball cap and a tank top, even though it was cold enough for a jacket. "You folks aren't from around here, are you?" he asked.

He didn't sound friendly. Alarm bells started going off in my head, but I couldn't tell if it was the paranoia I'd honed over years or a more well-founded wariness. I pushed it aside. "Our friend is hurt, and we need to get to a phone. Do you have one on you?"

"What's that boy wearing?" the driver asked, leaning forward over the steering wheel to peer past his freckled friend at Smith.

"If it's even a boy," said the guy hanging out the window.

"Like I said, we're not from around here," I said, my heart starting to pound as I tightened my grip on Zeke's shoulder. Zeke, who probably could have talked our way out of a situation like this.

"I can tell," the man said. "There's a good reason we don't got folks like you in North Carolina."

The South. Lovely. Neil couldn't have put Mom in a hospital in New York, or San Francisco, or anywhere else that no one would bat an eye at a petite black man in satin pants.

"We'll be gone as soon as we get to a phone," Finn assured him. "We're not trying to cause any trouble."

"What are you, his boyfriend?" the driver asked, looking him over.

Finn's clothes always looked more like an afterthought than a fashion statement, but the guys didn't seem to like his long hair, ripped jeans, and faded Third Eye Blind T-shirt.

"Someone you don't want to mess with," Finn said quietly.

I winced. Shit. Finn's words didn't even convince me, let alone two hostile locals.

"Is that right, pretty boy?" said the guy hanging out the window. "And what if I do?"

"You look smart," Finn said. "So I don't think you do."

"What are you doing?" I hissed through clenched teeth. Our only chance against these guys was hanging like a sack of potatoes between us. I glanced at the town with longing.

Come on, come on, I prayed silently. *Leave us alone. You don't really want to mess with us right here on the side of the road.*

"Tell you what," said the driver. "We'll see you out of town ourselves. We don't like your kind around here."

"You don't like my kind?" Huginn asked, dropping Zeke's leg and sashaying over to the car. I hadn't paid much attention to her body under that feathery layer, but suddenly it looked as if it were made of nothing but soft, rounded curves and sex. I gaped as she leaned against the door of the pickup and toyed with a silky strand of her hair. "You know, that's too bad. I see there are two of you, and I just so happen to have a twin sister. Some say you can't tell us apart."

The guy inside the truck looked like he had a peach pit stuck in his throat. "Y-you do?" he asked after a pause.

Her raspy voice dipped low, almost to a purr. "I do. She went ahead to make a call from the diner. If you don't have a doctor here, we might need a place to stay in town until our friend wakes up. You don't happen to have an inn here in town, do you? Or maybe some nice folks who would rent us a room for a night? I'll pay…somehow."

The guy's Adam's apple bobbed, and his gaze moved over the group. I recovered from my shock at seeing Huginn go into seductress mode, my mind racing ahead. If we couldn't find a doctor, we'd have to do something, but I sure as hell didn't want to stay with this creep.

"We might could make room for you and your sister," the driver said. "If she's anything like you, I'm looking forward to meeting her. Hop up in the back, and we'll take you down there right now."

Huginn jerked her head at the bed of the truck before she went on spinning her magic. I was a bit hesitant to climb in, but I figured if it came down to it, we could jump out. It couldn't be more than another mile down to the town. We scrambled in, heaving Zeke with us. Huginn climbed into the cab with the two men, and we started down the hill.

"These people don't feel safe," Smith muttered. "What's their problem with me? They don't like dwarves?"

"People in our world don't know about dwarves," I said. "They think you're gay."

Smith looked at me blankly. "What's wrong with that?"

"Nothing," I said. "Just, some people don't like it."

"They don't like…happy people?"

"Not that kind of gay," Finn said. "They think we're…romantically involved."

I wondered if that would bother Finn more than the other guys since he was so religious. But his sister was gay, and he'd never seemed to have any problem with her.

"Oh," Smith said, then repeated more slowly this time, "Ohhhh."

"People in our world don't usually dress like that," I said, gesturing at his flamboyant outfit.

"Like what?" Smith asked, glancing down at himself.

"Maybe we could find you something more like Finn's wearing."

"They thought he was gay, too," Smith pointed out.

"The important thing is that they gave us a lift," Finn said. "As soon as we get to town, we can find help for Zeke."

"Yeah," I said, my heart squeezing as I gripped Zeke's hand. "Let's hope that's where these rednecks are taking us."

Chapter Fifteen

Xander

When I got back to Valhalla, I walked into my room and stood there for a minute. This tight, itchy sensation had crept up under my ribs, like when I was a kid and I'd get a cough that lingered after a chest cold, and my lungs felt all itchy, but I couldn't scratch them. And just like that, this flash of memory smacked me in the face, the way memories of Mom always did.

I remembered stretching across her knees and letting my head hang down while she ran her nails across my back, trying to get that itch. I remembered thinking the whole world looked completely different upside down, and my imagination went where kids' imaginations go, and I started rambling to her about what life would be like if we all walked around on the ceiling. Mom just laughed and acted like I was the first kid who ever had that stupid idea, like I was so fucking clever.

If she could see me now, a flunkie with an itch to fight and get drunk and ride a motorcycle. I had to get out of this room, away from the closet reminding me too much of home. I needed my bike, a cigarette, and someone to hit. I didn't have my bike or a cigarette. But there was a whole field of guys who wanted to get hit right outside this creepy Hotel California.

I stepped out of Valhalla and onto the battlefield. I had a knife, and that would be enough. There must be some freedom to being able to die every day and come back in time for dinner. These guys didn't have to worry about what would happen if they weren't careful, if they got too drunk and knocked up a girl or ended up in jail for the night. They could beat the shit out of each other and kill each other, every single day. Talk about great therapy.

A little greasy dude with spectacles came my way, baring his teeth like an animal. "Better watch out, new guy," he said. "Wouldn't want to wind up dead."

He cackled like he'd told some great joke. I didn't know how he'd ended up here, but obviously the Valkyries had been feeling generous that day. This guy was no hero.

My knife was ready when he came at me. I didn't have to feel remorse for this sack of shit. He was already dead. He wasn't some guy who had hung out with my brother, some guy I'd seen at my house a hundred times over the years. He wasn't some asshole who irritated the shit out of me, but who I couldn't stop thinking about for some reason I didn't understand. Joaquin had deserved to die. He had to die. So why the fuck couldn't I get him out of my head?

A crazy, half-bear guy charged at me next, roaring something unintelligible and swiping his claws at me. He might feel real because ghosts up here weren't flickering phantoms. They looked as real as anyone in our world. They weren't, though. Before I could sink my knife into him, another guy threw himself into the bear-man's path. They locked together in a wordless struggle until the bear snapped him in half. He fell to the ground, screaming in agony, blood burbling from his mouth.

The bear charged into the melee, raking his claws across some guy with a sword. I went in with my knife, slashing like everyone else. If this was preparation for Ragnarok, I'd better get busy. Stopping it didn't seem high on anyone's priority list right now. I lost myself in the battle, fighting with knife and fists and feet. Before long, I was cut and bleeding and dirty like everyone else. I'd forgotten all about my mother, who wasn't part of this world any more than she was part of ours. I'd even forgotten about killing Joaquin—almost. To stay alive, I needed to crystal clear focus.

A blond guy who looked to be in his mid-twenties stepped into my path, and for a second, we sized each other up. There was something familiar about him, those wide-set eyes and that funny little mouth.

"You're not dead," he said, his words an accusation if I'd ever heard one.

"Yeah, but you are," I said, throwing a punch.

He ducked it and frowned at me. "You shouldn't be here."

"Tell me something I don't know, old man."

"Where is she?" he asked, blocking my next blow.

"I don't know what you're talking about."

"I heard you were here," he said. "You're the only living people in Asgard. The only gods to show up in years. What happens to her if you get yourself killed?"

"Who?"

"You know who," he said. "My daughter."

"Why do you care?" I asked, slashing with my knife this time. It tore through his shirt and left a red gash in his forearm when he raised it to block me. "She doesn't care."

"You're part of her," he said. "They say you're all part of one god. You know where she is."

"She left," I said. "That's where she is. She didn't even look for you. She doesn't care about you or me or anyone here."

"She'd remember me."

"She doesn't," I said, going in with my fist. When he blocked me, I jabbed my knife under his arm with the other hand. I saw the realization sink into his face, his eyes clearing for a moment. It was the same look she gave me when I hurt her, that flash of shock and anger. The look of a fighter, of someone who went down swinging. It wasn't the hollow, vacant stare of someone who pulled the curtains and lay in a dark bedroom all day, refusing to leave the house for weeks at a time. He'd gotten here by fighting, not by giving up.

I was supposed to find some gods, go home, and struggle through a life that held no more meaning than a football game. That's what humans did. I didn't get to stand on a cliff and think about just letting myself fall, letting it all be over. I didn't get to hide away and tell the world to fuck off, even when I wanted to. I had to buck up, son, keep on fighting the good fight like I was some kind of hero. But I didn't have hero's blood in my veins. The best I could do was get it on my hands.

Gwen's father fell at my feet, and my stomach churned. Someone knocked into me, but I didn't even feel it. I stared down at that glazed, frozen expression. For a second, it flickered, and Joaquin's face was grinning up at me like a skull. Joaquin wouldn't be coming back to have supper with me tonight and tell me I'd pulled a dirty trick on him, though. I stumbled back, blinking away the image. It wasn't Joaquin. He hadn't died gloriously in battle. He'd died by chance—the same way I would have if it hadn't been for Zeke. Zeke was the hero in our family, the one who'd pulled me back from the edge. I was the fuck up. No one expected more from me. I was my mother's son, after all.

I turned and shoved my way out of the fight, off the field. My knife slipped from my hand, but I didn't stop to pick it up. I should tell Gwen I'd found her father. I should tell her he was a hero. But she couldn't cut it in this world, just like she couldn't in ours. Of course she'd run away. My own mother couldn't deal with the shit that went along with being a Keen. Why would a girl who barely knew us stick around?

Chapter Sixteen

Gwen

We pulled up at the diner, and I hopped out, my heart pounding. The guys hadn't kidnapped us, so that was a start. I gestured for Finn and Smith to hurry. Together, we barely managed to get Zeke out of the truck and not drop him. Then we staggered into the diner, Zeke supported between us.

The woman behind the counter rushed out, wiping her hands on her checkered apron. "Oh, my word," she said. "What happened here?"

"Do you have a phone?" I asked, glancing back at the door. Zeke should have come around by now. I didn't know how long Huginn could entertain those assholes before they got impatient. I couldn't imagine what would happen then, but I didn't think it would be anything good.

"Why, sure I do," the woman said. She clutched a pen in one hand and an order pad in the other, as if she expected me to order chicken strips right now.

Impatience clawed at me, and I had to keep myself from snapping. "Can we borrow the phone?"

"You sure can." The woman seemed to come out of her daze. She rushed behind the counter and hoisted a black vinyl purse with gold studs onto a stool. After digging for a second, she handed me a phone.

I turned to Finn. "What's Neil's number?"

Finn recited the numbers while I punched them in, praying he'd pick up. Of course, he was a super rich business man who probably didn't want people calling him, so why would he answer a stranger's call?

Pick up, pick up…

"Hello?"

"Neil," I said. "We need help."

"Who is this?" he asked, his voice edged with suspicion.

"It's Gwen."

"Gwen? You're with your mother?"

"No," I said, my voice coming out sharper than I meant.

"You're calling from the same area code as Cedar Crest."

My chest burned with anger, but I didn't have time to accuse him of locking up my mom. I would take better care of his son than he'd taken of her. "We need help."

"What happened? Are you okay?"

I glanced at the waitress and edged toward the side of the diner, turning my back and lowering my voice. "No, we're not okay," I hissed. "Zeke's hurt, Finn can't be left alone because he might commit suicide, and I brought back a dwarf with a fashion sense that's caught the eye of some homophobes who seem really interested in when we leave this diner. Not to mention you put my mother in a loony bin. We need a hospital, money, a car…" I started hyperventilating, casting a quick glance over my shoulder.

The waitress gave me a wary but encouraging smile, like she hoped I wasn't about to lose it and was rethinking her generosity with the phone.

Neil didn't speak for a long minute. I could hear the clicking of a computer's keyboard on his end. Then he spoke in a hurried but businesslike tone. "An Uber will be there in five minutes. They'll take you to the clinic at Cedar Crest. They can help Zeke. Your mother has money. I'll be there in an hour."

I was too bewildered to speak. When I'd asked for all that, I'd expected him to tell me he was done with my family, that my mom was psycho, and that I was responsible for whatever happened to Zeke.

When I didn't answer, Neil went on, "Be careful. Wait with Zeke in the clinic until I get there. Then we'll go see your mom. I have to talk to you first."

I wanted to say so much more, to ask how he could lock my mother up like an animal, but I didn't have time to fight with him now. I simply thanked him and hung up.

"He sent a car," I said. "We'd better get Huginn."

The door flew open, and the two guys from the truck jostled the raven lady inside. They held her by her upper arms, marching her in. Her big, black eyes were so wide, I could see white all around them, and her hair was a wild mess. "Where's this sister of yours?" the man with the camo hat said.

"Now, we don't want none of that in here," the waitress said, clutching the phone I'd just handed back.

"I'm beginning to think you tricked us," the driver said, giving Huginn a little shake.

"I didn't," Huginn growled, wrenching to free herself. "She's out back."

"You think we're dumb?" the driver said. "You said she was in here before. I know a lie when I hear it."

"She doesn't owe you anything," I said, trembling as I stepped forward. "Including her sister."

"If she ain't got a sister, I'll take you," the other guy said.

"I don't think so," I said. I wasn't sure what we could do in this world with only three of us conscious and one laying on a table, but I could feel the buzz inside me increasing as my fear did. My human side might be scared, but my god side wasn't.

"Let me go," Huginn said.

The driver sneered. "And what if I don't?"

"She told you to let her go," Finn said quietly. "You should probably listen."

"Or what?" the driver said. "Your pansy ass is going to teach me a lesson?"

The guys both laughed, but no one else joined in.

Huginn lurched forward, throwing herself against the guys' grasp. They stumbled, fighting to keep their balance. Suddenly, there was a flurry of movement, an explosion of feathers, and a raven sailed out of the commotion.

"Shit," I muttered, grabbing Zeke's shoulders and shaking him. *Now would be a really good time to wake up,* I urged him.

The two guys from the truck yelled at each other, their faces stark with fear and bewilderment, and the waitress covered her ears, shrieking.

"Let's get out of here," I shouted to the others.

Finn and Smith grabbed Zeke, and we started for the door. The two guys jumped back like we might be carrying the plague.

"Wait," Finn said, and he set down Zeke's legs, turned, and delivered a deft blow to the waitress. She crumpled to the floor, as if boneless.

"What the hell," I yelled, dragging Zeke through the door. Finn picked up Zeke's legs and held the door as the raven swooped out. Then he let the door swing closed.

"She'll think she imagined it all when she wakes up," he said.

"There are two more witnesses," I pointed out.

"Let them think they've lost their minds," he said. "They deserve it."

"Who even are you?" I asked, staring at him.

He shrugged. "I practice martial arts. I can throw a punch."

"You? You practice martial arts? Since when?"

"Since I was a kid," he said with a little smile. "Didn't we talk about your tendency to assume you know people?"

"Yeah, but..." I trailed off, realizing that for the first time since we'd slept together, we were talking almost like normal. And then it all came back—the awkwardness, the realization I didn't know the boy I'd lost my virginity to at all. I thought he always froze in a crisis. Turned out, Finn could be a bit of a badass. Like everyone, I'd overlooked and underestimated him. He was always being brushed aside, and I was no different from everyone else who ignored him or counted his opinion the least of all his brothers. Shame washed over me, and I turned away, my throat constricting.

I would not cry, though. I had work left to do. I channeled my inner Peyton, tightened my ponytail, and pressed back the tears. Peyton never cried. She was always badass, even when she wasn't trying. I missed her to hell and back. Somewhere along the way, I'd started to rely on her to kick my ass when I was moping, to pick me up and dust me off. She wasn't just my stepsister. She was my soul sister.

A green SUV pulled into the parking lot, and a guy rolled down the window. "I'm the Uber driver," he said. "I'm supposed to not ask questions, and you're supposed to tip me well."

Finn shook his head but didn't say anything. Huginn trotted around the side of the building in human form and helped us climb in with Zeke across our laps. Huginn took the front seat, and ten minutes later, we were driving up into the hills. I could see where the hospital name came from—this must be one of the highest points in the area, and we'd passed from bare trees into a forest of dark cedars.

We stopped at a wrought iron fence at least twenty feet high. Behind it, I could make out a sprawling brick building that resembled a private estate more than a hospital. Gently sloping, manicured lawns surrounded the building. Everything was meticulously landscaped, from the walkways to the shrubbery to the cutesy herb gardens surrounding enormous oaks.

"That's a loony bin?" I choked out.

"This is as far as I go," the driver said. "This place is too fancy for me."

I wanted to tell him it was too fancy for me, too. I didn't belong with the Keens and their money, either. But I belonged with my mother, and she was behind those gates. The urge to see her was all me, but it was as strong as Heimdall's pull to be with my godling family.

A black SUV pulled up on the other side of the gate, and two hulking men climbed out. Finn slid out from under Zeke's feet and met the men at the gate. Whatever he said, it seemed to work because a minute later, the huge gate swung open. The men whisked Zeke into their car, and we climbed in with him. I should have been used to the stink of money hanging on everything the Keens touched, but it smacked me all over again now that I was back in Midgard. It was easy to think we were all equal when we were sleeping on the ground in grubby, second-hand leathers.

Even though Finn's style was uncalculated, he'd grown up with these privileges. He expected all gates to swing open for him, just like Xander and Zeke did. They all did. He'd never had a door slammed in his face in his life. I tried not to feel inadequate, but every inch we moved back into our world only reinforced it. I didn't belong here, not even as the poor, adopted stepdaughter.

I forced the thoughts away. Now was not the time.

"We'll take him into the clinic," one of the guys in the front seat said. "You can just check in and wait in the recreation area. The doctor will see him right away."

I breathed a small sigh of relief. Zeke would be okay. I wondered how much money Neil had donated to the hospital to make sure his son got seen first in a place like this. I didn't want to know. Probably enough that Mom and I could have lived comfortably in a decent apartment for a year. Apparently, Neil hadn't told him we were also visiting my mother because no one looked at us like we might be related to a mental patient.

We climbed out, and the SUV pulled around the back of the building. A part of me seemed to go with it, the need to stay with Zeke almost choking me. But I needed something else first.

I turned and followed the others, my hands feeling conspicuous and empty without Zeke to hold onto. "Don't we need a code to get in or something?" I muttered.

"Once you're in the gate, they don't restrict access to the common buildings," Finn said, further confirming he was familiar with the place. I wanted to ask about their mother, but I wasn't sure how.

"And they know you," I said, edging in on the topic. "From before."

Finn's shoulders stiffened. "Neil told them we were coming."

We stepped into the building through a set of oak doors at least ten feet tall. Inside, a crystal chandelier hung overhead, the light playing off the gold threads in the marble floor. I could almost believe I was visiting one of the Keen's relatives or a rich friend instead of a hospital.

The appearance of a pretty, twentyish woman in a navy pencil skirt and creamy silk blouse only increased the odd sensation. Her professional smile quavered as she took in Smith and Huginn, but she quickly recovered herself. She was at least six feet tall and looked more like the type who might work at a swanky hotel in Manhattan than a psych ward in the middle of nowhere.

"I'm here to see my mom," I said. "Olivia—Keen." I almost stumbled over the words, not used to the new name.

"Of course," the woman said. "We've just got a few forms for you to sign first."

"My brother is in the clinic," Finn said. "Maybe I should fill out his paperwork while you do that. Ezekiel Keen?"

The woman's eyes widened, and a genuine smile replaced her practiced one. "Finnegan Keen? Little Finnie the Poo?"

Finn flinched. "You couldn't have forgotten that in the past three years?"

"Oh my god, it is you," she said, pulling him into an embrace. She was just tall enough that when she cradled his head, it was pretty much squished up against her chest.

I tried not to care. It didn't matter that he was happy to hug this girl like she was his long-lost savior, but he couldn't even touch me without flinching.

"We have so much catching up to do," she gushed, releasing Finn at last. "Let me grab the forms, and we can talk over coffee. You can fill out paperwork in the café. Hey, I get off in an hour—maybe we can do ceramics." She sang out the last words like it was some secret she was teasing Finn about. She must have been at least five years older than us, but she had obviously been close enough to give him an embarrassing nickname and do crafts together. I'd missed so much of his life.

He shifted, shoving his hands in his pockets. "Okay."

"Remember when you made that lumpy mug with the saggy handle? I still have it."

"No, you don't," Finn said, his face reddening.

"I do so," she crowed, grabbing his arm. Jealousy flared up inside me, ugly and mean. She had her hands all over my Finn, and she'd known him before he knew I existed. And even though it was Finn, and I knew she hadn't been anything more than a friend to him, it still stung. She might have held his hand while he cried over his mother, comforted him in a time when he needed someone. A time when I hadn't been there. I couldn't compete with that.

"Um, I hate to break up this reunion, but can I see my mom?" I asked.

"Oh, of course," the girl said, adjusting her shiny brunette braid over one shoulder. "I'm Vanessa, by the way. I'm an old friend of Finn's. Your mom is so lucky she found Neil." She tilted her head, giving me a sympathetic smile. "She's doing really well."

"Great." I had always hated the pitying looks people gave me when they figured out my mom wasn't quite normal. I didn't know what to make of this place. It wasn't the loony bin I'd expected when Valerie said Mom was in a hospital, but I still couldn't see her liking a place with a locked gate. I had trusted Neil to keep her safe the way I always had, to keep her close. He hadn't, but at least he hadn't shoved her in a sterile psych ward with bars on the windows.

"She just got back from a swim," Vanessa said. "I think she's going out to do putt-putt in a minute. I'll take you up to her room right now. We don't want to miss her."

"Should you really let mental patients have golf clubs?" I muttered. "And a swimming pool?"

"Oh, this isn't that kind of place," Vanessa said, giving me a smile that was probably meant to reassure me.

"What kind of place is it?"

Finn gave me some side-eye. Was he embarrassed of me? That stung worse than his familiarity with her.

"The kind that has a confidentiality agreement to walk in," she said, ushering us to a small table. She opened a cabinet and took out a stack of iPads. "You'll just need to read over these and sign. It just says you won't take pictures, and you won't talk about what you see here with anyone else."

"What do you think I'm going to see?" I asked, leaving the iPad untouched. Mom had always warned me about giving out personal information, and I sure as hell didn't want to sign a gag order.

"Our guests are here to focus on rest and recovery," she said. "We can't have anyone selling stories of what they've seen. This form just makes sure your presence is not a liability."

I was getting the feeling that being sued by Cedar Crest might be worse than getting sued by the Keens.

"We don't have phones," I said.

"On us," Finn said, pushing the iPad across the table to Vanessa. "We didn't bring our phones in. Gwen is here to see her mom, not take selfies with whatever member of the latest boy band is here this time."

"Of course not," Vanessa said with a wave of her hand and a forced smile. "It's just a precaution, Gwen."

I didn't like the way she said my name, like she didn't trust me not to run screaming down the halls disturbing all their "guests," which even I could figure out was a fancy word for *patient*.

Finn stood, resting a hand on my shoulder. His fingers cut in, and I wished again I could read his mind. Was he warning me about her, or telling me to behave myself like a good little Keen?

"It's their policy," he said. "She's not taking your soul. Just sign it."

"Fine," I said, reaching for the iPad.

Before I could read the fine print, the carved double doors at the far end of the room burst open and a tall, curvaceous woman, wearing nothing but underwear and a bra, came careening through. "I am the high priestess," she screamed, her long hair flying out behind her. "Feel my power!"

Two women in scrubs rushed in through the door after her. The two security guards who had taken Zeke came running in through another door, staccato bursts of instructions coming through walkie-talkies clipped to their belts. And just like that, the carefully curated image they'd tried so hard to maintain was shattered. No matter the trappings they put on it, this was a home for the mentally ill.

"Sadie," one of the nurses said, rushing for the woman.

"Gods," Sadie bellowed, throwing out her arms. The nurses tried to seize her arms, but she yanked free and sprinted toward us. The security guards stepped in front of her, but she dodged one way and then the other, the slap of her bare feet on the marble floor echoing in the enormous chamber. The walkie-talkies were still going off, and everyone was yelling at everyone else.

I jumped up from my chair, aware of a strange crackle in the air. It wasn't quite like when I'd first met the Keens, but it was enough to make the hairs on my arms stand. Finn froze, and Smith pressed in against our shoulders. The familiar buzz of our bodies connecting comforted me. It was no longer scary and new. In the face of the unknown, our connection had become a sign of safety.

"I am the great healer," Sadie screamed over all the noise, her eyes wild as she darted away from one of the nurses. She was as tall as Vanessa and might have been twice as pretty if her face weren't twisted with a strange mania.

Sadie dove for an opening between her pursuers, and suddenly she was flying at us. My hands shot up to defend myself, but she'd already barreled into me. Her body hit me so hard it took me a second to process she wasn't attacking me. Her arms wrapped tightly around me.

"Oh, my," Vanessa said, taking a few mincing steps back, so she wasn't in danger of being touched.

"Don't let them lock the door," Sadie said, her voice low and urgent, so only I could hear her over the commotion. "They'll never let you go."

A chill exploded down my spine as one of the nurses stepped up behind her and popped the cap off a syringe. "Help me," Sadie whispered in my ear.

The nurse plunged the needle into Sadie's shoulder, and a second later, she stumbled back, her arms flopping loosely at her sides. One of the guards caught her under the arms, her limp body sagging against his. Her eyes were glassy and unfocused as she grinned at us. "I had cats."

"Um, cool," I said, cutting my eyes at Finn.

"Now, Sadie," said a black nurse with a kind face. "You know you can't come down here when you haven't taken your meds. It's against the rules."

"That's not my name," Sadie said, her lip jutting out in a pout like a small child. "And I know all the rules. I'm the high priestess."

"High, all right," the nurse muttered. "All the way up in outer space."

"I have panthers," Sadie insisted. "They're coming to take me home."

"Space panthers," the nurse said, shaking her head with a smile. "What will you come up with next?"

The guards dragged Sadie away while she ranted and mumbled about panthers. As they were stepping out of the room, I heard a sentence clearly and my stomach dropped.

"I rode a rainbow," Sadie said in a dreamy voice.

I turned to Finn, but Vanessa interrupted. "Sorry you had to see that," she said. "Sadie is by far our most eccentric guest. Don't worry, she doesn't interact with the other guests. Now, where were we?"

"Can I talk to her?" I asked, a new urgency gripping me. I didn't care if Vanessa thought I was nuts. I needed to find out what Sadie knew. What she was.

"Olivia's on the third floor," Vanessa said. "It's just this way."

"No, I mean Sadie."

She gave me a strange look. "Our guests are here to focus on their healing. We only allow family to visit them on the grounds."

"Come on," Finn said, taking my elbow. His grip was firm, almost painful. Again, I couldn't tell if he was upset at me or warning me. Had he felt the strangeness, or was he caught up in being who he was expected to be in Midgard? After all, he had wanted to come back here all along. Maybe he liked this place for reasons I hadn't considered. I couldn't blame him. Who didn't want to be rich, to have every door swing open at the mention of your name?

I decided to play along for now. I wanted to see my mother first, to make sure she was okay. Then I could talk to Finn in private and figure things out. For now, I knew two things for sure. That woman didn't belong in this world, and I was going to find out why.

Chapter Seventeen

Peyton

When Xander finally showed up, he looked like he'd been picked up by a tornado and set back down in his room. I jumped up from the bed, where I'd been waiting with Eliot and Alvan.

"Oh my gods, what happened?" I asked, reaching for Xander's shredded leather jacket.

"Just doing a little prep work for Ragnarok. I'm fine." He shrugged out of his jacket. His T-shirt was slashed and sticky with blood.

I planted a hand on my hip and glared. "Says the guy who is obviously not fine."

"Chill, Cheerleader," he said. "No need for the drama."

"Yeah, what you need is a doctor," I said. "Or all of Heimdall."

"Where's Zeke?" he asked. "I need to talk to him."

I snorted. "You can just ask about Gwen. That's what you really want to know."

Xander wheeled around, his eyes dark with rage. "Fuck Gwen," he said. "She's just like all the fake friends, and parents, and other assholes who can't be counted on. She doesn't matter anymore."

"Nothing matters to big, bad Xander," I said, irritation getting the better of me.

"We matter," he said, his voice low but edged with ferocity. "The five of us. We don't ditch each other, and we don't run away. Gwen left."

"Yeah," I said. "She did. And Zeke and Finn went with her."

Xander grabbed my shoulders. "Finn? You let her take Finn? Are you fucking crazy?"

"No, and please get your hands off me," I said. "I'm not one of your desperate girlfriends who will let you treat her like shit for a scrap of hope. I'm your sister, and I will happily punch you in the nuts."

Xander dropped his hands and glared. "Finn is suicidal, Peyton. Remember what that means? Or are you too busy looking on the bright side? He'll try again. Zeke and Gwen don't know how to stop him."

My throat tightened, and my heartbeat sped up a notch. "You aren't the only one who lost Mom," I said quietly. "Zeke was there with us, too. He knows how to handle Finn."

Xander stared back at me for a minute before he spoke. "Zeke couldn't stop Mom."

I knew he wasn't saying what he really meant. He didn't blame Zeke for it. None of us blamed each other. We loved each other too much. And I loved him too much to see him getting chopped up in a stupid battle that wasn't meant for us. I loved him too much to see him keep blaming himself. He hadn't even been home when she died. He'd been off at court with Dad.

"You couldn't have stopped her, Xander," I said. "Nothing could have."

He turned away and peeled off his tattered shirt. "I saw Gwen's dad."

A gasp escaped my lips. "What?"

"On the battlefield. Because he died heroically fighting a fire giant, remember?"

I could barely swallow. My eyes stung, but I wasn't a crier. I couldn't have survived growing up with four brothers if I had been.

"Did you…" I swallowed the whole pineapple that seemed to have lodged in my throat.

"No," Xander said. "I didn't see Mom. Wake up, Peyton. Just because she's your hero doesn't mean she's a real hero."

"She fought heroically," Eliot said from the bed.

"If she's not here, she'll be in Helheim," Alvan said. He didn't say it like it was something to be ashamed of, and I was flooded with affection for the big oaf. To him, it was just another place. Despite Xander's worries, I was glad Finn wasn't there. He would have freaked at the idea of Mom being in Helheim, although he was probably the first who'd say she'd gone to hell. Helheim seemed a little different. To the elves, it was just another one of the Nine Worlds. It was no more shameful than Alfheim, although definitely less preferable.

"You mean, we can find her?" I asked.

"Why would you want to?" Xander asked. "She left. She doesn't want to see us."

"Are you suddenly psychic?" I asked. "You don't know what she wants, and I want to see her. She's still my mom."

"Do you really want to revisit that time?" Eliot asked, but his tone was neutral instead of resentful. "It was hard enough losing her the first time."

"Then you guys don't have to come," I said, crossing my arms. "I want to know why."

"I know why," Xander said.

"Oh, yeah? Enlighten me, oh Wise One. You can't know someone else's reasons."

"Life hurts too much for some people," he said with a shrug.

"And what if it's more than that?" I asked. "What if it's not a coincidence that literally all of our parents were messed up? Finn's birth mother killed herself. And when Finn tried, it wasn't like he was alone in thinking up that solution. He had some encouragement."

"Let's find the gods first," Eliot cut in. "If we finish our mission, we'll have our whole lives to visit other worlds."

He usually looked excited by things like that, but even Eliot looked subdued by our conversation. He seemed to shrink a little, like he was becoming the shrimpy, nerdy preteen he'd been when she died. Since then, he'd found plenty of female love to make up for what his mother wasn't there to give. A different kind of love, sure, but my shrink said sometimes it worked like that. Love was love, after all.

"You're right," I said. "What had happened to our parents in the past won't change, but what happens to the rest of the world depends on us."

We still had Dad, and Gwen had her mom. We had to protect our world for them and for ourselves. I had to remember to focus on what I had left, not on what I'd lost.

"Did you talk to Gwen's dad?" I asked, taking a seat on the bed again.

Xander stepped into the closet to find another shirt. His voice echoed out from the depths. "I killed him."

"Wow," I said. "I don't even want to know what a shrink would say about that."

"You probably shouldn't tell Gwen," Eliot said. "Even if he's alive again by tonight."

"Where are the others?" Xander asked. "Did she take Smith and Valdan, too?"

"Smith, yes," Alvan said. "Valdan will be back."

"I am here." The door burst open, and Valdan posed heroically in the entrance. His body was covered in dirt, blood, and soot—and not much else.

"Yes, you are," I said. Even a lesbian could appreciate that hunk of man.

A feather-clad figure hovered in the shadows behind him. At least we had a guide on this mission.

Xander emerged in clean clothes and another one of his leather jackets.

"Together, Valdan and I can heal your wounds," Alvan said. "Your god is too divided."

I jumped up and clapped my hands together. "Great. Let's get our guys healed. Then we go god hunting."

Chapter Eighteen

Gwen

The hallway of the third floor was as wide as a runway. The doors on either side were decorated with tiny wreaths made of fresh daffodils. I wondered who had made them, and more importantly, how much someone got paid to make miniature daffodil wreaths in a place like this. I didn't want to ask Vanessa, though, and Finn had stayed downstairs to fill out some admission forms and wait with Zeke. Since the others weren't family, they had stayed with Finn. I wanted to see Mom alone, anyway, so I could ask her what really happened.

"Olivia is doing so well," Vanessa said. "Her meds have helped stabilize her outbursts, and with daily yoga and meditation, she's learning to live in the now and adopt a more positive mindset."

Was she freaking kidding? Giants were about to take over our world. Positive thinking wasn't going to make them change their minds, turn around, and make their merry way back to Jotunheim.

My thoughts were interrupted when Vanessa stopped and opened the door to Room 309.

"Mom," I cried, rushing in and throwing my arms around her. I didn't need Neil's permission to visit my own mother. He could explain himself later. For now, I needed to see my mom, to ask her the questions that she might not be willing to answer in front of her new husband.

Her body swayed like she might topple if I didn't steady her. She was still wearing a swimsuit, the straps showing above a damp towel wrapped around her. "Gwen," she said, patting my back a few times. "You came back."

"I promised," I said, pulling back to study her. "We never break promises to each other."

"We never do." She gave me a dreamy, vacant smile. Her eyes looked like they did after a vision that wasn't quite bad enough for her to run screaming down the street or go catatonic.

I turned to Vanessa. "How long has she been like this?"

"Since we nailed down the right combination of meds," Vanessa said. "It takes a few weeks to find the right dosage, but she's been wonderful since then."

"I'm an all-star guest," Mom said. I halfway expected her to pull out a sticker chart with stars on it.

I wheeled around to face Vanessa. "She's been like this for two weeks? You let her swim when she's like this? She looks like she might fall asleep in the swimming pool. She can barely sit up."

"We have a lifeguard on duty at all hours," Vanessa said, drawing up, so she could look down her nose at me. "As well as attendants all over the grounds. I assure you, she's safer here than she's ever been."

That little dig about me not keeping Mom safe hit me right under the ribs. Anger bubbled up inside me. I'd done the best I could all those years, even if I hadn't made the right choices. At least I'd tried. All they'd done was shut her down with a bunch of drugs. Vanessa could assure me all she wanted, but I knew my mom. I'd come too far to let an ordinary human intimidate me. No matter how high on her heels she perched, she couldn't make me feel small.

"My mother is not your smiley puppet," I said. "This isn't her. Whatever you have her on, you need to take her off."

"That would be a mistake," Vanessa said. "We've just started on her path to recovery, but you can see how well she's adjusted already. It would be a shock for her to go back to her disordered thinking."

"That's what you call well adjusted?" I asked, my fists clenching. "She can barely say two words. I thought you gave her meds, not a lobotomy."

It was one thing for this bitch to flirt with Finn, another thing entirely for her to mess with my mother.

"If you're concerned about her medications, you can speak with her doctor," Vanessa said, giving me a syrupy smile. "You have nothing to worry about, Gwen. Nothing at all. Her doctor came highly recommended from one of the best restorative health facilities in California. They say he's the best in the business."

"The drug business?" I asked, gesturing to Mom. "I've never taken prescription drugs in my life, and even I can see she's doped out of her mind."

A stitch pulled tight between Mom's brows as she looked at Vanessa as if she was trying to remember who she was. "No fighting," she said. "This is a happy place."

"You hate hospitals," I said to Mom. "How is this your happy place?"

"I can see my daughter here."

"That's right," Vanessa said. "She's been talking about you coming to visit since she got here. She's so excited about it."

"Yeah," Mom said with a bright, childish smile. "And now you can find Freya."

A charge zinged up my spine. "What?"

"Now, none of that, Olivia," Vanessa said. "We've talked about this. Sadie has a case of identity dysmorphia. It's not real."

"The woman in the lobby?" I asked.

"She ran into her one day," Vanessa said. "It's nothing to be concerned about. I'll make a note for Dr. Scott. He'll want to know she's still fixating on their encounter."

I fought the urge to grab my mother and shake the answers out of her. I knew it was more than anyone suspected. If Vanessa was in on some plot against my mother, though, I didn't want to let her know I'd caught on. I smiled and forced myself to stay calm, not to sound like I'd bought into one of Mom's conspiracy theories. "How do I check her out of here?" I asked.

"There's no need," Vanessa said. "Our guests are just that—guests. They can come and go as they please."

"Can we have a moment alone?" I asked.

Vanessa gave me that bright, plastic smile. "Certainly," she said. "There's a button on the phone you can hit if you need someone. We're just a moment away."

Her phone chimed, and she slipped it out of her pocket and frowned down at the screen. "It seems you didn't complete your visitor form," she said. "You'll need to finish that if you want to stay. If you don't want to sign, I'm afraid our security will have to escort you off the grounds. I'm sorry, Miss Keen. I didn't realize you hadn't signed. I've never had any trouble with your family before, so I didn't check as carefully as I should have."

"Fine, I'll sign your stupid form," I said. "Where is it?"

"There's an iPad in the desk down the hall," she said, eyeing me like she thought I might attack her. Taking a deep breath, I tried to remind myself she was just a normal human in the human world, and that to her, all this red tape seemed necessary. My signature was a small price to pay for talking to Mom in private.

I strode down the hall after Vanessa, stopping at a small desk that was obviously not supposed to look like a nurses' station, though that's exactly what it was. "Where do I sign?" I asked, holding out a hand.

I didn't bother to read the fine print. If it said I was committing myself, so be it. Since the others had signed, at least I'd be with them—and Mom. I handed over the iPad and hurried back toward room 309. Vanessa followed close behind, but when I stepped into Mom's room, I pulled the door shut behind me. I rushed to Mom, fighting the urge to wrap my arms around her and sob. After all we'd been through, I wanted her to hold me and tell me it was okay. But Mom had never been that type.

"What did Neil say to make you commit yourself?" I asked, taking her hands in mine.

"I came here so you would come visit," Mom said, that moony expression on her face again. "And look, you did." While I'd been gone, she'd changed into dry clothes, but they seemed to hang too loosely on her. Even her voice was different, higher and slightly slurred. It was like talking to a child who had stayed up way past bedtime.

I didn't know if I could get answers from her, but I had to try. "Mom, what's going on here?" I asked. "Sadie is Freya? How did you know?"

"I saw it in my dreams," she said. "I used to call them visions, but the doctor says that's bad. We're supposed to call them dreams because they aren't real."

"And you came here to find her?"

"Oh, no," she said, her eyes widening. "I came here so you would come. I knew the ravens would find me. They always do."

"What else have you seen?" I asked, trying not to think about how many times my mother had quit her job and taken off because she saw a raven. How many times had they been nothing but ordinary ravens?

"Nothing," she said with a pout. "I'm not allowed to have dreams anymore. The doctor says they're bad. He gave me medicine to make them go away."

"I know." My throat tightened as I looked at her innocent, blank face. If I'd gotten her help years ago, maybe she wouldn't think every raven in Midgard was a messenger of Odin. Maybe she was better off in a mental hospital disguised as a swanky resort. But then I'd never have found Freya, or even my fellow godlings.

"How long have you been here?"

She screwed her mouth to one side and squinted at the ceiling for a moment. "I don't know," she said at last. "Neil came for Christmas. I like Christmas. The lights are pretty."

I could hardly breathe. A knot had formed in my chest. She'd been here for months. Waiting for the ravens to see her—ravens that never came. They hadn't been watching her at all. They'd only watched her because of me, and once I was gone, they'd abandoned her, too. All that time, she'd been waiting for me to come back for her. She'd gone through so much for me.

Because I couldn't think of anything else to say, and because tears had pooled in my eyes and I didn't want her to see me cry, I wrapped my arms around her. She didn't pull back. "I'm sorry," I whispered. "I'm so sorry, Mom."

"The doctors think Freya is crazy," Mom said with a little giggle. It was so unlike her my heart broke a little. How could this be better for anyone?

Finn had reminded me I couldn't assume I knew people just because I had a certain idea of them, though. I had to extend the same courtesy to Mom.

"Do you like it here?" I asked.

"She's not crazy."

"I know, Mom. She's not crazy, and neither are you."

I sat holding her for a long time. She used to pull away, not comfortable with physical touch. But now she sat limp in my arms. I wondered how scrambled her brain was—not from her visions, but from whatever they'd done to her. I wondered if Zeke's head would be okay after the blow he'd received and if the doctor could be trusted not to fry his brain, too. Neil would be on his way by now. He'd make sure Zeke got the best care in the world.

He must have known why my mother wanted to come here. She'd known I would need to find Freya. I no longer blamed him for putting her here, since I knew how hard it was to argue when she had a vision. I'd thought she was weak and sick. But maybe she was stronger than any of us. She knew what she wanted, what needed to happen, and she made it happen. Even if it meant running down a street screaming until I said, "Okay, okay, you win. I didn't like Cleveland that much, anyway."

Neil may not know that—I didn't even see it that way until now. But whatever he thought of the episode that convinced him to send her here, he should have monitored her care more closely.

"I'm going to get you out of here," I said. I didn't actually know how these places worked, but I would figure it out. They might refuse to release her into my care, since I was a minor, or maybe they'd let her go of her own free will.

Suddenly, the ridiculousness of worrying about those rules hit me. Who cared that I was sixteen? The rules of our world seemed so arbitrary. I wasn't keen to freak out the whole human race by revealing we weren't alone in the universe, and that there were eight other worlds we could slip through doors into, but still. If I had to make a few waves to get my mother away from this creepy place, I'd do it in a heartbeat.

As my mother gathered a few belongings from her drawer, I went over the steps in my head. I liked planning. The orderliness was like a map. These were the steps.

I was in charge of Mom. Finn was watching over Zeke. I had to talk to Mom's doctor and see what meds she was on, then make sure it was safe to take her off them immediately. If not, we'd ween her off them slowly. Neil would help me get Mom out without drawing attention. He was her husband, so it was all legal. He had a car, and a home, so they couldn't complain she wouldn't have proper care. We'd take Zeke and Mom home to recover. Then I'd go back with Finn, Smith, and Freya to help the others.

That was the weak link. I knew she was human, and her name was Sadie, but that was about as far as my knowledge went. Where had she come from, and how had she ended up here? Where was the rest of her? Heimdall had told us that one human wasn't strong enough to contain a whole god—even two huge Viking elves had to split Thor. So where were Sadie's other pieces? Since it had taken all nine of Heimdall's pieces to cross Bifrost, I had to assume only whole gods could do it. That meant we'd have to somehow convince Cedar Crest to release Sadie into Neil's care. And then we had to find the other parts of her. And all of Frey.

Just trying to keep up with all we had left to do overwhelmed me so much, I wanted to take Mom and run, like we always had. But I'd promised myself I'd stop running from the hard things, and I wasn't going to break that promise now.

I squared my shoulders and strode to the door. But when I tried to turn the knob, nothing happened.

My heart lurched into my throat, and Sadie's words came back to me. *"Don't let them lock the door. They'll never let you go."*

But I hadn't let them. It wasn't like they'd asked me. I turned to my mother, my pulse quickening. "The door is locked," I said. "Mom, why is the door locked?"

"So you can't get out," she said, turning from the dresser. The duffle bag she'd taken to pack her things hung empty in her hands.

"I'm not a patient here," I said, trying not to completely freak out. "Why would they lock me in?"

My mom hated locked doors, and she wasn't dangerous. Why would they lock her door?

"Then maybe it's to keep other people out," she said, a weird smile forming on her lips.

"What do you mean?" I demanded. "It can't lock from both sides."

"Sure it can," she said, dropping the bag. "Money can buy anything, Gwennie. Didn't Mommy tell you that?"

Chapter Nineteen

Gwen

The faraway look disappeared from Mom's face, and she straightened, her mouth twisting into a grin my mother was not capable of. She stepped toward me, almost leering. I stepped back, shaking my head. My brain refused to comprehend what I saw. It couldn't be true. If it was true, that meant my mother was the enemy, and that was not possible.

"Money can even buy a little privacy," she said, slinking toward me. "Isn't that what you asked for, Gwennie?"

"You're—you're not my mother," I said. "Where's my mom?"

"Good girl," she said. "You're getting smarter. That's why I had to use a better disguise." Her face stretched grotesquely like a character in a scary movie coming to life.

"You paid someone to leave us alone here? To lock me in with you?"

I backed into the door. Closing my eyes, I let myself freak right the fuck out for one second. This time, I knew what to do, though. This time, I wouldn't wait until I was tied up and bleeding before I called them. I didn't know if it would work when they were in another world, but I drew on all the god strength inside me and screamed with all the terror of Midgard behind it. Then I opened my eyes again. When I did, I almost wished I hadn't.

My mother was gone, and in her place was the boy I thought we'd killed. I sagged against the door. At least he hadn't inhabited her body. He must have shapeshifted like Eliot said he could or cast some illusion. Which meant my mother might be okay, wherever she was.

"You're the one who asked to be alone with me." Joaquin grinned and slunk forward another step, pressing his body to mine. "We have all the privacy you wanted. I don't need to talk this time, so it'll be quick. Unless you want me to take my time with you. After all, this has always been a little like a game of cat and mouse, hasn't it? And I do enjoy playing with my food before I eat."

Where are you?

I startled at the clarity of Smith's voice inside my head, then cursed myself when Joaquin narrowed his eyes. I couldn't let him know anything was going on beyond what was right here in this room.

"How did you know all that stuff about my mom?" I asked. Sure, there had been flaws, but he'd had me convinced.

I'm in room 309. With Loki.

"You told me yourself," Joaquin said, stroking my hair behind my ear. "The first time we did this little dance, you told me all about her. Don't you remember, Gwennie? I remember. I can still taste you when I close my eyes."

"No." I started shaking my head, wanting his words not to be true. But they were. I'd told him everything about her, from her episodes to her fear of ravens. I'd given him all the ammunition he needed and enough information for him to impersonate her. I pushed Joaquin away, frantically searching the room for a weapon. "My mother's not here at all?"

Come on, Smith. Hurry!

"Now, Gwennie, how would I know where your mother is?"

"Does Neil know you're here? Does he know you're not really Olivia?"

"Don't feel too bad," Joaquin said. "You're not the first one I fooled. And you didn't tell me everything I needed to know. Some of it I could only learn from first-hand observation." He stalked closer, and I edged along the wall. I needed time, and distance, and a fucking key.

"Where is she?" I demanded. "You said she wasn't here."

"Did I?" he asked. "I don't think I said that. You're not a very good listener, Gwennie, are you? I'm a good listener, though. I learn all sorts of things. I'm what they call a quick study. Too bad you're not as smart as me. Maybe you could have lived longer."

He slid his hand into his pocket and pulled out a familiar, folded knife. My heart quaked in my chest, and my knees went liquid with fear.

"Why me?" I whispered, cowering away.

I'm coming.

Smith could hear me and answer me silently. He was my best hope.

"Oh, Gwennie, I thought you'd gotten smarter. You're the heart of Heimdall. When you're gone, he'll have to wait until the rest of them die before he can start over and build a new team. By then, it might be too late."

"What about Freya?"

"Oh, her heart will find her eventually. That's why Sadie is here. To lure her in. I tried to get Finn back here, so I could lure you away from the others, but you had to go and follow us and fuck all that up, didn't you?" He tossed the folded knife in the air. It spun upwards, end over end, painfully tempting. Joaquin caught it and grinned, enjoying his tease. "It wasn't my idea, you know. He wanted to jump. I was just going to bring him here."

I would not take the bait. I knew what he'd done. He couldn't twist the truth any longer. "I thought you were dead," I said. "We knocked you off a cliff."

Joaquin threw his head back and let out a maniacal laugh. "You're not strong enough to kill me," he sneered. "You're all weak and pathetic. You still live by Midgard's laws. That's why you're going to die here, and I'm going to walk out a free man."

"You should be dead," I said, anger bubbling up inside me. "If you hadn't changed into a falcon, we would have killed you."

"And that's your mistake," Joaquin said, flicking his blade open. "You can't think beyond your own world and what makes sense here. I'd be dead if I was human? Fine, you're right. But I'm not human. You didn't think of that because you're just a tiny fraction of a god. I'm a giant. One who can take the form of a falcon when I feel like it. It's really quite convenient."

He leapt forward, smashing me backward against the wall. A cracking sound echoed through the room as my head hit, and plaster dust scattered at my feet. I fought for consciousness, gripping Joaquin's arms to fend him off and steady myself at once. When my vision cleared, his nose was inches from mine. "You're not brave enough or smart enough to do what needs to be done to survive in another world. Or this one."

I choked back a scream as his knife slashed across my collarbones, splitting my skin open. Panic set in, and I thrashed in his grip. "Xander's strong enough to throw you off a cliff," I said. "He's on his way now. He'll break down the door. He'll kill you."

Joaquin snorted. "Xander didn't throw me off a cliff. He's a pussy who's afraid to get his hands dirty, just like the rest of you." He leaned forward and licked my neck. I squeezed my eyes closed, willing the tears not to spill. Joaquin lifted his head and grinned, his teeth streaked with red. "You bumped into me and I fell. You could just as easily have knocked Finn off. You wouldn't be bragging about how brave you were then, would you?"

While he was gloating, I gathered every ounce of fear I had and brought the side of my hand down on his wrist. The knife skittered across the floor. Instead of going after it, Joaquin slammed his forearm against my throat. "You think you can get rid of me that easily? Wouldn't that be convenient? You get my death all wrapped up in a tidy package, and no one has to feel bad about it. Too bad life isn't that neat. And neither is death. It's messy, and dirty, and bloody." He pinned my shoulders to the wall, gripping my hair and sucking at the cut he'd made in my skin.

"It's a little harder taking other shapes, but I studied your mom long enough to convince you, didn't I?" He grinned like he was so proud of himself. Now, his chin was streaked with gore, too. "I had to get clever to get you here. I couldn't lure you in with one of your fellow godlings, so I had to go with the next best thing."

I wanted to spit in his face, to claw and gouge his eyes out. I couldn't die without knowing my mother was okay, that she wasn't tied up in a closet somewhere while he took her place. "Where is she?" I asked again. "Why play games? You said no one was coming to get me out, right? You've won. Just tell me she's okay and I won't fight."

Joaquin ground his hips against mine, pressing his nose into my neck while he gripped my hair to keep my head back. I turned my face away, my skin crawling from his touch, my body trembling with pain. "Where's the fun in that?" he asked. "It's so much more satisfying when you put up a little fight. Then it feels like a real victory. If I wanted a piece of meat on a plate, I could just order a steak."

Revulsion overpowered my rational mind. I shoved Joaquin's hips away, a shudder wracking my body. I'd held him tenderly for five minutes, maybe ten, thinking he was my mom. I'd cried in front of him. Rage burned in my chest. "Don't touch me," I growled through clenched teeth.

Joaquin grinned and wiggled his eyebrows. "That's more like the Gwen I know. I was beginning to think you'd lost your fighting spirit. Are all those guys wearing you out? It must be exhausting satisfying them all every night. Even if you take two or three at a time."

Where was Smith? This was no time for his impeccable manners. Surely, he wouldn't just accept it when they told him he couldn't come up here because he wasn't a family member. And what about Finn? Had he heard me? Had Vanessa tricked him, too?

"Is Vanessa in on this with you?" I asked. "Is she a giant?"

Joaquin's lip curled in disgust. "Don't insult giants. Vanessa is a pathetic human who would sell the whole of Midgard for the chance to be noticed."

"So, she is working with you."

"She's gullible enough to be useful," Joaquin said. "That's enough talk. Let's kick this party into high gear." He swiveled his hips as he stepped toward me again. Apparently, he'd forgotten the last time I'd had such easy access. I hadn't. I brought my knee up directly between his legs.

He howled in pain, but before he dropped to the floor, his fist shot out and connected with my nose. Blackness rushed over my vision and then receded, replaced by a blinding veil of pain. In all the worlds we'd entered, I'd never felt anything like being punched in the face by a giant. Not when I was fighting the other giants, or he was cutting me, or when I'd been bitten by a dragon. It knocked the breath out of me, as if I'd slammed into a brick wall. I fell to my knees, nausea rolling over me in waves.

"Gwen," someone called outside.

"Finn," I cried, groping at the door and forcing my knees to hold me.

"I'm here," he said, his voice so close he must be pressed against the other side of the door. "I'm going to get you out, Gwen. I promise."

"Too bad your god only enhances your human gifts," Joaquin said from where he knelt on the floor, his hands over his groin. "That door is built to withstand a full-sized human hopped up on crazy-juice. Your puny little boyfriends will break that down the day singing can bust through iron." He threw his head back and laughed.

Fury exploded inside me, and I swung at him with all the rage that had built while he spoke. Joaquin's hand shot out and clamped around mine. He slammed me to the floor and leapt onto me, his fist smashing into my face at the same moment someone threw himself at the door.

The knife was out of reach. I was in a place where probably every potential weapon was confiscated upon arrival. I didn't have enhanced strength. I needed my godlings.

I threw up my hands, blocking Joaquin's next blow. He cursed and twisted my wrist, and a splintering pain ripped up my arm. I screamed out loud this time.

Heimdall, help me, I urged silently. But he'd told me he wouldn't come once we'd found all our pieces. I had to find him inside me. If he enhanced natural abilities, what had he given me?

Joaquin grabbed the hair at the crown of my head and leaned down to lick blood off my mouth. I was going to shave my fucking head when I got out of here.

Not bothering to struggle as he slurped blood off my face, I tried to gather strength and energy as I thought through what to do. I had the ability to communicate telepathically with Smith, who couldn't break down the door. I had sent some kind of signal to the others, too. Eliot was in another world, though, and Finn was outside the door. He couldn't help me, either.

Which left Zeke.

Wake up! I screamed inside my mind, channeling all my energy toward the thought of Zeke. Zeke, who was strong enough to stand up for whoever was being picked on, whether it was Xander cutting me down or me unfairly attacking Peyton. Zeke, who was strong enough to withstand the pain of his own heartbreak if it meant Finn and I could be happy. Zeke, who was strong enough to leap ten feet and catch Xander by one hand when he'd fallen off a cliff.

Joaquin leered down at me, then dug his fingers into the cut he'd made. Agony gripped me, and my body clenched in terror. But I wouldn't flinch. I wouldn't even cry out. Nothing could distract me from Zeke.

"Lucky me, I have a little advantage over the crazies in this place," Joaquin said, licking his fingers clean. "I can make myself look like I'm wearing whatever they want me to wear. They don't have to see my knife."

He leaned over, reaching for the knife. The second I felt his weight shift, I bucked my hips, throwing him off balance. He sprawled on the floor, and I rolled away. But he came up with the knife in one hand, triumph written all over his bloody face. I had no weapon, no way out.

There must be something. I had to keep it together. I would not panic.

And then I heard my mother's voice. "Gwen? Gwen, where are you?"

"Mom," I cried. A wave of fear swallowed me whole. I rushed the door, forgetting Joaquin. A second later, I was ripped backwards and thrown to the floor again. The impact and the shock of pain knocked the breath from my lungs. Joaquin jumped onto me, a sick grin twisting his face. His thighs tightened around my hips as he straddled me.

No, no, no. If he killed me, I'd never see her again. This time, I screamed the word, as if she could save me from this monster. "Mom!"

Fists pounded the door. I flailed under Joaquin like a drowning man in open water, grabbing handfuls of water and finding nothing solid to hold, nothing to save me. Pure panic ripped all thought from my mind.

"This is even hotter than when you sat on the bed holding me," Joaquin said. "I was totally popping a boner, but I figured that might tip you off that I wasn't your mom."

This was too familiar, like the last time I'd been under this creep, when he'd lured me to his apartment and shoved me down on the bed. I'd sworn I'd never fall for the trickster again, but here I was. Anger pierced through the panic, stilling something inside me. I was more than a mindless zombie soul in Helheim. I was part of something real and powerful. Something strong.

Even if I was the only one in this room with Loki, I wasn't alone in this fight. I would never be alone again. The others, the rest of Heimdall, they were a part of me, part of this, whether they knew what was happening or not. If Loki took out Heimdall's heart, the rest of them would be missing a part of themselves for the rest of their lives. I wouldn't let that happen.

Loki had said we weren't strong, but he hadn't accounted for more than the physical. We were all strong in different ways. My strength was the pull I had toward the others. I'd fought it for so long, fought the attraction, the need to be with them. Now, I stopped fighting it. I opened myself to it, letting the need turn my heart inside out. Something inside my chest felt like it was ripping, like I'd swallowed Joaquin's knife. But I didn't stop.

I gathered all the want of my whole life into this one moment, concentrating on the group. On the unfairness of Midgard, on the impossibility of being with my stepbrothers. On the stark pain of wanting them all, wanting them to be happy, and not being able to give any one of them all of me. The ache of yearning for what I could never have consumed me like a disease, and I screamed again.

"I hear the heart is the best part," Joaquin said. He grabbed my throat with one hand and brought the knife down on my chest with the other.

Chapter Twenty

Eliot

It was odd going into another world without being a complete god. Now that we'd found each other, it seemed logical that we'd stay together. But we couldn't be sure when Gwen was coming back, and we needed to find the gods sooner rather than later. So, we gathered on the grassy hillside in front of Valhalla and took stock of our situation.

Besides Peyton, Xander, and I, the two elves had stayed, and we now had a knowledgeable guide in the ravens. One of them fluttered down in bird form and perched on Alvan's shoulder.

"Where to, Raven?" Alvan asked, holding out a hand. She hopped into his palm, her black wings spread.

"Where's the other one?" Peyton asked.

The raven transformed into Muninn before our eyes. It still startled me when she did that. Feathers swayed gently around her body as if they hung from her skin itself. I couldn't actually tell if her feathers transformed into a conveniently shaped garment or if she had feathers even in human form.

"My sister went with the rest of Heimdall," Muninn said. Her voice was so sweet and lilting that it was almost a lisp. It was hard to look at her and believe that baby's voice came out of a tough-looking woman like her. I'd never seen the ravens wear anything but their skimpy feather covering, but I could imagine her in black leathers wielding a battle ax.

"Why?" Xander asked. "I thought they were helping us find Freya and Frey, not Gwen's mom."

"Maybe her mom is Freya," Peyton said, throwing the idea out like it was nothing.

"No," Xander said. "We would have known."

"How?" Peyton asked, a hand planted on her hip.

This was going to be a long mission without Zeke there to make peace between the three of us.

"Let us not argue," Alvan said. "We must stay focused on our quest."

Even Xander didn't push the argument. He might be a big man on the campus of our tiny school, but Xander was no match for the crazy Viking elves. Even he could see that.

"I'll take you to Frey first," Muninn said. "You're lucky. They are already on a quest."

"What?" Xander asked, turning to our raven lady. "Who is *they?*"

"Frey's pieces have already assembled, just as you have," Muninn said. "They are in Vanaheim on a mission from Frey."

"That is lucky," I said. "They're in the other world of the gods?"

"Suspiciously lucky," Xander muttered.

Muninn smiled serenely as if nothing could ruffle her feathers.

"Just because it's convenient that Frey is together and that he's in a world run by gods, that doesn't make it a trap," Peyton said. "It's about time we had a lucky break. I'll take it over going back to Jotunheim where the inhabitants think we're good snacks."

"It's not a lucky break," I said. "There are dozens of gods. It would be arrogant to think we're the first to find out."

Xander glared.

"The carriage awaits," Valdan said, scooping Peyton into his arms.

"Um, my legs work just fine," she said.

"I know," Valdan said as he deposited her in the carriage. "I just wanted to get you moving."

"Jerk," Peyton muttered, crossing her arms and slumping back in the seat.

Valdan shot her a grin and turned to us. "Do you also require an escort?"

I thought Xander was going to throw a punch, so I stepped in front of him, separating him from the elf who could probably break our necks with a single twist. "He's right," I said. "Let's get going."

When we were seated in the goat-drawn carriage, Muninn transformed into a raven, and we followed her up into the sky, slipping into the dense fog within minutes. I was dying to know what would happen if something fell while in the fog. It was supposedly between worlds nothingness, but my rational human brain had a problem with the concept of *nothing*. Then again, human logic had nothing to do with ninety percent of what we'd been through since Gwen showed up on our doorstep, so I couldn't rely on that any more than I could rely on stories holding true a thousand years after they'd been told.

"Has anyone been to Vanaheim?" I asked as the goats flew on.

"It has been many years," Valdan said. "Last time we visited, it was not a friendly place. It was a world at war with itself."

"See?" Peyton said, throwing out an arm toward Xander. "You couldn't just say it was going to be easy, and we'd gotten lucky, could you?"

Xander smirked at her. "You think I made an entire world go to war by saying it was too convenient that we'd find a god there? Damn, I am powerful."

"Powerfully annoying," she said. "You jinxed us."

"Let's talk about Vanaheim," I said. "In the stories, it's the home of the Vanir gods. They specialized in wisdom, fertility, and the ability to see the future."

"Aww, just like you," Peyton said. "No wonder you're excited about it."

"Very funny," I said. "Just wait until you get there and have to hike through a jungle. It's supposed to be all natural and lush—fertile land, after all. It's probably crawling with animals we've never even dreamed of."

"Okay, you made your point," Peyton said with a shudder.

"Someone looking on the bright side would have asked if there were any unicorns," Xander said. "You're off your game, little sis."

Before they could get more heated, Muninn swooped back and perched on the edge of the carriage, transforming into a human after a second. I watched her feathers dancing in the air currents, trying to see if they were attached.

Peyton elbowed me. "Stare much?" she hissed.

"It's not like that," I said quickly.

"Sure it's not," she said, rolling her eyes. "You totally weren't trying to see up her skirt."

"I totally wasn't," I said through gritted teeth.

Muninn showed no signs of embarrassment or annoyance. "This world, like yours, has many diverse landscapes," she said. "Frey is in a more populated area right now. Be prepared to meet Vanir descendants."

"What does that mean?" I asked. "The gods have kids?"

"You said it was the land of fertility," Peyton said.

"The population is made up of demigods," Muninn said. "Most are many, many generations away from being pure gods, though."

"What are they?" I asked. "Human?"

"Yes, human," she said. "Also dwarf, elf, faerie, giant, god, goblin, witch, shapeshifter, and anything else you can imagine."

"This should be fun," Peyton said as we soared through a clear rectangle that opened from thick fog into a bright, clear sky.

"I'll guide you in," Muninn said, a twinkle in her eye as she gave me a suggestive smile.

I felt my face warm under the intensity of her flirtatious gaze, but then she turned into a raven and disappearing over the edge of the carriage. I shook myself free of her odd spell and leaned over to take in my first glimpse of Vanaheim.

Below, I could make out a city, everything in it made of sharp angles of grey and silver. As we descended, I gaped at the foreignness of it. It was a city made entirely of metal. The buildings were like upside down pyramids with flat metal roofs. The streets were smooth metal with strange symbols etched into them. I couldn't make out a single space for people. No sidewalks, no courtyards, not even a tree with a chair under it. A unicorn sighting would have been easier to believe than what had become of Vanaheim.

This was the furthest thing from fertile land I could imagine. It was the exact opposite of everything I'd read. We seemed to be the only living things in the entire city. As Valdan landed the carriage, the symbols on the street lit up with a silvery purple hue.

"Frey is here?" Peyton asked, standing and giving the angular city a skeptical once-over. She stepped toward the edge of the carriage, but I grabbed her arm before she could step out.

"Wait," I said, feeling silly for the wave of anxiety that washed over me at the thought of leaving the carriage. Not that a goat-drawn carriage made of tattered wood and flying a hundred feet above the ground would pass any safety inspections, but this world was a complete unknown. Everything was a variable to solve before we knew if we could even step out of our ride.

"Don't be paranoid," Peyton said, hopping out of the carriage. The symbols on the steel surface underfoot glowed more brightly nearest her feet. Xander stepped out behind her just as a raven landed on the street in front of us. Her body unfurled, growing like some kind of super-speed video of a plant going from seedling to blossom stage in seconds.

"This way," she said, gesturing ahead. "We don't want to dawdle here. Humans are so soft and vulnerable."

"Where are all the other humans?" Peyton asked.

A soft pop came from the inverted pyramid beside us, and a metal door lowered open from the overhanging wall.

"Make haste," Muninn said over her shoulder, already striding down the street. I hopped out of the carriage, noting the brightening symbols when my feet hit the smooth metal surface of the road. Beside us, the door had lowered to touch the ground, forming a steep ramp. As much as I wanted to see what was in there, I knew that anything that sent Muninn scurrying was better avoided. I jogged to catch up to the others, who had followed our raven guide.

I glanced back over my shoulder in time to see something egg-shaped and roughly coffin sized sliding down the ramp. It was about ten feet tall, with large panels fitting together to form the sleek body, and glowing symbols forming a circle near the top. It was the only thing I'd seen since landing that wasn't made of metal, and the white surface of the machine stood out even more against the endless sea of silver and grey. It bobbled when it reached the steel surface of the road, and then began to whirr as it zoomed after us.

"Holy shitballs," Peyton yelled, breaking into a sprint.

Muninn ran to the next building, ducking when she was close to the base. Xander and Peyton joined her, crouching at the lowest point under the inverted pyramid. The elves charged after them, and I brought up the rear. Behind me, I could hear a low, electronic buzz as the pod-like vehicle approached, and the hair along my arms stood on end.

"Eliot," Peyton screamed, jumping toward me. Valdan blocked her way. Alvan spun, grabbed me by the shirt, and dove to the ground. We slid across the smooth metal and crashed into the others. Valdan and Peyton toppled onto us.

"Freaking idiot," Peyton said, sitting up and slugging me in the shoulder.

"Ow," I said, rubbing the muscle. I sat up as the pod stopped, bobbing against the overhang of the building like a buoy against the side of a boat. It was too tall to go further.

"What the hell is that?" Peyton asked. "Please tell me it's not an egg that's going to hatch out some weird alien baby that wants to eat us."

"It's obviously a vehicle," I said. "I can't speak for what's inside it."

"So much for catching a break," Peyton muttered as the side panel of the pod lifted with a soft pop like opening the lid of sealed jar. It hovered a few inches above the opening instead of swinging open like a car door. The panel swiveled toward us, the pod turning with it. The image of a face shimmered into view on the panel—a computer generated face. It looked like a 3-D rendering of an attractive blonde woman with her hair pulled back.

"Congratulations, citizens," a pleasant electronic voice said. "Your electromagnetic signals indicate a high level of otherwise unspecified dweomercraft aptitude, or OUDA." The acronym came out in an especially robotic tone.

"What's that?" Xander asked, glaring at the screen like he thought it was a real person.

"Magic," Muninn said.

"Per the laws set down by the Nornir Empire, you are to be escorted to the queen's court for testing and absorption," said the pod lady. I couldn't tell if she was artificial intelligence or controlled by someone. I'd assumed it was a vehicle with someone inside, but now I wasn't sure.

"Are you serious?" Peyton asked, throwing her hands up. "I totally called it. I told you they'd want to eat us."

"You will not be harmed," the AI woman said. "Joining the court is an honor reserved for those with similar aptitude."

"We're pieces of Heimdall," I said to the digital woman, hoping maybe whoever was in charge would get the information and maybe even help us. "We're honored, but right now we're on a quest to find the godlings who make up Frey."

"Don't tell them that," Xander growled.

"Should we fight them?" Alvan asked. "We can smash them with Mjolnir."

As much as I wanted to see that, I didn't think attacking one of their vessels would help. I started to say so, but I was interrupted by the arrival of four more pods.

"Oh, hell no," Peyton said, yanking her elven dagger free of her belt. "I'll stab their motherboards if they try to take me."

"Do you even know what a motherboard looks like?" I asked.

"No," Peyton said. "Which means you're about to see a stab-happy lesbian go to town on an artificial egg. Good thing Dad's not a politician. He'd never live that down."

"Get back," Xander said, throwing out a hand like he could fend off the interest of the new pods. They all stopped when their tops bumped against the overhanging roof of the pyramid. They swiveled to show us five identical, digitally rendered faces.

"Each of you will ride in comfort to a holding area to await an official summons from the queen," the AI lady said.

"That's a hard no for me," Peyton said.

The pods began to rock, and after a few seconds, they fell backwards, their bottoms facing us. A circular doorway spiraled open in each, and the pods raced toward us. Peyton screamed, slashing with her dagger as the machine sucked her in. Xander hit at his and ducked aside, but the pod turned with him. Steel cables shot out of the next one, wrapping around me like silver snakes. I tried to pull away, but they drew me into the third vehicle before I could begin to work myself free. They released me inside the pod, and I rolled over, looking for an exit. The machine slid forward, then tipped upright. I grasped the walls, trying to get my bearings.

The inside of the vehicle consisted of a plush leather seat and not much else. I had no choice but to sit in its cocooning arms. In front of me, three panels showed three scenes. I tried to focus on them instead of the coffin-like size of my surroundings. One was a mirror that reflected my startled, wide eyes and disheveled hair. The next showed the road outside, though I couldn't tell if it was a projection, screen, or window. The third panel showed a stainless-steel room with five guys sitting along one wall in almost identical poses, their elbows resting on their knees, their hands hanging limp.

I wasn't as interested in the scenes as I was the machinery. I ran my fingers over the smooth, cool material of the panels, but I couldn't find any clues about what they were showing me, how to see anything different, or how to stop the vehicle. Soon enough, it glided to a halt.

"You have arrived," it said, sounding eerily like my GPS at home.

"Where have I arrived?" I asked, casting around to see if I could get a feel on any of the others. My stomach dipped as if I'd started upwards in an elevator.

"Holding area one-three-seven." The door opened with the sound like a vacuum seal being broken, and my ears popped. I jumped out the door of the pod and into a huge stainless-steel room that was obviously the same one I'd seen on the wall of the pod. It was gloriously large after the suffocating ride.

The rest of my group was stumbling out of the doors of their pods, each of which was set into the wall in something like an elevator shaft. I scanned the group quickly, making sure everyone was there before I could breathe again. As soon as we stepped out, the pods closed and dropped down the shafts with a quiet whoosh.

Along the wall sat the five guys I'd seen on the screen. They had perked up, and one of them had even gotten to his feet. They were all wearing skinny jeans, flannel shirts, and beanies. Too bad our pieces didn't look quite so normal. These guys would fit right in back in Boston.

"Hey, I'm Erik," said the one who had stood. He came over, the rest of his group trailing after. Our group drew in closer to form one unit with Muninn orbiting like a satellite.

"Eliot," I said, holding out a hand to shake. The moment our hands linked, a current of electricity crackled up my arm, making every hair on my entire body stand on end. I jerked my hand back at the same moment he did, and we stared at each other.

"Even I felt that," Peyton said. "But we're complete. He can't be one of us."

"Frey," I said, my gaze traveling between the guys. "Right?"

"Yeah," Erik said. "We were supposed to find his sword, and our clues led us here. Unfortunately, we were detected by Her Highness, who has as fondness for gods in her court."

"Same," Peyton said, eyeing the guys. "Does she also have a fondness for hipster boy bands?"

"Apparently," Erik said.

"You laugh now," said another one. "Just wait until they pick out your clothes."

"And make you wax your body hair," said another with a shudder.

Peyton snorted and rolled her eyes. "Are you serious?"

"It seems we require a lot of prepping before having an audience with a queen that we never asked for," Xander said.

"We need to get Frey's sword," Erik said. "But we're kind of stuck here. Why are you here?"

"We need to fix Bifrost," I said. "We came looking for you."

"Well, good luck," Erik said. "When the queen chooses you to be part of her court, it's not optional."

Suddenly, something yanked tight inside me. "Gwen," I said, choking on the word. The pull increased until I thought I'd be torn inside out. "Gwen," I said again, grasping my chest.

"We need to get to her," Xander said. "Now."

"What do we do?" Peyton asked, her panicked gaze flying around the steel room.

"You can't do anything," Erik said. "We can't get out."

Chapter Twenty-One

Gwen

If I'd thought the pain of being punched in the face hurt, I'd been crazier than Sadie. I thought I'd vomit, but I was frozen, rigid with agony, helpless to move. Something inside me jerked to a more even level, as if I'd clipped into a steadying harness. An anchor. But it was too late. My mind was already moving past the pain, past my body. Joaquin yanked the knife free from where he'd stabbed me and licked the blade.

The door flew inward, bouncing off the wall with a deafening crash. Zeke lifted Joaquin into the air and slammed him onto the floor. Finn pulled me into his arms, tears streaming down his face. His lips were moving, but his voice was distorted, as if he were speaking underwater. And Smith was there, pressing his fancy shirt to my chest, soaking it in blood. And my mother was there, my real mother. She was okay.

I closed my eyes, but someone slapped my cheek, and my lids rose halfway. My vision swam with Xander's face, though he wasn't here. He couldn't be. My eyelids were heavy. I needed to rest. Just for a second. But when I closed my eyes, I saw Eliot. And Peyton. I had something I needed to say to her. I fought to remember what, to find the words, but nothing came.

I was losing the parts of myself belonging to them, one by one. But wait, there were more people in the room, people I didn't know. I struggled against the end, trying to force away the image of the twins leaning over me. Then, at odds with all the other faces, the frantic face of Sadie appeared and disappeared. Before my eyes closed a final time, a familiar white-robed figure showed up, her wings extended in full glory. I tried to scream, to tell her I wasn't going, but nothing came. The Valkyrie leaned over me, and a blinding white shroud swallowed everything.

*

When consciousness returned, at first I was only dimly aware of many voices murmuring at once. An urgent tug inside me awoke. I had to get back. I had to get back to my people. My family. My heart. I might have been Heimdall's heart, but they were mine.

It took a few seconds for vision to return after that. Sight came swooping down over my eyes, and I blinked at the random shapes in front of my eyes—an elbow, a shoulder, the place behind an ear. I opened my mouth to speak, but I could barely draw breath. I was being crushed, but that didn't account for the throbbing arrow of pain in my chest.

Someone chanted in another language, and someone else shifted against me. The sensation brought a flame of heat shimmering through my bones, igniting my blood. I needed. I needed to be near and nearer, to be whole with them again. The chanting continued, but it seemed far away. The urgency of needing to be closer to the others swallowed everything else, even the pain. A buzzing vibration filled the room, filling me up, racing over my skin like a chill.

They were crushing me. It was one of the elves' elbows I could see and the side of Eliot's neck that always made me want to lean in and kiss it. Had I done that on the hill in Asgard? I couldn't remember. I'd waited so long for that kiss, and I didn't even know if I'd given it. Someone even lay under me, the rise and fall of his chest pushing me up into the person on top of me, the vibration of his voice buzzing through me. Xander's shoulder was right in front of my face, pressed to my mouth. I could smell him, the faint tang of smoke and sweat and leather. His pelvic bone crushed painfully into mine, and I could see the vein in the side of his throat pulsing.

I couldn't seem to move, not even to turn my head and clear my airway. I managed to draw a breath past the pain and the crushing weight on top of me.

"Am I dead?" I asked. No one answered. After a minute, I wasn't sure if I'd spoken aloud or just thought the words. I didn't remember what my voice had sounded like. They kept chanting in another language, all of them together. Had I been out another three months or longer, long enough for them to learn a new language?

There was no fear in me. If anything, I was slightly irritated that no one had answered me, and they were squishing me between them like the jelly on a sandwich. I was ready to get on with my life, like I had been when I woke after the dragon bite. But I wasn't sure if I had a life anymore. Valerie had come to me at the last moment—did that mean I'd fought bravely and died with honor? I didn't give a rat's ass about honor. I wanted to be alive.

"Am I alive?" I asked, making sure to hear myself this time, to feel the words tickling my vocal chords. My voice was hoarse and croaky, but I'd spoken aloud. When they kept chanting, I squirmed to drag one arm free. Bracing my hand on Xander's shoulder, I shoved him as hard as I could. He barely moved.

"Get off me," I growled, struggling harder.

"Let her up," Zeke's voice said from under me, and the bed shifted. People rolled away, and I could breathe easier, but Xander's chest still crushed me.

"Don't be a psycho," Peyton said, yanking at Xander.

He looked down at me, his eyes an unfathomable, dark grey. "Fuck you, Gweneviere Keen," he said. "If you ever pull this shit again, I will kill you myself."

"Noted," I said, shoving at him.

After a second's hesitation, his mouth pulled into a smirk. He took his sweet time rolling off me. I sat up, surveying the pile of people on the bed with me. My god family. The pieces of me. The two giant elves lounged on the bed, smiling despite our close call. Peyton sat on her heels in the crook of Alvan's body, biting her lip as she studied me with her big, blue eyes that showed so much depth even when her mouth was always moving, always finding something mundane or cheerful to say. My patient, curious Eliot lay right at Zeke's side, gazing up at me with interest and relief. Colorful Smith, who brought a bit of lightness to the group, was on Zeke's other side, watching warily as I took him in.

Xander had turned his back to me, but he hadn't stalked out. He hadn't run. At last, he had stayed with us after the moment of crisis was over.

And there was Finn, propped on his elbow, his eyes so intense and vulnerable and full of pain that it always took my breath. I wanted to reach out and touch him, to pull him back to me again. There was still so far to go with him, so much that needed to be mended, if only I knew how.

Zeke sat up, his arms circling my waist, his long legs on either side of mine. He pressed his nose into my hair and inhaled, his arm tightening around me. "You're alive," he murmured into the back of my neck, his voice sending a warm shiver through my body.

But we weren't alone in the room—not even close. Not only were my other stepsiblings and godlings present and accounted for, the room was full of other people. A handful of scruffy, hipster-type guys stood gaping at us near the door. Vanessa gripped the doorknob, her mouth hanging open and her face stark white. Valerie stood over the bed, watching us with open curiosity. Sadie sat cross-legged in the middle of the floor, now wearing what looked like two baggy T-shirts—one as a top, the other as a skirt. Huginn and Muninn stood near the window. Joaquin lay motionless in the middle of the floor. And Neil stood in the corner with his arm around my mom.

"Mom," I said, climbing off the bed. My legs were shaking, and my head swam with dizziness. My chest still ached, but I lurched across the floor toward her. She looked a little freaked out, and I realized how weird it must be for all these people to witness our healing ritual. It had freaked me out at first, and I was one of the participants. For our parents to see all nine of us piled up on the bed loving on each other while I was bleeding to death—it must have taken a lot of trust for them to let the others heal me instead of calling a doctor.

"I'm okay, Mom," I said, holding out my arms. When I looked down at myself, I wasn't a very comforting sight. My shirt was slashed and soaked with blood. Mom looked like she was about to fly off the deep end, but the expression on her face settled me. This was really my mom, fragile and strange, a woman I didn't even fully know after sixteen years of living with her. Maybe only another person whose mind worked that way could understand her.

I dropped my arms to my sides. I couldn't blame her for not wanting my blood all over her. At least not completely.

"What happened?" I asked. "How did you end up here? Assuming you actually are here, and that's why Joaquin could pretend he was you…"

"I'm a guest," Mom said, licking her lip in the familiar, anxious gesture that made my chest tighten. But her eyes were wrong, still glassy as they had been earlier. "When Neil goes away on business…"

I turned to Neil, my eyes narrowing. "You left her?"

"I had a few business trips in the past few months," Neil said. "I told Olivia she could come with me if she wanted." He looked the same as when we left—tall and thin, with black hair sprinkled with a few strands of silver. But he'd definitely worked on his tan while he was on these trips. A seed of anger grew inside me at the thought of him frolicking on a beach somewhere while Mom was in a hospital.

"I saw that you'd need to find Freya, but I couldn't tell you where she was," Mom said. "I told you that just a few minutes ago, before the giant locked us out. Didn't I?" She narrowed her eyes, as if searching for a memory.

"That was you?" I asked, the wheels turning in my head. "He must have changed places with you when I went to sign the form with Vanessa."

"I got a call that Neil was downstairs, and we were all going to meet together," she said, smiling at the ceiling. "I went downstairs."

"You did the right thing," Neil said, slipping an arm around her and squeezing her to him. For a second, I stared at that hand resting on her waist. It was a possessive gesture, one of ownership.

My own protective instinct flared. My mother didn't belong to him. She belonged to me. I'd gone to literal Hel to get here and save her from his mistake. But as I watched Mom shift her weight in his direction instead of pulling away, I reigned myself in. She liked his hand on her hip. Maybe she even *liked* him, as weird as that was for me. Peyton had told me before they got married that Neil had been lonely, and my mother had married him, after all. I couldn't be too weirded out if they'd started sleeping together. I wanted her to be happy, to be loved, just like I was. Even if it meant she got her hugs from him and not me.

"I didn't think he could hurt you in this place," Mom said after an awkward pause. Neil hadn't put her here. She'd come for me—for all of us. She'd put herself in the place she hated worst in all the world to stop the end from coming, doing her part even when it terrified her. So maybe she had taught me something about bravery. And now, it was time I went back and finished doing my part.

"Bastard," I muttered. "He tricked us both."

"Loki is the trickster," Neil murmured.

I shook my head and took Mom's hands. The pain lingered in my arm from where Joaquin had twisted my wrist, but it was quickly fading. My chest still throbbed, but if I knew anything about Heimdall's healing powers, it would be gone by morning.

"Are you okay?" I asked, studying Mom's face, her mannerisms. It should have been so obvious that Joaquin wasn't her, even with his disguise. But he had been right. My brain was programmed from a lifetime of Midgard, where people didn't change forms, where a sixteen-year-old boy couldn't look like a forty-year-old woman when it suited him. That, combined with her new drug-induced dreaminess, had been enough to convince me when I was in such a desperate panic to see her.

"This place is good when Neil's not home," Mom said. "I can leave when I want, but when he's gone, and you're not there... I'm safe. Freya believes me. She's the only person besides Neil."

"And me."

"And you," Mom repeated.

"You hate hospitals."

"I was scared at first but then I adjusted."

"To your meds," I muttered.

Mom gave me a vacant smile. She probably didn't even realize I was coming home, or that months had passed since I'd seen her last. I'd forgotten how spacy she could be, how much of her mind was just... gone. The drugs hadn't helped.

During the past three months, I had imagined our homecoming, how Mom would welcome us and be loving and excited and all the things a normal mom would be.

Now that she had someone who believed her, I'd thought she might recover some. She hadn't been miraculously transformed into a normal mother, though. Even on drugs that calmed her, she was still Mom, with all her flaws and faults. I'd been worried I'd missed so much while I was gone, that Mom would be so different, but nothing much happened to change her life. That had been wishful thinking.

I was the one who had changed. I couldn't blame her for that, even if I couldn't help but feel a little let down. I sighed and backed up, sinking onto the edge of the bed. Zeke put an arm around me and squeezed me against him. This was my family now. Not just Mom, but all my stepsiblings, all the pieces of Heimdall. They gave me everything she couldn't—clarity and concern, physical affection, presence of mind. With them, I didn't have to be constantly vigilant, constantly on a state of high alert and fear. They protected me the way Mom never could.

"What happened?" I asked, nodding at Joaquin. "Is he dead?"

"He's not dead," Neil said. "Now that you're awake, we should probably get a real doctor up here."

"How did he get here?" I asked. "Is he a patient?"

"Yes," Mom said. "He appeared soon after you left, on my first visit here."

I imagined Mom freaking out, running through the place trying to get someone to listen to her, insisting a giant was in their midst. No wonder she'd made fast friends with Sadie.

"This place is like a halfway house for believers in Norse mythology," I muttered.

"I was keeping an eye on him," Mom said. "If he was here, watching us, then he couldn't be there, hurting you." She smiled with so much pride and hope that I couldn't bring myself to tell her the truth. Joaquin hadn't just been watching her as she watched him. He'd been going back and forth. We'd ditched him so many times, but I hadn't stopped to wonder where he was when we'd eluded him. Along with a new workout routine, I was going to have to work on not being so completely gullible.

I'd wanted to believe Joaquin was at least halfway good, that he was halfway human. While I was giving him the benefit of the doubt, he was going back and forth between worlds, scheming. I may not have been a good judge of character, but some of the others were. I should have listened to Peyton and Xander. They had wanted to get rid of him all along. It had taken a knife in my chest to finally get it through my head. Joaquin may have been a good person without Loki, but he wasn't just Joaquin. He was both. And Loki seemed to be the one in charge.

I suddenly remembered what he'd said. He wouldn't die in a freak accident. If we wanted to get rid of him, we had to do it ourselves. The thought of killing another human being made me nauseous. But he wasn't human. He'd told me as much himself. I might have been half human and half god, but I only had a little bit of Heimdall. If all of Heimdall had been inside me, wouldn't he have completely overridden my small human influence? If giants worked the same way, there was precious little Joaquin inside the body on the floor.

"We have to kill him," I said. "We have to get rid of Joaquin, so Loki will go back to that cave in whatever world he's supposed to be in."

"Gwen," Neil said, frowning at me. "You're talking murder."

"I'm talking self-defense," I said, balling my hands into fists. "He tried to kill me. He would have, if the others hadn't been here to heal me. I'll do it. Where's the knife?"

Neil turned to the others, searching for allies. As I followed his gaze, my conviction was strengthened. Eliot gave me a curt nod. Peyton bobbed her head in agreement with me. Even Finn didn't scold me. The strangers and those I hardly knew didn't protest, either. In fact, no one looked horrified by my suggestion except Vanessa, who sank to the floor and pressed her forehead to her knees and started rocking back and forth. After today, she might end up a patient here instead of a receptionist.

"No," Xander said, stepping in front of me. "I'll do it. I thought I already did. I'm used to the guilt."

"Guilt?" I asked. "You feel bad about that?"

"I'm not a psychopath," he said.

"I know that," I said, shrinking back from his angry eyes. "But that wasn't your fault."

"Yeah, well, this one will be," he said, taking a step toward Joaquin's body.

"No one is killing this kid," Neil said, intercepting Xander.

"He's not a kid," Peyton said, jumping up from the bed. "He's tried to kill us, like, fifty times. Did you see Gwen?"

"An eye for an eye, and the whole world ends up blind," Neil said, his voice firm.

"He stabbed her in the heart, Dad. And he tried to make Finn commit suicide. Believe me, there's a reason the gods chained him up for all eternity," Xander said.

"In this world, he's human," Neil said. "And so are you. No child of mine is going to kill a man while he lies defenseless on the floor. Not if I have anything to do with it."

A shout sounded down the hall, and running feet approached.

"Where's the knife?" I hissed. I was sure I could still do it. If I had to spend my life in prison, at least the others would be free of Loki. Prison would seem like a luxury compared to some of the places I'd lived. I'd have food and shelter, a bed with a blanket, and heating in the winter. The others could go back to their rich, free lives.

Two orderlies rushed in with a stretcher, almost tripping over Vanessa, who had started keening quietly to herself. They jostled us aside and loaded Joaquin onto the stretcher.

"Where is it?" I asked, turning to Xander.

"Why do you think I have it?" he asked, holding up his hands. "If I had it, I would have used it by now."

"Maybe it's a magic disappearing knife," Peyton said.

I knew better. Joaquin said he could look however he wanted, and that included disguising his knife. Right now, he wasn't using a disguise. I scanned his body, looking for signs of it, but there was no bulge in his pocket big enough to be the knife. There were going to be serious questions when the cops showed up and found a bloody knife, blood all over the floor and bed, and me without a scratch.

"Are you sure he's not dead?" Peyton whispered to Zeke, sounding hopeful. Apparently, I wasn't the only one who had been changed by our experiences in another world. I couldn't go back to the way I had been, and Peyton wasn't all unicorns and rainbows anymore.

"I choked him out," Zeke said. "He passed out. He wasn't dead."

"Knowing him, he's faking it," Xander said. "He's probably listening and trying to find his next angle."

Dread sat heavy in my gut at the thought. What if Xander was right? Would we never be rid of Joaquin? After all, Loki would die at Ragnarok like all the other gods. Regardless, we'd missed our chance. We watched in sober silence as they carried him down the hall. We couldn't just tell an ordinary human Joaquin was a giant, and we needed to kill him. And I didn't really want to stab him while two hulking orderlies carried him. They'd probably stop me before I got close, anyway.

Xander stepped between the bed and the others, and a strange silence fell over us. Sadie joined the hipsters, and they all started talking at once, like long lost friends who had just been reunited. Valerie and the raven girls turned to examine the window with great curiosity. Neil and Mom argued quietly on the other side of the room, probably talking about whether it was okay for us to kill people now.

"What happened?" I asked, breaking the silence in our little group of nine. "How did everyone get here? And who are the hipsters?"

"That's Frey," Eliot said. "We found them in Vanaheim. Muninn is awesome."

"I'm sure," I muttered.

Eliot grinned and slid an arm around me. "Not as awesome as you. You ripped a doorway from there to here and pulled us through."

"What?" I asked, my breath catching.

"Apparently, your super power is to summon us," he said, grinning.

I shook my head. "Loki said the god only strengthens the abilities we already have."

"That explains why I was able to break down the door with these guns," Zeke said, admiring his muscles as he flexed.

"Your head," I cried, feeling selfish for forgetting his injury in all the commotion.

"Good as new," he said with a grin. "Though I was feeling pretty woozy until we were all together doing the golden healing magic thing."

I smiled in relief, relaxing back against him again.

"You must have some kind of mental communication," Peyton said to me.

"Have you seen me try to communicate?" I asked.

"You called us before," Eliot reminded me. "We were in this world, but we definitely heard you. And you called the goats one time."

"In the giant's house, you called us to come to the door," Xander said.

"Gwen's power is to make us all come," Eliot said. "That's convenient."

"Shut up," I said, heat flaring in my cheeks.

"I heard you calling me to wake up," Zeke said.

"I've heard you," Smith said.

"I can hear you, too," I said, turning to him.

He gave me a small smile. "I thought you could."

My hands itched with the urge to touch him, to pull him closer to our group. I took his hand and squeezed, my heart thudding in my chest. I'd never had much physical contact with him, and my blood pulsed hot at the rightness of it.

"Really?" Eliot asked. "Just you two? That's interesting."

"Do you answer her when you hear her?" Smith asked.

The others looked around at each other. At last, Finn shook his head. "I don't."

The others shook their heads, too.

"Cool," Peyton said. "It's like telepathy, only we have to do it with intention. Oh my god, my childhood self would have *killed* for that ability. I wish we'd known each other when we were kids. We would have gotten in so much trouble." She laughed, but a twinge of sadness found its way into my heart. We'd missed so much of each other's lives. So much time we could have been together as a family like we were now.

"Like anything else, you're probably getting better at it with practice," Eliot said, pulling me out of my gloom. "You saw how strong you can really be in a desperate situation."

"We should be careful with that," Peyton said. "That's a pretty impressive power—ripping into other worlds. Holy shit, Gwen."

"Are you sure I did that?" I asked. "Maybe I just called you, and one of you broke through."

"Maybe," Xander said. "But I wouldn't try it again just to find out. We don't actually know if these holes between worlds are a good thing."

"We have strength and healing abilities," Alvan said.

"And we're fireproof," Valdan said. "But we didn't make that opening."

"Eliot's got spidey senses," Zeke said. "He can sense danger. I've got super strength. Finn can see the future or warn us of what could happen if we don't act. Gwen can communicate with her mind. Maybe Peyton or Xander made the hole."

"Xander does that protection thing," Peyton said.

"What protection thing?" Xander asked, glowering like she'd insulted him.

"The thing you're doing right now," she said, rolling her eyes. "Look, no one in the room is paying any attention to us. You're like... making us invisible. Except we're not invisible. Just people suddenly found other things more interesting. Don't you think it's weird that Gwen's mom isn't over here freaking out about her?"

"Maybe she's a shitty mom," Xander said.

"Don't even," I said, glaring at him.

"Fine," Peyton said. "Xander, sit down on the bed and smile at Dad. He'll be over here in two seconds, wanting to know all about our experiences. He hasn't seen us in months."

"Maybe he's a shitty dad."

"Either do it or admit you're keeping them away."

"Is anyone honestly surprised Xander's strength is pushing people away?" I asked. "I mean, I barely know you, and I'm slapping myself for not figuring that one out."

I remembered the weird things that had happened, how sometimes I felt like Xander and I were the only two people in the room—in the world. Had he been pushing people away, even without meaning to, giving us privacy? He'd walked off with me at the giant's house, and she'd just let us go with her blessing. We'd talked at the campfire one night without waking anyone, and he'd even fended off the falcon that had attacked us on Bifrost. Instead of coming back, it had just flown away. I found it ironic that a guy who could draw so much attention in this world now had the ability to turn it away with his mind.

"Well, this is lame," Peyton said, bouncing on the edge of the bed. "Everyone gets a superpower but me."

"Your superpower is being awesome," Zeke said, putting an arm around her shoulders.

"Consolation prize," she muttered. "I've always been awesome."

"We'll figure it out," I said. "Maybe you made the opening. But right now, we need to get Freya's other pieces and get across that bridge. Then we can come back here for good. Our parents really do need some answers. And I need to spend some time with Mom." I glared at Xander as I said the last words, but he met my gaze with blank indifference.

If he didn't want to work on his relationship with Neil, that was his problem. I was definitely looking forward to time with Mom. Maybe I'd never live a normal life, and she'd never be a normal mom, but that didn't mean we couldn't enjoy a few simple pleasures when we weren't running from giants and ravens. I could even invite Peyton along and have a spa day.

Peyton hopped up from the bed, adjusted her ponytail, and skipped over to her dad. She looped her arm around him. "We'll be back," she said. "But for now, we should probably get out of here before the cops show up."

"True," I said, joining her. "They're bound to get suspicious when they see all this blood."

"Nose bleed," Zeke said.

"What about Joaquin?" I asked.

"I'll talk to the staff," Neil said. "This isn't a place for violent offenders. He'll need to go elsewhere."

"He's probably loving it here," Finn muttered. "Good food, soft beds, an attentive staff."

I got the feeling the staff wasn't quite as attentive to Joaquin as they were to Finn. He'd obviously been able to slip away into other worlds pretty often. And how he could afford this place was another mystery altogether. Last I'd seen, he lived in a fleabag apartment, and his diet consisted mainly of hot sauce and grape drink.

"You have to admit, it beats an acid cave," Eliot said, glancing around the spacious room.

Peyton planted a hand on her hip. "It beats any of the other worlds we've been to. You can sign me up for a stint in rehab next time we get called up for a mission."

"How are you going to convince the staff that Joaquin needs to go to prison when there's no one here?" Eliot asked. "I mean, it's going to look weird when someone shows up with questions. Joaquin's the only one hurt, and we won't be here at all."

"Does it really matter?" I asked. "We need to go. We can't risk one of us getting arrested."

"She's right," Xander said, resting a hand on my back. "We stick together. Say what you need to say, but we won't be sticking around for it."

A swell of warmth filled my chest so full I could hardly stand it. Sure, we'd kissed a few times, but this was the first time Xander had included me when he said the family stuck together. It was like he'd just claimed me as one of his own. His hand on my back seemed to heat my whole body. I wanted to swoon back against his strong chest and give myself over to the god raging inside me, yearning for closeness with the one piece of this whole thing who had been the hardest to win over and the one who challenged and pushed me to grow like no one else. At last, he was accepting me as one of them, and I wanted something to seal it in stone, some unbreakable bond. I wanted to give myself to him in a way I'd never done with anyone but Finn.

Unfortunately, the room was full of people. And then sirens sounded in the distance.

Chapter Twenty-Two

Gwen

Neil's solution to our Joaquin problem was, "We'll figure it out. We always do."

I remembered what Joaquin had said about money buying privacy. Figuring something out probably meant figuring out who to give money to. In a weird way, I would always relate to Joaquin in a way I couldn't relate to my siblings. I hated that still, even now, I could understand that part of his life.

But having sympathy didn't mean being gullible. I was done with that. Sympathy was what we *didn't* have in common. Like Xander had said, we weren't complete psychopaths. Just because Joaquin was hosting an evil giant didn't mean we couldn't feel sympathy for him or guilt for hurting him. What set us apart was that we still felt those things. All he knew was trickery and blood lust.

I wrapped my arms around my mother. "We'll be back," I said. "We won't be long."

"The hole is at the window," Peyton said. "I'm going through. Don't take too long. There's a lot of us."

"Make sure Loki doesn't get to my mom," I said to Neil. "If you can't get him out of here, get her out."

"I will," Neil said. He cleared his throat and nodded. "Take care of my sons and my girl."

The ravens, the twins, Sadie, and the guys who shared Frey had climbed through now. My stomach bottomed out at the thought of stepping through the window of the third floor. Which was crazy, really, when I thought about what I'd just been through.

Zeke climbed through the window and disappeared into thin air. I balled my hands, anxiety eating away at me. I didn't know where we'd come out. As the room emptied, it seemed more and more cavernous. There was less to look at, too. It became harder not to stare at the blood-stained floor and at the hole in the drywall where Joaquin had bashed my head.

When only a handful of us remained, Xander turned to Finn. "You go next," he said. "I'll be close behind you."

"I'm not going," Finn said quietly, his eyes locked on me.

My throat tightened, and it felt like Joaquin's knife was in my chest all over again. "What?"

"I'm staying here," Finn said. "Heimdall didn't say we all had to cross more than once. We did our duty."

"Part of it," Smith said. "We didn't gather the gods."

"He didn't say we had to be together for that part," Finn said. "We just had to cross it together one time."

"Is—is this about…" My voice caught in my throat, and I could feel tears pressing behind my eyes. Was he going to make me say it in front of our parents?

He glanced from them to me, and then nodded toward the door. "Can we talk out there?"

As I walked toward the door, I felt like I was marching down death row. I'd lived through his rejection before. I knew how much it hurt. I wasn't looking forward to a repeat. Dread knotted in my stomach in a hard, heavy lump. As soon as we were in the hall with the door closed, I turned to Finn. "Don't draw it out," I said, steeling myself. "Just tell me."

"Gwen…" He looked at me with tenderness bordering on pity.

My temper responded. He knew he was hurting me, and he was doing it anyway.

"Finn," I said flatly.

He shrugged out of his flannel and swung it around my shoulders. I stood stiffly, letting him pull it closed. My traitorous body didn't care about my anger. It hummed in response to his touch, aching at the closeness. His gaze fixed on his hands where they lingered, holding the shirt closed around me. The heat of his body sent my pulse racing and quickened my breath.

Memory folded in on itself, reliving the last time he'd touched me. I was swept under by the sensation of his hot, bare thighs against mine in the cold night, my satin dress bunching under us as he braced his knees on the ground, the painful heat between my legs as he struggled to push into me.

Finn gasped and stepped back like I'd burned him. Shit. Had I telegraphed those images to him? My whole body flared with an inferno of embarrassment.

He raked his hand through his hair, his fingers tangling in the bun he'd knotted on top of his head. "What was that?"

I crossed my arms over my chest, letting his shirt hang off my shoulders like a cape. "I don't know what you're talking about."

Smooth, Gwen. Real smooth.

"Nothing," he said. He stuffed his hands in his pockets, hunching his shoulders. He took a deep breath before continuing, his words sounding rehearsed. "I don't want you guys to have to babysit me. You don't need a liability while you have all the rest of this stuff to deal with. And I need to stay here and get... help."

"Here?" I asked. "You're staying here? At Cedar Crest?"

"Yeah," Finn said. "I'm sorry I can't go with you. It's just... I need to do this right now. For me, and for... for all of us."

Stupidly, selfishly, the image of Vanessa popped into my head. And just as stupidly, it popped out of my mouth. "Is this about that girl?"

"What girl?"

"It's okay if it is. I get it. You have a past with her. She was here for you when your mom died, and I wasn't." As I spoke, my words formed a knot in my throat, pulling tighter and tighter. I finished in a croak, "I can't make up for all the years I missed with you, Finn."

"Don't you think we feel the same way?" he asked. "Don't you think we all feel responsible for the way you grew up, the way you lived? We could have saved you."

"I didn't need saving," I said, hugging myself tighter. We stood there in the ridiculously wide hallway with the stupid door decorations, silence echoing around us. At last, I had to admit the truth. "I could have used a little help, though."

"And now I can use a little help," Finn said. "Don't be angry. I want to get better. I want to be better for you, Gwen."

"I want you to get better, too." Tears pressed in, aching behind my eyes. "I mean, not that you're not good enough, because you are, Finn. You're too good." I pressed my hand to his chest, feeling the rapid beat of his good, good heart. I had to bite my lip to stop the trembling. Despite everything that had happened since, I could never be sorry that he had been my first.

"Then let me do this," Finn whispered. "For us. All of us. Not just you and me."

"I'm sorry," I said, laughing at myself even as the tears spilled over. "I'm a hypocrite. You should do this if it's what you need. You're brave, and if it's just for you, that's fine. It's more than fine. I want you to be happy, no matter where you are or who you're with."

"What are you talking about?" Finn asked.

"Nothing," I said, knowing I'd said too much of the wrong things yet again. "It's just that you never said what you wanted when I said I liked all of you, and…"

I couldn't finish. It hurt too much.

"I told you I loved you," Finn said, his hazel eyes earnest and breathtakingly vulnerable. "I don't say that to just anyone, Gwen. I don't say it to anyone, period. Do you think I only said that—in the heat of the moment?"

I bent my head in shame, letting the tears spill down his flannel shirt. He could have accused me of worse suspicions, and I couldn't have denied them. I didn't deserve his tactfulness.

"I didn't," he said quietly.

I nodded, still unable look at him.

"Did you?" he asked after a long moment.

My head jerked up. "What? No." I stepped forward, taking his face between my hands without thinking. I hadn't touched him since that night, not really. Not intentionally. The intensity of our connection blossomed into life again, and I had to fight not to shrink back from it. It was so strong it scared me. "Finn, no."

He nodded, his lips tight. "Then this is what I need to do. I need to be here right now."

"Okay," I whispered, searching his gaze. "And you know I need to be there, or I wouldn't leave you like this."

"I know." He stepped forward, taking my face in his hands. He bent toward me, his body grazing mine, and a dart of longing shot through me like a flare. It burst in my chest, filling it with so much warmth I could hardly breathe. For a long moment, neither of us moved.

"I love you, Finn," I whispered, lifting my mouth to his. I dropped my hands to his arms, my fingers curling around his biceps as I pulled him closer.

"I love you, too," he said, his breath teasing my lips. "You're my forever, Gwen."

"And you're mine."

He folded me in his arms, pressing his heart to mine. Another tear snuck out the corner of my eye, as I rested my head on his chest. For a minute, he stood, stroking my hair back. I could hear his heart beating, the rise and fall of his chest, and all I wanted was to stay here, engulfed in his arms again at last.

"You'd better go," he said. "I'll look after your mom while she's here. Her and Joaquin both."

I stepped back, sliding my arms into the sleeves of his flannel shirt and wiping my cheeks, an embarrassed laugh escaping. I must be a splotchy mess, with my tear-stained cheeks and runny nose. As I turned toward the door, he caught me, pulling me back. And then his mouth was on mine, his hand tangling in my hair. My lips parted against his, and his tongue pressed gently inside, finding the warmth within. I melted against him, a helpless gasp of pleasure caught in my throat. A shudder went through him, and he tensed, abruptly breaking away.

"I'm sorry," he said. "I can't."

"It's okay," I said, linking my arms around his waist and looking up at him, my pulse still racing. "You don't have to apologize. I want you to be happy, Finn. I want you to be comfortable with this. If that means we never kiss again, then I'm okay with that."

The words tore at my throat as I said them, no matter how true they were. When we'd been intimate, I'd wanted to bring the group together, but I'd be lying if I pretended that I hadn't also wanted to bring *us* together. I had wanted him, and I still did. The thought of never being close in that way made my chest clench with pain. But the thought of Finn being unhappy was a thousand—a trillion—times worse. I'd do it in a heartbeat, I'd do anything, to make him happy again.

He gave a small, sad smile and smoothed my hair. "You taste like the ocean."

"It's called being a crying mess," I said with a breathless laugh, remembering what a wreck I must look.

"You're not a mess," Finn said. "You're perfect."

I swallowed past the lump in my throat. Somewhere down the hall, I could hear heavy footsteps in the stairwell. My heart beat double time, and I clutched Finn tighter. I felt time running out with every footfall coming nearer.

"I want to say I love you again, but maybe that's overdoing it," I said. "This isn't goodbye."

"I love you, too," he said. He looked different somehow, felt different. He wasn't the boy who had walked on the beach with me the first morning I'd spent on the Cape. And it wasn't that he was pulling away. It wasn't distance I felt. It was something else, a determination that hadn't been there before. He'd resolved something inside himself and he wouldn't break.

"Don't take the fall," I said. "If they think you hurt Joaquin—"

"Joaquin's not hurt," he said, the muscle in his jaw clenching. "You're the one who was hurt."

"Still," I said. "You're the only one left."

"Go," he said. "It's time."

I wanted to kiss him again, but I knew once I did, I wouldn't want to stop. I didn't have time to linger another moment. I slipped into the room just as the footsteps reached the top of the stairs. Xander and Smith stood at the window. From here, it looked so ordinary, like any other window. The thought of stepping through it into thin air still made me nauseated.

"I'll step through with you," Smith said, holding out a hand. He offered me a shy smile and my heart stilled. I knew my fear of heights for what it was now. Irrational. I could reason my way through it. I took Smith's hand, my lips tugging up in response to his. I barely knew the guy, and I felt shy, too. Shy but determined. "Okay."

Smith's long, warm fingers held tightly to mine as we climbed through. Only when I was halfway out did I really believe I wouldn't fall. And then we were through, standing in a strange room smelling like rust and looking like it was made entirely of stainless steel. The whole group who had left Room 309 stood staring at us.

"What took you so long?" Peyton demanded, rushing over and grabbing my free hand. "We thought you got caught. We were debating who should go back through."

A moment later, Xander stepped into the room from out of nowhere. "I guess we're all here," he said, turning to the raven women. "Can you help us find the rest of Freya?"

Sadness rippled through me. We weren't all here. Finn wasn't here, and he wouldn't be. I remembered Heimdall telling us we'd lose a piece. I guessed this was a better way to lose someone than the definition humans used. If one of the nine died, I thought I'd probably spontaneously die from grief. At the very least, I'd become a shell of a person, like my mother.

I felt a pang of sympathy for Neil, but also admiration. He'd kept it together even after losing the love of his life. He'd done the best he could for his kids. There were so many parents like my mom who couldn't be as strong as he had been. Sure, he'd made mistakes with Xander, but it could have been so much worse. He could have simply checked out. Instead, he'd kept going for them. At last, I felt myself relax away from my fear for Mom. She'd made it this long without me. In fact, she didn't seem to have taken it hard at all. And Neil was far more capable than I'd given him credit for.

My years of taking care of Mom were over. It was time to take care of myself.

Chapter Twenty-Three

Gwen

We allowed ourselves one day in Asgard to finish healing. Zeke's head injury seemed gone, but I wanted to make sure he had time to really recover. My own wound had been so severe that it took longer to heal than anything I'd had before—except the dragon bite, of course. Heimdall's eight remaining godlings spent the day together, trying to pretend we were a complete unit. Without Finn, the group felt broken, though, as if an essential piece was missing.

It was.

What choice did we have, though? We had to go on, had to finish our task before Bifrost went back to the ghost of itself that it had been when we crossed. It was strong now, but we knew it wouldn't hold. If we wanted it to last, we had to make sure it stayed in use. We had to figure out where Heimdall had put the horn we needed to blow, and we still had to follow the ravens into the other worlds to help Sadie find her pieces.

The second morning, we climbed into Thor's chariot with the elves. Huginn had volunteered to take us to find the first piece while Muninn went ahead to scout out the next one. With the addition of Sadie and the loss of Finn, our group dynamic had changed. It was no longer a group of guys with me and Peyton as the only females. Now we had almost as many girls in the group as guys.

"This is so exciting," Sadie said, running her fingers along a strand of her long brown hair until it began to resemble a dreadlock. "Maybe I'll find my cats. I had cats, you know. Big cats."

"We know," Xander grumbled.

I wasn't sure how much help Sadie would be in finding her own pieces, and I could only hope some of her mind would return when Freya was complete.

"We are home," Alvan said as the chariot emerged from the fog and descended into a vaguely familiar, agricultural landscape.

"Alfheim," Peyton squealed, clapping her hands as if she'd forgotten all her complaints about the elven world.

"Maybe we'll see Gracelyn," Eliot said, looking way too hopeful.

"Bro," Zeke said, elbowing his brother. "Not cool. Gwen is right there."

Eliot blinked at me as if he'd never considered that I might not like his attachment to the badass elven chick who had rescued us more than once. I owed her a lot, and I really didn't want to be jealous of her. I decided to leave that comment alone.

We swooped down past a lot of fields and conical elven dwellings before landing at the base of a rocky hill. Scrub trees and bushes dotted the landscape, reminding me of the vegetation I'd seen from the car window when driving through New Mexico with Mom. The thought of her, of being in the same world as her again, made my throat tighten with homesickness.

After a few days, it became clear that going home was a very real possibility—and much sooner than I'd expected. Following the ravens' guidance, we were able to find the next piece of Freya in just four days. I couldn't help but be a little bitter that we hadn't had such an adept guide throughout our whole ordeal. It made things so easy it was almost like cheating. Sure, we still had to overcome a few obstacles in each world, but knowing where we were going was a huge help.

Seeing Mom hadn't curbed my anxiety about her at all. In fact, it had renewed my determination to get home. When we'd found the elf to add to Sadie's piece, we headed on to collect the next piece, which Muninn had already scouted for us. Valdan drove this time, and we slipped into the thick, between-worlds fog, a swirling white so dense I could hardly see the others in the chariot with me.

"This is where we say goodbye," he said at last, urging the goats downward.

"You're going home and leaving us your chariot?" I asked.

"Oh no, you don't," Peyton said. "You're not going to pull a Rosa on us."

"I'm just following the raven," Valdan said.

"We cannot visit your world without risking detection," Alvan said.

"Wait, we're going back to Midgard?" I said. "How do you know that's where the next piece is?"

"I have spoken with the raven," Alvan said, a satisfied smile on his face.

"I bet you have," Peyton said, smirking at him. "I bet that's all you were doing with her, too."

Alvan only smiled wider. They had never answered my confession that I was drawn to all of them, so I took this to mean that Alvan was not keen on being one of my boyfriends. In truth, my bond with them was from our shared god and shared experiences only. I didn't have the kind of human attraction to him and Valdan that I had to the Keens. Maybe it was because they hadn't been there when we'd found out we were godlings, or because they also hosted a second god, or because elves were so different that it was hard for me to connect with them on a human level. Or maybe it was just that the heart wanted what it wanted, and mine wanted Peyton and my stepbrothers.

"Why are we back at Bifrost?" I asked as we descended over the shining, roaring, blazing bridge. We had done that. Not only that, but there was only a handful of giants still on the far bank, and instead of jeering and throwing things, they paced glumly as if they knew we had already won.

We were so close.

"There's an entrance to Midgard in the cave," Alvan reminded me as the goat-drawn chariot blasted through the windy center of Bifrost. It tore at us so violently I thought we'd all fly out of the chariot and be swept up to Asgard, but a second later, we landed in the cave, windblown and breathless.

"You told me the window opens into a cave in Midgard," I said. "But is it close to another of Freya's pieces?"

"Aye," said Muninn in her sweet, baby voice. She stood beside the doorway in her human form, the black feathers of her garment swaying gently against her skin. "When the gods entered the human worlds, many of them stayed near the doorways they entered through. Like yourselves."

Heimdall had come through the entrance on Yggdrasil that led into Boston. The rest of the Keens had stayed close, but I hadn't. Mom had taken me everywhere but Boston. Even so, I hadn't been able to outrun fate.

We didn't dawdle on our goodbyes this time, even though we were leaving the elves behind. We knew what to expect in our world. Or so we thought.

*

We stepped into a blackness so complete I felt like I must have passed out. My heart hammered, and I reached out, my fingers grazing a sandstone wall. Someone stepped through behind me, and I stumbled forward, bumping into Zeke, who had gone before us.

"Not cool with this," he said. "It was daylight on the other side."

"It's not nighttime here," Eliot said behind me. "We're in a cave."

A light blinked on, and Zeke sighed in relief. Eliot scanned the walls with the beam, and Peyton let out a shriek and buried her face in Zeke's chest. "Was that a bat?"

"No," Eliot said. "It's lots of bats."

"Oh my god, get me out of here," Peyton said, her voice muffled in Zeke's hoodie.

"This way," said a bubbly child's voice from the darkness on our left. It took me a second to remember our guide had come through first. Eliot swung the light in her direction, and we filed along through the cave, stooping to waddle through a low spot before scrambling up some boulders. At last, the light of day filtered in, and we climbed up into the mouth of the cave.

The first thing I noticed was that it seemed ominously familiar. I mean, it was just a shallow stone overhang with a forest around it and a black hole at the back where we'd emerged. There must have been hundreds, maybe even thousands, just like it in the United States alone. And yet, I knew this cave. I remembered this cave.

"I—I've been here," I said, crossing my arms against the chill that had nothing to do with the brisk, damp wind in the air. The trees outside the cave were still bare, but I could see a few tiny green sprouts coming up through the leaves on the forest floor, little white flowers huddling close to the ground.

"What do you mean?" Eliot asked, pushing his glasses up and fixing me with his curious stare.

"Mom took me here," I said, running my fingers along the stone wall, the tiny shelf of stone that jutted from the wall. I had swept off the dirt and kept my books there, though they'd gotten damp when it rained. We'd spent an entire month here, sleeping on a bedroll, eating granola bars and canned tuna. Then one day Mom had seen a wolf and a raven together, and she'd had one of her scariest fits ever. That was the end of our caveman days.

"That makes sense, right?" Smith asked. "You said she had visions about the other worlds."

"Usually she was trying to keep me from them," I said. "Or so I thought."

"Maybe she knew one day you'd have to find Freya here," Peyton said.

The group of us took stock of the tiny cave. It still made me feel a little strange to have the Keens see the way I'd lived, the crazy things my mother had put me through. But that was part of letting them in, so I didn't rush them out of the cave. Eliot, Xander, Peyton, Zeke, and Smith examined the cave, studying the little fire ring we'd left, the dirt on the floor. It didn't look like anyone had come through the cave since we'd left.

Muninn, Sadie, and the elven piece of Freya, now wearing Zeke's beanie to hide her ears, didn't seem as interested.

Suddenly, all three of them gave a start. Muninn's head snapped up, and she pointed to a tree. "There," she cried.

"There what?" Peyton asked, frowning.

"That's her," Sadie said, jumping up and down and clapping her hands like a child.

"That...bird?" I asked as a large black bird swooped over us, then rose to circle above the trees.

"Wait, are you saying she's some kind of raven?" Peyton asked, planting a hand on her hip and giving Muninn her no-bullshit look. "Like you?"

"A shapeshifter," Muninn said. "Not a raven."

"Here?" Peyton asked. "In our world? Since when do we have shapeshifters?"

"Since long before you hosted a god," Muninn said with a little smile. "Their ancestors may have come through this very doorway to populate your world."

"Okay, shapeshifters don't populate our world," Peyton said.

"There are many beings in your world that hide in plain sight," Muninn said.

For about a second, my mind balked, full of skepticism. Girls could be birds in other worlds, not in ours. But then the ridiculousness of that thought hit me, and I shook my head, silently laughing at myself. If a girl could be a god in our world, why not a bird?

"Let's go find her," I said, stepping from the cave onto the carpet of crunchy, dry leaves on the forest floor. I remembered walking here before, when we lived here. I remembered rounding a bend in a nearby bluff and coming face to face with an enormous white tiger. I had stood there blinking, sure I was dreaming. It had been so close, no more than a dozen feet away. Terror had frozen me to the spot, and I hadn't moved as it regarded me with huge, golden cat eyes. At last, it had turned and loped off down the mountain. My mother had said it didn't matter, that it wasn't important. Her indifference had been enough to make me think it had been nothing more than my imagination, but I'd never forgotten that moment. Had that been Freya? Or one of her cats?

I found my heart hammering as we tromped through the woods. Fear and excitement coursed through me at the knowledge that even our world was so much more than I'd ever known.

At first, I could see the bird still circling high above, but after a while, I lost sight of it. Finally, we came to a narrow dirt road and stopped to regroup.

"We still on track?" Eliot asked, turning to Muninn.

"I don't have a connection," she said. "I observe just like you." She directed her attention to Freya's two pieces.

"That way," Sadie said, pointing down the road.

We had nothing else to go on, so we started along the road. A minute later, a figure stepped from the woods into our path. I stifled a cry. She'd materialized from the woods like a ghost. One second, there had been only forest on either side of us, and the next, a girl with startling, stark white hair stood before us. She looked a bit older than me, maybe eighteen or twenty, and everything about her appearance was slightly disheveled, from the rumpled T-shirt to the twig caught in her hair to the way one ankle of her jeans was tucked into her brown boot.

"Who are you?" she demanded, planting her feet wide as she faced us on the road. It gave the impression she was blocking our way, especially when she crossed her arms and added a fierce frown to her pretty face.

I opened my mouth to answer, but I wasn't sure how to answer that. Who were we? Gods? Humans, ravens, dwarves, and elves? Rich kids, poor kids, kids with bruised bodies and battered minds?

"I'm the high priestess," Sadie volunteered. "I'm part of Freya, and I'm looking for another piece. She was in a tree when we got here. She's a bird. I like birds."

The girl's eyes narrowed, and her lips twisted to one side as she surveyed us. "What do you want with her?" she asked at last.

"We need her help," Peyton said. "Do you know her?"

"What are you?" the white-haired girl asked.

"We're people," I said, not sure how much we should share with someone in this world. "What are you?"

"Of course you're people," the girl said. "But you don't have a car on this road, which means you either hiked here from over the mountain or you came from the cave. And you didn't hike here over the mountain."

"How do you know?" Xander asked.

"We have patrols."

I shivered, remembering that tiger in the woods. Remembering strange noises in the forest when we'd slept at night. "Creepy," I muttered to Peyton.

"They say nothing good ever comes from that cave," the girl said.

"Who says that?" Peyton asked.

"The people in the valley," the girl said. "I'm Stella. You'll need to meet our leader before you ask for anything from our people."

"Your leader?" Zeke asked.

"Yes," Stella said, tossing her white hair back. "Is that a problem?"

Since we wanted Freya's other piece, we followed Stella along the road. She turned down a drive that looked less like a road than a place where a few people had turned their cars off the road and driven straight through the woods. But eventually, we reached a clearing where a dozen people stood facing us as if they'd been waiting for our arrival.

"Double creepy," Peyton muttered.

The guy at the front of the group broke away and strode forward to meet us. He was tall, with tan skin, black hair, and eyes like silver moons. "I'm Harmon," he said, offering a hand. "We've been expecting you."

*

Harmon led us to a pavilion at the far end of the clearing. I was grateful that he hadn't taken us into a house or compound. Being outside felt safer. We could run if we needed to. We sat along one side of a long, wooden picnic table. Stella and four guys from Harmon's group sat across from us, one of them cradling an orange cat in his arms. I stared at the cat, wondering if it could change sizes. If that was the tiger I had seen that day in the woods. But it only stared back at me with round yellow eyes, the pupils as thin as a slash of black ink.

"How long have you been expecting us?" Eliot asked right away. "Just since your spy saw us? Or longer?"

"The cat," Sadie said, pointing at the boy holding the orange tabby. "I want the cat."

The boy holding it scowled and huddled protectively over his pet. If that's what it was. Now, I had to question everything I'd known of the human world all over again. If even animals could be suspect, who could we trust? Anyone could be in a disguise as convincing as Joaquin's. The thought made a shudder of fear grip my entire body.

Harmon fixed me with those disconcerting, silvery blue eyes. "I think we'll ask the questions," he said. "Since you welcomed yourself to our territory and demanded one of our people."

"Whoa, wait," I said. "That's not what we're doing. We're looking for someone, that's all."

"Give me the cat," Sadie said.

Harmon quirked an eyebrow and looked at me like he'd just proved his point.

"No way," said one of the other boys. "Astrid is ours."

"No one is taking your cat or anyone else," I said. "We just want to talk to her. Assuming that is who we're looking for."

Harmon held up a hand. "Hold on," he said. "Why don't you start by introducing yourselves and telling us why you're here and what you really want?"

"And what you are," Stella said, her nostrils flaring as she pointed at Muninn.

"I'm a raven," Muninn said with a serene smile. Apparently she had no idea how to play this game.

Stella nodded thoughtfully. Beside Harmon, she looked small and pale, but she had a calm assurance in her presence, as if nothing in the world could ruffle her feathers. Like that tiger I'd seen in the forest looking back at me with such unfathomable stillness. Or maybe it had been Harmon, who had a white stripe in his black hair like a tell-tale sign of his second nature. And then there was Astrid, the orange cat with the golden eyes. When I stared at her, she looked away first.

"Let's just tell them," Zeke said. "They have a point. We barged in and asked for one of their... friends. Or whatever she is."

Sadie got up and circled the table. "Give her to me."

Harmon tensed, watching like he was ready to pounce the moment Sadie crossed some invisible line. Unfortunately, I didn't know where the line was or what Harmon would do if we stepped over it. The boy at the end of the table stood, blocking Sadie from getting to the one with the cat.

I looked to the elven piece of Freya, but she couldn't speak our language, and without our own elves, we had no translator.

"Sadie," I said. "Come and sit down. Now."

To my surprise, Sadie sank back on the bench beside her other piece. It was now or never, and I wanted to get home. I was tired of stalling. "Fine, we'll show our hand first," I said. "We're part human, part god."

"God?" Stella asked, drawing back. "We don't have gods here."

Harmon's jaw twitched, and I caught a flicker of annoyance on his face before he smoothed his features. "Where are you from?"

"Here," I said. "I mean, this world."

"We travel between worlds, which is how we came through the door in the cave," Eliot said.

"We're on a quest from our god, and we can't go home until we finish it," I said. "We need to assemble the pieces of the goddess Freya, and Astrid is one of those pieces. We'll bring her back unharmed. As far as I know, we'll never need her again. I can't promise Freya won't, but we aren't trying to take her, or keep her, or do anything against her will. We just need her help. We need your help."

"Astrid is a shapeshifter," Harmon said. "I don't know any goddesses."

"She hasn't done anything strange?" I asked, cutting my eyes at Sadie. "Does she act strange, or have dreams, or visions or... a gift?"

"She's a very gifted shifter," Stella said.

I didn't know what that meant, how you could be better or worse at being what you were. Before I could ask, though, the boy holding the cat scooted back. The animal elongated, fur melting into skin, body growing into a human shape. Within seconds, a girl sat where the cat had been. A very pale, very naked girl with auburn hair that fell all the way to her hips when she stood. "I'm Astrid, the shifter queen," the girl said, raising her chin slightly as if daring anyone to contradict her.

"Whoa," Zeke said, turning to Muninn. "How come you get to keep your clothes and she doesn't?"

Muninn just gave that serene smile and spoke in her strange voice. "Magic."

The rest of us gaped at the sudden transformation of a cat into a stark naked human. Yes, we'd seen the ravens shift, but they seemed less human somehow, as if their feathery garments were part of them. Maybe they were. Even in human form, they seemed half animal. This girl appeared one hundred percent human.

Finally, Eliot recovered himself and stood, giving a slight bow. "You look every inch the part."

And we could see every inch of her. My jealousy was raging, but what was I going to do—cover five sets of eyes so they couldn't look at this perfect girl? Give her my shirt and expose my own ugly scars, the ones from the burns and the hideous green track left down one arm from the dragon's bite? I settled on doing nothing.

Peyton choked on air, and Smith startled. He shot to his feet and bowed deeply at the waist. "Your Majesty," he said.

"Nice to meet you, Your Majesty," Peyton said, a hint of laughter in her voice. I glanced sideways at her, wondering why she sounded so amused. She liked girls, too. Even I couldn't deny that Astrid looked freaking amazing standing there like a nudist queen. Hell, I wished I was that unselfconscious. The girl didn't even seem to realize she wasn't wearing a stitch of clothing.

"Astrid," Stella said with a sigh. "Clothes."

"Sorry, sorry," Astrid said, turning and searching the row of guys beside her. One of them handed her a bundle, a big grin on his face, and she pulled on a thin cotton dress before turning back to us. "So, I'm the queen," she said as if nothing weird had just happened at all.

"And we're a god," I said. "All of us except Muninn. She's a raven."

Astrid's whole face lit up with childlike excitement. "Oh, neat! You must be named after Odin's ravens," she said, clapping her hands in a way that reminded me way too much of Sadie. I didn't know if we could handle another person who shared Sadie's mental state.

"I am Odin's messenger," Muninn said, sitting straighter on the bench.

"No way," Astrid said, her fingers flying to her mouth. "You must be like a thousand years old."

Muninn gave a little smile, a dimple sinking into her cheek. "Older."

"Wow," Astrid said, her eyes wide.

"You know Norse mythology?" Eliot asked, looking almost as excited as Astrid had.

"Yeah," she said. "My mother—well, I've read lots of books. I know all the myths."

"Yeah, not really myths," Zeke said, rubbing the back of his neck.

"Wow," Astrid said, slumping down on the end of the bench. She reached across the table, seemingly without awareness, and took Sadie's hand. "You're those gods? Which one is Freya?"

"I am," Sadie said. "And this elf. She only speaks elven."

"And you," I said. "At least, we think you are."

Muninn nodded, back to looking slightly bored and lounging on the far end of the bench.

"Me?" Astrid asked, sitting up straight, her eyes widening so far I could see white all around her irises. "But I'm just a shifter."

"You can do spells," Stella said quietly.

"Mother Dear taught me those," Astrid said.

"Tell them about the tears," said the guy next to Astrid. He took her hand, lacing his fingers through hers.

"I… I cry golden tears," she said.

"What?" Stella asked, drawing back like she'd been slapped. "You never told me that."

"I didn't think you needed to know," Astrid said before turning back to us. "You know who else cries golden tears?"

"Freya," Eliot said, a smile spreading across his face.

Astrid held his gaze for a second or two longer than necessary, her own smile matching his. "I'm a goddess," she said, then repeated it with a squeal. "I'm a goddess!"

"Yeah, you are," said the guy next to her. He wrapped his arms around her and kissed her on the mouth before pulling away, a big smile on his face, too. A second later, she jumped up and started dancing around, singing that she was a goddess. All four guys on the bench beside her got up, too, and they all laughed and hugged and jumped around while Stella and Harmon watched with indulgent smiles.

"Huh," Peyton said. "I wonder if that's the normal reaction to finding out you're a god."

"Maybe we're more fucked up than we thought," Xander said, staring at the celebration going on before us.

"You're just now figuring that out?" Smith asked.

Sadie and the new elf joined the happy group, and Astrid pulled them both into an exuberant embrace that was about as far from poised and queenly as you could get.

"I don't think there's a normal way to react," Eliot said. "None of this is normal."

"You guys are nuts," Zeke said. "I was stoked when I found out."

"So, uh, I guess this is as good a time to ask as any," I said to Stella and Harmon. "But does this mean we can borrow your queen for a while?"

"Ask her," Harmon said. "She's her own person. That's completely up to her."

"Can we get ice cream?" Astrid asked, returning to the table with flushed cheeks and sparkling eyes. "And see the ocean? Oh, and ride a rollercoaster?"

"Now she sounds like a queen," I muttered.

"Any other demands, Your Highness?" Peyton asked.

One of the guys plopped down beside her and whispered in her ear. "Cotton candy?" she said, leaning away and wrinkling her nose. "What's that? Is it really made of cotton?"

"Is she serious?" Zeke asked.

"I know this is the middle of nowhere, but don't you have, like, a county fair?" Peyton asked. "Who doesn't know what cotton candy is?"

"Astrid has lived a very sheltered life," Harmon said, glaring like we'd, well, insulted his queen. "We wouldn't be comfortable sending her with you without an escort."

"Sorry," I said. "We're not criticizing. I grew up very sheltered, too."

"Please tell me you've had cotton candy," Peyton said.

"I know what it is," I said.

"Oh my god," Peyton said.

Another guy came and sat on Astrid's other side. "Can I be your escort?" he asked, giving her a big grin and a wink before adding, "Your Highness?"

Astrid blushed, but she was smiling, too. "Okay."

"Wait, I don't want to miss her first trip out of the Three Valleys," said one of the others.

"Can I bring all my boyfriends?" she asked, peeking at us from under her lashes.

I almost choked, and I could feel my face flushing. "You have boyfriends? More than one?"

"Four," Astrid said, her smile widening into a giddy grin.

"Me, too," I said. We stared at each other for a second, and then she burst out laughing.

"Do I get to meet Thor? Ooh, and Loki?"

I shuddered. "Thor is waiting for us to come back with you."

"So cool," she breathed. Even though Stella had deferred to Harmon and made us come meet him, and though he had told us that Astrid could make her own decision, Astrid still turned to Stella before giving us an answer. "Can I go? I really want to," she said, clasping her hands in front of her and giving Stella a pleading look.

"No pressure," Peyton said. "Not like it's a matter of life and death."

"For the entire world," I added.

Stella frowned for a long moment before nodding. "Take the Whiskey Boys with you," she said.

Astrid squealed and jumped up, flinging her arms around Stella.

"Then it's all settled," I said. "When can you be ready?"

"I'm ready," she said, grabbing the hands of two of the boys. As we started walking, she bombarded us with questions. "Where are you from? Have you ever been to a city? Are the people scary? Have you ever had spaghetti?"

We tried to answer as well as we could, but I was already overwhelmed by the time we reached the cave. The next days didn't change that much. She was strange and wide-eyed with wonder about every little thing, which could sometimes get annoying. At times, she was more like a small child than a grown woman, but she was no more challenging than Sadie. Having another piece of Freya also helped us locate the remaining piece, as they felt the same draw to become complete that we had. After another few weeks of searching, we had found the last of Freya and returned to Bifrost.

"We're supposed to blow a horn," Eliot said. "That was Heimdall's last instruction. Blow a horn, and the other gods will cross Bifrost."

Peyton groaned. "You've got to be kidding me. Are we going to have to go searching for a horn now? We're never going to get home at this rate."

I looked around at the others as we gathered at the base of Bifrost. Alvan and Valdan had joined us, along with Frey's group, who had been camping in the cave. They couldn't cross Bifrost yet, and neither could Freya. Across the lava river, only three giants remained on the far bank, one of them watching us while the other two sat with their heads hanging as if in shame. We had already defeated them.

They'd given up, but we couldn't risk leaving our task incomplete. My eyes moved over the group, from my cheerleader Peyton to my challenger Xander, from my protector Zeke to my mystery Eliot and my two burly elves. At last, my gaze settled on quiet, flamboyant Smith who could surprise us with his snark at the strangest times. Smith, who sang loud and sweet enough to call to my soul.

"Smith is the horn," I blurted out, not knowing where my certainty came from but knowing the truth without question.

"What?" Smith asked, jerking to attention.

"Your singing," I said. "It's what calls the gods across the bridge."

"But I'm not even a good dwarf," he said, as if that were somehow relevant.

"You don't have to be," I said. "You just have to be a good god."

"You think it'll work?" Smith asked, uncertainty painting his expression.

I took his hand and squeezed. "I know it will."

"Then let's go," Peyton said, grabbing Smith's other hand. "Sing until every one of those crazy bastards can gallop across the bridge like an eight-legged horse." We stepped onto the bridge, joining hands as we rose up through the flame and wind and water. When we reached the highest point, I squeezed Smith's hand.

"Now," I said.

He opened his mouth, and the first notes of his song trickled out, as sweet as spring water over stones in a brook. He shot us an uncertain glance, but we all nodded. Peyton had tears in her eyes, and on my other side, Eliot gave my hand a gentle squeeze. Smith continued, his voice growing louder, soaring through the clouds and echoing in the canyon below. It wrapped around us, enveloping us in every spine-tingling, soul-tugging note. It reached so deep inside my chest that it ached with sweetness and loss.

Far below, Astrid stepped up to the bridge and into the flames. A dart of panic squeezed my heart as I imagined her bursting into flame. Instead, she began to rise.

"You're doing it," I said, giving Smith's hand a shake. Now I knew the elation Astrid had felt when she found out she was a goddess. I might not have been ecstatic about that, but I was sure as hell happy to have succeeded. A rush of pride filled me, along with so much love and gratitude for my fellow godlings that I nearly choked on it. Relief flooded me next, and I gripped Smith's hand so hard he faltered.

"Don't stop. Keep singing," I cried. "They're coming."

And they did. One by one, Freya's pieces came marching up Bifrost, followed by Frey. From the other side, we heard cheers. We turned to see a crowd of slain warriors gathering on the Asgard side. They were cheering for Vali and Vidar, who were making their way in our direction from the hillside in Asgard. They were cheering for us.

Behind the honorable dead, I saw two men standing back to watch. One of them had a long white beard mingling with his long hair, an eye patch over one eye. We'd barely seen Odin since we arrived, but now he looked down and smiled. He held up a hand in a gesture that I could interpret even from here. With a lifted hand, he gave his acknowledgement of our hard work and success.

A second later, he disappeared. I looked at Peyton, who grinned back at me. She'd seen him, too. We'd done well, and the All-Father was proud of us.

I almost turned away before I caught sight of the other man lingering on the edges of the crowd. He looked familiar. More than that, he looked like me.

"Dad," I gasped. I hadn't remembered what he looked like, not in the way you remember a picture. But the second I saw him, there was no doubt in my mind. This was my father, a man I remembered in other ways besides surface appearance. I remembered him swinging me around. I remembered him carrying me. I remembered him yelling at Mom to take me and run while the house burned around us.

Without thought, I released the hands of my stepsiblings and ran down the far side of Bifrost toward my father. My job here was done. We had found all nine of Heimdall's pieces. We had crossed the bridge and strengthened it until it could hold the other gods. We had found other gods and figured out how to play the note to summon the gods to cross the elemental bridge. We had finished our task.

Now, it was time to return to my parents.

Chapter Twenty-Four

Gwen

It took two weeks of crossing Bifrost with the gods to bring the bridge to full strength. At last, though, the day came when it grew no stronger from our presence. I felt the presence of Heimdall rise up inside me in a swell of triumph before settling back. It wasn't absence I felt, but more like he'd sighed and gone to sleep after a long day of hard work. For the first time since I met the Keens, I wasn't worried about why I felt the way I did or whether it was right. After all we'd been through, we would be bound together, even if Heimdall slept inside us for the rest of our lives. We had shared something no one else ever would, and no one could even begin to understand.

I didn't worry about which part of me was Heimdall and which was Gwen. Heimdall was part of Gwen. He was part of who I was, of who we all were. That part was no less real than the awkward book nerd who devoured romance novels, or the girl who had to step up and take care of her mom when times sucked. It was all me.

The last morning in Asgard, Heimdall's nine godlings woke, said our goodbyes to the All-Father, his ravens, and Valerie, and headed for the bridge.

"So, this is it," I said, as we hurried down the grassy slope. I couldn't believe it, but I thought I'd actually miss this. I'd miss being with my stepsiblings without judgment, without worrying what anyone thought. I'd miss Valerie and the ravens, and even more, I'd miss the elven twins, who couldn't pass for human in our world. I would *not* miss eating goat every night for weeks at a time.

"We're going home," Peyton sang, skipping past me and spinning around, her arms out and eyes closed, letting the morning sun dance off her glossy skin and blissful face.

My throat tightened at the sight of her joy. Everything we'd been through was worth it for this one moment.

"We'll come back and visit you," I said to the twins, an ache in my chest when I turned to them. I wouldn't miss them with the unbearable anguish of being separated from the other pieces of our god in a time of need, but I'd still miss them. They were funny and warm and kind.

"About that," Xander said. "Now's probably a good time to tell you we agreed to help Frey with something."

"What?" I asked, turning toward him, my heart hammering.

"It's true," Peyton said. "But hey, we did tell him we needed a month at home first."

I jerked around to see the others. "Since when?"

"When you guys went to find your mom, we went to find Frey," Eliot said.

"I remember," I said, glaring at him.

"Well, I guess they've got a quest, too," Peyton said, gathering her hair and looping it through a hairband. "They said they'd help us in exchange for our help."

"Does everyone else know about this?" I asked.

"I didn't," Zeke said.

"Me, neither," Smith said.

"He lost his sword," Xander said. "Apparently, it's a big deal."

"Honestly, I'm kind of okay with doing more stuff like this," Peyton said. "I mean, now that I've been to some other worlds, I don't know if I'm going to be happy just going to boring old high school in a tiny town. I'm not that sheltered anymore."

"What about your Starbucks?" I asked, turning to her at the foot of Bifrost. "And your clothes, and shampoo, and all that stuff you've been missing?"

"You know, maybe it wouldn't hurt to be less materialistic."

"What did you do with Peyton?" Zeke asked. "Are you really Joaquin in disguise?"

"Fine, I totally don't mean that part," Peyton said, laughing. "But hey, now I know what to pack. Razors and a healthy supply of flavored coffee are on top of that list."

"Yeah," Eliot said. "I wouldn't mind visiting some other worlds. And if we're always going to be half god…"

"I don't think it will take all nine of us," Xander said. "It's not a quest for Heimdall, so we shouldn't have to be complete to do it. If some of you want to stay home where it's safe…"

I couldn't believe it, but I realized as he offered to leave me behind that I didn't want my tiny human life anymore, either. As ridiculous as it sounded, that world was too small for us now. There were eight other worlds out there. How could we be content to pretend nothing but humanity existed? I had longed for a normal life, but that would never be mine. And I didn't want it to be. I wanted more. More than to be normal, more than my familiar world.

"I'll go," I said. "After we spend a month at home. I need to see Mom for more than five minutes. And Finn."

A beat of silence passed. I had said the word we tried not to speak, though the ache of missing him was always with us.

"Me, too," Peyton said. "And I still need to officially break up with my girlfriend."

My ugly, jealous streak flared, but I forced myself not to react. I knew Peyton was mine, despite her inability to break up with Alejandra. We'd been in another world—it wasn't like she'd meant to ignore or disappear on Alej, or fall in love for that matter. I had nothing to worry about when she went to see her ex, though. I trusted Peyton more than anyone, if only because she was a girl. I'd grown up trusting my mom, so maybe it was some weird kind of instinct. Most of what I knew about guys had been gleaned from romance novels, and let's just say those guys were not the most trustworthy.

"Alej hasn't heard from you in four or five months," Eliot said to Peyton. "I'm sure she's gotten the message."

"Still," Peyton said with a shrug. "She deserves closure, even if I can't give her the real answers."

"What about you?" I asked the twins. "What are your plans?"

"We'll cross with you and then say goodbye," Alvan said. "Until next time."

"We will keep crossing the river every day," Valdan said.

"And going back and forth between Alfheim and Asgard?" I asked. I was sorry to leave them, but now that our mission was complete, it wasn't a crippling sorrow. It was just the regular regret of leaving someone I'd shared so much with.

"We'll make sure the gods are using Bifrost, so it doesn't dim," Valdan said.

"Now, come and give us a hug, pretty human," Alvan said, opening his muscular, golden arms.

"You don't have to say goodbye yet. We haven't even done our final crossing." But I stepped into his embrace, anyway. To my surprise, my throat tightened. I would miss these big, horny Vikings. Valdan stepped up behind me and sandwiched me between him and his brother. My sentimental feelings were quickly erased by their wandering hands. "You should really find a girl or two of your own," I said, laughing and swatting their big paws away. "I think you could use it."

"There's a pair of hot raven chicks flying around here somewhere," Peyton teased. Since they weren't going to be in our world, and our connection wasn't quite the same as my connection with the others, I hoped they would find some worthy partners of their own. I would always be connected to them through Heimdall, and beyond that, from what we'd been through together.

We turned to the roaring, soaring arc of the Bifrost bridge. This time, I stepped onto it without trepidation. We'd been crossing it multiple times a day to strengthen it, and my fear had all but disappeared by now.

"This is so much fun," Peyton yelled, splashing in the water beside me. She spun around, kicking up spray with her perfectly tanned, shapely legs, now clad in a pair of running shorts. "I'm going to miss it."

Zeke ran up the streak of fire on my other side, pumping his fists and singing "Eye of the Tiger," like he had the very first day we crossed. Eliot and Smith were doing flips in the air portion of the bridge. Pain rippled through me as it did every time we formed a group without Finn. But just as I started to feel sad, Xander ran up behind me and grabbed me around the middle, lifting my feet off the ground.

"I claim you tonight," he growled in my ear.

Before I could ask what that meant, Peyton kicked water onto us. Xander set me down and ran after Peyton like nothing had happened, like he hadn't said a word. My head was spinning, and I could barely keep my feet. The heady sensation of falling gripped my belly, but this time, it wasn't from the height of the bridge. My knees trembled as I watched Xander race toward his sister in a half-crouch, a rare smile on his face. His catlike movements only emphasized his tall, muscular build, and that smile... Damn, that smile. I'd give anything to see that smile every morning of my life.

Xander grabbed Peyton the same way he'd just grabbed me, playfully and full of excitement. Maybe I'd read too much into his words, read something he hadn't meant. If he'd meant what I'd thought, was I ready for that?

As Peyton squealed, kicking at Xander, the elves ran over and scooped me up. They tossed me into the air, ignoring my shriek of protest. But just like the very first time we'd met, their strong arms were there to catch me, unwavering in their strength. The eight of us probably didn't make a very godlike spectacle. There was no somber dignity in our ascent. We were like giddy children, except instead of Christmas morning, we were excited about the prospect of going home for longer than a few hours.

I didn't care, though. No one was watching us. And despite what we'd been through, most of us were still teenagers. I wasn't sure about the elves, who were basically immortal.

When we reached the apex of the sloping bridge, we paused in our revelry and gazed down over the worlds. It must be some kind of god power allowing us to see beyond the human eye's capacity. Above and behind, Asgard stood sentry over the other worlds. Below, through the swirling fog, I could make out the towering spires of Alfheim, though I knew it had to be farther than it seemed. On the other side of the bridge, I could see what must be Vanaheim, the other world of the gods, where we'd found the last of Freya's pieces. It was as if we were standing on the exact spot that let us see through a multidimensional window into so many of the worlds at once. Turning forward, we could see Midgard, the trees and cities, even the beach, as if we were seeing it from an airplane. The sun shone over it all, filtering through the layered worlds.

"Wow," I breathed.

"Yeah," Eliot said, his hand landing on my hip. A jolt of electricity rocked through my body. That part hadn't changed, even with Heimdall apparently satisfied and dormant within us. My attraction to my stepsiblings was still alive and well. I hoped it always would be.

"Last one down is a rotten egg," Peyton taunted like a kid.

Zeke and Xander took off at full speed, racing down the far side.

"Let's show the boys how it's done," Peyton said, reaching out a hand.

I slipped my fingers between hers, a grin spreading across my face. "You might have to show me how it's done."

She took off running, pulling me with her, our laughter echoing into the abyss below. And then she dropped down onto the water and slid, pulling me with her. I screamed, but it was mixed with laughter. Exhilaration and terror gripped me as we slid faster and faster, passing the guys, dropping at heart-stopping speed until everything around us was a blur, and I was sure I would pass out. Instead, I joined Peyton as she shrieked with joy. I let the feeling open its jaws and swallow me, let the realness and immediacy of the present moment be all that existed in the world, no more and no less.

We spent our last day at Bifrost playing on the bridge like children, twirling through the air, rising on the fire like sparks, and sliding on the water. Valerie and the ravens joined us for a while, as did Freya and Frey's pieces. Apparently, gods were totally okay with playfulness and didn't take themselves too seriously. At last, we said our goodbyes to the others and descended to the far side of Bifrost, where the cave in the canyon wall waited, and inside that, the window into our world.

When we stepped into the cave, we were all laughing and sparkling with energy and the golden glow of Heimdall. The giants that had once populated the banks of the lava river were gone now. With the bridge repaired, they had no reason to believe they would be crossing any time soon. Satisfaction settled in my belly, and I found myself smiling. We'd done it. We'd saved our world, and even if no one in Midgard even knew giants existed, let alone they'd been in danger from them, it didn't make our success any less real.

"Let's stay," Peyton said.

We all hesitated, staring at her.

"Forever?" Zeke asked.

"Not forever," she said. "Just tonight. Let's camp here one more night. I just…I don't want it to end just yet."

I couldn't believe it, but I found myself agreeing. As much as I loved the soft beds in Valhalla, as much as I wanted to go home and see my mom again, I didn't want my freedom to end just yet. The others seemed to feel the same way. After all that time we'd spent trying to finish so we could run home, now we found ourselves lingering in these last moments of being a complete god.

"Hey." A strong, firm hand slipped into mine, and I looked up to find Xander towering over me. His usual scowl was gone, as was his earlier smile. His eyes burned into me with liquid heat, making me tremble all the way to my core. I remembered his words on the bridge.

I claim you tonight.

I swallowed, my eyes dropping to his full, unsmiling mouth. Every angle of his face was breathtaking, as perfect as if it had been specially crafted by the gods themselves.

"Hey," I breathed.

The corner of his mouth tugged into the tiniest smirk, as if he knew he'd caught me swooning over his beauty but wasn't going to rub it in this time. "Want to get out of here for a few minutes?"

"Right now?" I asked, my pulse fluttering in my throat.

He cocked an eyebrow.

I glanced at the others, like they were going to step in and object, but no one was paying us any attention. Damn Xander and his power of redirection. Not that I didn't want to be alone with him. I did. I wanted to be alone with him so much it terrified me.

Just watching his tongue slip out and quickly wet his lip as he waited for my answer made me pulse with need. I had held myself in check since Finn, been so careful. Even with Eliot, I had clearly laid down the boundaries when we'd been alone. It had been fine with him, but Xander was not Eliot. Xander didn't do casual sex. Or sex at all.

If I laid down boundaries with Xander, he'd blow by every one of them. I'd want him to. I would probably beg him to. And I didn't know if either of us were ready for the fallout. It had taken long enough to get him on my side. I couldn't let my traitorous body ruin the connection our minds had made just to find some relief from the ache building inside me every time his eyes raked over me and settled on mine with such hunger it made my thighs clench.

When I'd let my body lead, it had broken my heart. Even worse, it had broken Finn's. Last time I'd snuck off at night with one of my stepbrothers, he'd taken my virginity and left me alone in the forest in a world full of giants. We might have been on our way to something better than the smothering agony of awkwardness when we looked at each other, but I didn't know if I could withstand that excruciating distance all over again.

"No?" Xander asked. His usual expression of bored disdain was nowhere to be found.

I didn't know if he could withstand the rejection, though. That's what had turned him into the angry, hard person he had been when I met him. Dealing with his father's rejection on top of the loss of his mother and the complete shattering of his world at school had left scars in him so deep, I didn't know if I could ever heal them. But I knew I didn't want to add to them.

"Okay," I said, nodding.

He turned to the others in the cave. "We're going for a walk," he said. "We'll be back... late."

My face flamed with heat at how obvious he was being. Before anyone could respond, Xander pulled me around the wall of water covering most of the mouth of the cave. Neither of us spoke as we walked along the bank of the river. The silence buffeted my nerves, building inside me until I could hardly breathe. My heart was beating so fast I thought I might pass out, and my knees were so weak I was sure I'd crumple to the ground in a heap with every step.

Without warning, Xander stopped and swept me off my feet, scooping me into his arms. The heat of our bodies pressing together was almost unbearable. His muscles shifted against me as he strode up a small slope toward the canyon wall. His breath came fast, and I could see the pulse in the vein at the side of his neck with every heartbeat. The shifting of his body against mine made every part of me come alive. I couldn't stand it another moment. I leaned up and pressed my lips to his throat, over his pulse.

A low moan escaped him.

He stepped into another cave, this one smaller and as hot and dry as the air outside. He set me down, his body never losing contact with mine. This was it. I was already melting, and he hadn't even kissed me yet. I could feel the tightness of his abs pressed against mine, the tension buzzing through him like anger. But it wasn't anger.

As I looked up into his eyes, I knew I had done this. As weak as I felt, as helpless over my own body's reaction, it wasn't one-sided. I had the power to make him feel this way, too. His eyes were hazy with desire, almost mad with it. My fingers closed around his muscular arms, trembling with need. When I inhaled, my breasts pressed against him, and a shudder rippled over him. He thrust his hands into my hair, yanking my face up. His mouth crashed into mine, my teeth cutting into my lip. I tasted blood, and then I tasted him. His tongue rasped against mine, and this time, I was the one who moaned, helpless to stop myself.

I didn't want to stop. The sound built inside me like power, and I let it out again, longer and slower this time, marveling that I could elicit such a primal response in Xander. He growled into my mouth, and I felt his hardness throb against me. As my knees gave, he caught my weight, pushing his hips slowly against mine. I didn't care if he knew how he affected me. Not only did I have the power to make him that hard, I contained sensations and powers I'd never felt before, ones I'd only begun to explore.

I had my whole life to discover and uncover and experience them, but I had only tonight to have Xander this way before we had to go home and hide. I tightened my arms around his neck and wrapped my legs around him, twining my feet together. With a sharp intake of breath, he broke our kiss, struggling to free one arm from his jacket. I helped, wrenching it off one shoulder at a time, peeling back the leather and burying my fingers in his warm, damp T-shirt. It wasn't enough. Hooking my fingers in the back of his shirt, I pulled that up, too, dragging it off and dropping it to the cave floor.

A sigh of pleasure ran through me. I hadn't realized how much I'd wanted this, how long I'd waited for it, until I could touch him at last. I skimmed my fingers over his sleek, golden skin. It was hot, filmed with a thin sheen of sweat in the darkness. I sank my lips to his shoulder, breathing in the masculine smell of him—sweat and leather and Xander. My tongue swiped across his collarbone, tasting the salt of his skin. A dart of pure lust pierced through me, settling in an ache between my thighs.

"What are you doing to me?" Xander said, his voice ragged.

"Everything," I said. "It's our last chance."

"Don't make promises you can't keep, Little Girl."

"I'm not a little girl," I said, raking my nails over his sculpted chest and his six-pack abs that made my thighs quiver. I circled a nail around his belly button, and a tremor wracked his body.

"If you keep that up, I won't be the gentleman you deserve."

"I didn't ask for a gentleman," I said.

Xander closed his eyes and swallowed, his nostrils flaring. When he opened his eyes, he lowered himself onto his knees, my legs still wrapped around him. After spreading his jacket, he laid me on my back and settled himself between my thighs.

"Is this what you want?" he asked, slowly rolling his hips against mine.

"No," I said, my voice barely escaping. "I want more. I want everything."

"Everything?" Xander asked, taking my hand and pulling it down to the front of his jeans. He slid my hand along the rigid length of his erection. "You want this inside you?"

My whole body seemed to throb at once, burning like a fever for him. "All of it," I whispered.

"Good," he murmured, dipping his mouth to my neck. "Because there's no halfway about it."

His lips found the fluttering pulse at my throat, his breath sending waves of heat over my body. I clawed at him, wanting him closer, faster, now. I undid the button of his jeans, my breath catching when I remembered the last time I'd done that. He'd stopped me.

Suddenly, I remembered how long it had been since he'd done this. He had more experience than Finn, more than me, but I didn't want to push him too fast.

"Is this okay?" I asked, pushing back the need consuming me every moment. I had to think about him, too, not just me.

"Yes," Xander said, his voice almost choked. He sat back and his hands slid over my hips, dipping into the curve of my waist and then farther, pushing my shirt up. A shiver went through me when he drew my shirt off. His gaze fell on my exposed skin. For once, I didn't try to cover my scars. I wanted him to look at me, all of me, exactly as I was.

"This isn't too much for you?" I asked. "You can tell me if you need to stop for a minute."

Xander's trademark smirk tugged at his lips. "You think I'm going to lose control and be done in two seconds?"

"No, but—"

"Fucking Finn," he said, shaking his head.

"Don't say that," I said, my face heating even more. "We figured it out."

"I haven't had sex in three years, but I remember how good it was," Xander said. "Trust me. I know how to control myself."

"Okay," I breathed. I reached for his jeans, my heart fluttering in my chest, adrenaline trembling through me. This time, he didn't stop me. This time, he reached for my jeans, too. His fingers shook as they slid inside, warm against my soft skin. He drew a shuddering breath, his eyes falling halfway closed. And then his mouth was on mine again, his lips taking their time and tasting my mouth. His fingers were gentle but insistent, skillfully pushing me toward the edge as his tongue tormented me with the same rhythmic motion as his fingers.

"Wait," I whispered, turning my face from his and squeezing my thighs closed. That only increased the pressure of his hand, and I could hardly hold myself back. "I don't want it to be over that fast."

He chuckled breathlessly into the hollow of my shoulder. "Over?" he said. "This is just a warm-up."

"Really?" I asked, hardly daring to hope for more.

"Again, I'm eighteen, and I haven't had sex in three years. I'm thinking we'll be here until morning."

"Oh, thank god," I whispered, unclamping my knees.

Xander chuckled, pulling back to watch my face as he began again, pushing me toward the brink and then over, and over, and over.

Chapter Twenty-Five

Finn

I had been at Cedar Crest for a month when the distance became too much. I couldn't do it anymore. Every day I was away from them, a part of myself wore away until I could hardly remember who I was. The suicide watch had ended after a week. The twice-daily head shrinking, the group sessions, the art, all of it was only healing a part of me. Another part died a little more each day. Finally, I left my room one night to find Vanessa doing her rounds.

"Are you here to keep me company on the night shift?" she asked, giving me a smile that always made me a little uncomfortable. I couldn't tell if I was like a little brother to her or like a crush. When Mom had been here, I'd been a stupid kid with a crush born from the need to forget what was happening. Vanessa had been the front desk girl, just out of high school but sensitive enough to pretend she didn't notice and treat me like a real friend.

I wasn't a kid anymore, though. Since I'd been with Gwen, something inside me had been turned on, and I couldn't turn it off. It must have been the dying of my innocence that did it. Like Adam and Eve, once I'd seen, once I knew, I couldn't erase that knowledge.

"Does your key work on every door in this place?" I asked.

"Some of them," Vanessa said, eyeing me with suspicion, like I was any other patient. "Why do you ask?"

"Let's get out of here," I said, starting down the hall. Whenever she had the night shift, I'd sit up with her at the desk, talking and watching. But tonight, I wanted more.

"You don't need a key for that," Vanessa said, falling into step beside me. "Your dad can check you out any time."

"I don't want to check out," I said. "And I don't want to do something sanctioned by my *father*." The word still tasted bitter on my tongue. Maybe it always would. But it didn't matter right now.

"Why, Finnegan Keen," Vanessa said. "I didn't know you had it in you."

"There's a lot of things about me that would surprise you," I said, stepping closer to her. I didn't know where the words came from. It was like my brother—any one of them—had stepped into my body. I wondered if this was how it felt to be them. Determined, reckless, brave.

"Is there, now?" Vanessa asked, her mouth twisting in a coy smile.

"There might be." I didn't feel good about what I was doing, but I'd stopped using that as a barometer for what I should and shouldn't do. It didn't matter how I felt about it. It mattered that it needed to be done, and I was the one who had to do it.

We stopped at the desk where the staff on night shift sat. There were more night watchmen on the other floors and in the clinic, but Vanessa had the third floor. I leaned my elbows on the desk while she checked off her rounds.

"Is there a way out that no one would see?" I asked, nodding to the small bank of monitors showing various parts of the third floor, the stairs, and the entrances.

"No, silly," she said. "Of course not."

"Could we make one?"

"You are being bad tonight," she teased.

When I didn't laugh, her smile changed. I couldn't say how, just that some understanding passed between us.

"And what would we do out there?" she asked, almost smirking now.

I smirked back at her. "I can think of a few things."

It came out of my mouth like I'd said it a hundred times, as naturally as my own name. Maybe I'd always been like my brothers, who could use people without a second thought. I'd hidden it, unwilling to admit I was just another Keen male, but it hadn't changed the truth of the matter. The using came easy.

I stepped around the counter and watched over her shoulder as she showed me the cameras. I asked questions until I found the one I wanted. It was that simple. She shut off the camera covering the end of the hall and the door to one stairway. It didn't matter that she left on the one covering the actual stairs. It was probably better, in fact. When she turned, our bodies were almost touching. Instinct, or maybe habit, told me to step back, but I didn't. We stood nose to nose, so close I could feel her breath on my lips. I'd never been this close to anyone but Gwen, and it was stirring up all sorts of fucked up feelings.

"Finn?" she whispered, though we were alone at the desk.

"Yeah."

We stood there, neither of us willing to take the plunge. I might not have felt bad about doing this to her, but I felt like shit about doing it to Gwen. Using Vanessa was a means to an end. Even if the end justified the means, I didn't want to hurt Gwen. She was the one thing good in my life. She was the light at the end of this dark tunnel, my sunshine on a cloudy day, the reason for everything.

She's the reason for everything, I repeated to myself. Even the reason for what I had to do now. Someday, she would understand.

"Are you going to kiss me?" Vanessa asked.

I'd let myself think too long, had hesitated too long. Now, she was questioning things. I couldn't allow that. Next, she'd be doubting my motives.

I licked my lips nervously. "Yes."

"Have you ever kissed a girl before?" Vanessa asked, looking wary now.

I slid my hand behind her back and pulled her against me. "Yes."

"Okay," she said, letting out a nervous, relieved laugh. And then her hands were on my face and we were kissing. That was easy, too. I'd only kissed twice before in my life, but it was like instinct, moving my mouth with hers. It was nothing like kissing Gwen. That hadn't been easy. It had been torturous and maddeningly wonderful at once. It had been all I could do to hold myself back. This time, I barely felt it. It was clinical, like a doctor searching her mouth for signs.

I pulled away first. "Let's go outside," I said, nodding to the monitor showing us standing at the desk together. "More privacy."

Thirty minutes later, we were slipping back through the side door. My heart pounded in my ears as we climbed the stairs. I needed a reason to keep Vanessa from the cameras, a reason that didn't include her going to my room. That invitation had only one meaning, and things had gone far enough already. I would never give her what I'd given Gwen. Never that. I still had a few morals left.

We reached the top of the stairs, and I held the door open for Vanessa. She gave me a shy smile that was so practiced it made me feel like I was the one who'd been used. How many times had she done this with the pop singers and movie stars who came here to detox and recover from "exhaustion"? We'd barely done more than kiss, and it was obvious she had a lot of practice with both the kissing and the *more than* parts of it.

I shook my head to clear it. What did it matter what she'd done with what guys, and how good they were, and how good she was? We were all playing a part. My motives were less pure than hers, and I needed to focus on why I was standing in the unmonitored hall at one in the morning. This was the moment I'd been waiting for, planning for, setting up for the past month. Since the moment I stepped through the door into Room 309 and saw a knife in Joaquin's hand and Gwen drowning in blood.

"I'm just going to duck in the ladies' room and freshen up," Vanessa said.

My chance. I hadn't even had to find an excuse to keep her away from the desk.

ASCEND

"I'll see you tomorrow," I said. I leaned in and kissed her, my hand slipping to her hip where her keycard hung by a clip. My fingers pinched it open, and then it was in my sweating palm, and I turned away. My heart pounded heavy and hard in my chest. With each step, I expected her to call out, to ask what I'd done.

I forced myself not to look back. I couldn't screw this up. It was the perfect opportunity, but it wouldn't last long. I had to move fast. I slipped inside my room and ran for the dresser. Under my clothes, instead of a forbidden magazine or a pack of smokes, I kept the knife.

I was halfway certain when I opened my door, I'd find Vanessa in the hallway. I didn't bother with pretending everything was normal. I didn't have time for that. As quietly as I could, I ran down the hall. Using Vanessa's keycard, I slipped into Room 309 and switched on the lamp.

Sleepy eyes blinked up at me. "Finn?"

Joaquin lay on his back under the blanket, his arms by his side. Joaquin, who had stayed at Cedar Crest after the attack, since no one could prove he did anything wrong. Joaquin, who had taken Olivia's room when she went home with Dad. I'd watched over him for the past month, waiting for this night. I'd been his best friend every waking moment.

"It's time," I said, drawing back the blankets.

"Time for what?" He pushed up on one elbow and rubbed his eyes as if trying to dispel his confusion.

"Time to go home," I said, pulling the knife from behind me and slipping the blade under his ribs. It was easier than I expected—easier than kissing Vanessa. My hands didn't even shake.

273

Joaquin fell back on the bed, his face contorted with pain. He grabbed my wrist, choking out his words. "I thought we were friends."

"Me, too."

He didn't struggle much. I had expected more. I'd been ready to wrestle him for control of the knife. I'd been ready to give my own life in the fight if I could somehow take his as well. But I'd prepared myself needlessly for that possibility. He couldn't fight back with a knife in his heart. I had hit the mark as easily as I'd done everything else tonight, as if I'd been born for this moment.

We stared at each other for a minute. The sheets around him were wet and red. He'd asked for this room when Olivia went home, and that was just too dangerous. The window to the other world was here. I couldn't watch over it when he was in this room with the door closed.

"I didn't think you had it in you," he croaked. He gave a weak cough, and blood speckled the white pillows.

"Don't worry," I said. "You're not the only one who underestimated me."

"It's always the quiet ones," he whispered. Blood bubbled between his lips when he spoke.

I waited until he stopped breathing, and his pulse was gone, before I gently closed his eyes and stepped through the window.

Chapter Twenty-Six

Gwen

For a while, it was enough to kiss Xander. But eventually, I wanted more. I'd never let myself go so completely with Eliot, though we'd spent a whole night together. With Eliot, I had been shy to the point of selfishness. I had let him lead, and he'd shown me what I'd been missing. I hadn't dared to let myself explore him, even as he explored me. I'd been too afraid that he'd find me lacking. How could I be anything but inadequate with a guy who had as much experience as he did?

With Xander, I was different. I was still shy, but I was curious, too. I didn't want to just watch and experience. I wanted to please him, to understand him, to learn what made him groan and gasp and growl. And he let me, giving me time to explore him in all the ways he was exploring me. But at last, we found ourselves lying on his jacket on the stone floor, our breath mingling as we stared at each other. I could feel him pressed against my belly, insistent and demanding, even as his eyes remained locked on mine with such intensity I trembled.

"Are you ready?" he asked.

We could have stopped then, and neither of us could have claimed we were leaving unfulfilled. But though my body might have found satisfaction, my curiosity hadn't. I'd done this just once, and there had been so much at stake. I couldn't say I regretted it, or that it hadn't been amazing. This time, though, I felt like I was in control, like I was making the decision by choice and not out of desperation. Last time, I had felt helpless over the circumstances and even my own body. This time, my mind was clear.

"Are you scared?" I whispered. Despite the past few hours, nervous tension coiled in my belly. This was a step that couldn't be untaken.

We were at the moment of no return, and it felt like the first time all over again.

Xander's fingers closed around mine, holding on for dear life. "Terrified," he whispered, his breath hot against my flushed cheeks.

I'd slept with Finn, done what I had to so our god could be whole. But this wasn't for some noble purpose. This time, I had no reasons, no excuses. I simply wanted Xander. Somehow, that felt even more momentous.

This decision moved my sexual history from past to present. It was no longer something I'd done once out of desperation, something I regretted in a lot of ways, and didn't want to risk again. This was the moment where it went from "I've had sex" to "I'm having sex." Once we did this, it would be an option every time I was with any of them. It would be something I wanted again, and not just with him.

I closed my eyes and took a long, slow breath to steady myself. "Are you going to run away?"

His fingers tightened, and he pulled me even closer against him. "Only if I can take you with me." His lips pressed against mine, already swollen and hot from the past hours. "But we don't have to go further if you're afraid."

I wanted to say it was fine, I was fine, and that I wasn't afraid. But I wouldn't lie to Xander. We'd worked too hard to get where we were. When I spoke, my lips felt frozen despite the heat. "What if it changes things between us?"

"It will," he said. "Any guy who tells you differently is lying."

I gulped, grateful for his honesty, even if the answer was hard to hear. "You're okay with that?"

He pressed his forehead to mine. I could feel his heart hammering against mine, our bare skin glowing at every point of contact. "Yes."

"You still want to?"

His voice dropped, coming out husky. "More than anything."

"Even if it won't help us fix Bifrost or summon our missing pieces?"

"Especially then."

"Why?" I pulled back a little, searching his face. He'd been the one to tell me this couldn't happen because his brothers might get upset.

"There are some things you should do for other people, but this isn't one of them," he said. "So you'd better be doing it for you. Not for Heimdall, and not for me."

"Is that allowed?"

"More than allowed," he said. "Required. I'm doing this because I want you, Gwen. That's the only reason to ever have sex."

"Not because you love someone?" I whispered.

"Not because you love someone," he said. "You can do lots of other things because you love someone, but not this."

"You don't care whether or not I love you?"

"I care," he said. "But it doesn't change how much I want you."

"It changes how much I want you," I whispered, slowly sliding my knee all the way over his thigh.

A tremor shuddered through his body, and his hands closed around my narrow hips. Despite his confession of fear, his grip was sure and strong. Holding me locked against him, he rolled onto his back, pulling me with him. His eyes raked over me from my knees to my hips astride his. They lingered, then moved up my scarred torso, over my small breasts, to my swollen lips, at last locking onto my gaze. "How much?" he asked, his voice a smooth murmur that made the very root of my being quake. "Show me."

As I moved with him, I could feel our connection binding us tighter. We were irrevocably bound now. We would never go back to the way we had been. Warmth swelled inside me, filling my chest until I thought I'd burst. With it, an incredible power surged through me. It was the power of a god, the power of a woman, and the power of love wrapping around us like the hot night and the shimmering golden light enveloping our bodies.

Xander sat up, sliding an arm around my waist and bracing the other on the floor, helping me move until we both reached completion. For a long time after, we sat wrapped around each other, catching our breath as the sweat dried on our skin.

At last, Xander gave a little half-laugh into my shoulder. "I lied," he said.

"About what?" I asked, my heart nearly stopping in my chest.

"I didn't remember how good it was," he said, maneuvering us down onto the jacket. His palm covered my shoulder, his thumb drawing a circle on the top of my breast that sent a shudder of longing through me again. "Or, more accurately, I had no idea it could be that good."

"Oh," I said. Because what else could I say? I had no words right now, no fears, no insecurities. I was completely content.

Until a few minutes later when I noticed a raven standing at the entrance of the cave.

"How long has that been there?" I asked, jerking my head toward it.

Xander grinned. "Want me to ask?"

"No," I said, burying my face in his shoulder. "I don't want to know."

"What do you want?" Xander asked the bird.

It transformed into the figure of Muninn. "We carry news from all over the Nine Worlds to Odin," she said, plucking a loose feather from her garment. "Believe me, that was nothing extraordinary."

I snorted, which made Xander shake with suppressed laughter.

"Humans always think they are so unique in their exploits." Her baby voice made the words slightly disturbing. She sighed. "The others began to worry that you'd been attacked when you were gone so long. Shall I tell them you're doing well?"

"No," I said quickly. Who knew what she would say to them. She'd probably tell them exactly what she'd seen, since to her, it seemed about as exciting as watching a tree grow.

"We got it," Xander said. "We're on our way back, anyway. Thanks for letting us know. You can go watch someone else have sex now."

"If that's your thing," I said. "No judgment."

Muninn smiled serenely. "Humans are much less dull when I can talk to them instead of just watching," she said. "I hope we meet again."

"Me, too," I said, and I meant it. We'd met so many fascinating people in the other worlds, some of them thousands of years old, all of them vastly different from humans. I wished I'd gotten to know them better. The gods, elves, dwarves, Valkyries, slain warriors, and ravens had been at least helpful, at most undeservedly kind and generous. Even some of the giants had shared their home with us. It was surprising to look back on it and remember that the good people—of every type—had far outweighed the few scary ones. I wasn't sure I could say the same for the humans I'd known in my life.

As we dressed, I teared up with gratitude thinking of all the amazing people we'd met. Just a little. I blamed the post-sex hormones.

Muninn took off in a flurry of wings, her black raven body disappearing into the dark sky above. Xander and I stepped out of the small cave and started back toward the large one at the foot of Bifrost, making our way along the bank lit by seams in the lava flow. At night, it seemed to flow sluggishly, the top cooling enough to turn black, with the hotter, molten lava still glowing from beneath the surface. Xander walked along the edge, his profile faintly lit with our godly glow.

For a while, neither of us spoke. The heat seemed oppressive suddenly. I willed Xander to speak, to say something. To say the right thing. But in the end, I was the one who broke down. I needed him to say the words. "So...what does this mean for us?" I asked, when we were halfway back.

Xander's chuckle came out of the near darkness. "Don't be such a girl, Gwen."

"Sorry, that's what I am," I said, crossing my arms and fighting my irritation. "I didn't notice you complaining about it an hour ago."

He laughed again, reaching out and tugging at my wrist. "Finn's the psychic," he said. "Why don't you ask him?"

"Because he's not here, you jackass," I said, glaring sideways at him.

But I let him pry my arms apart and link his fingers through mine. I wanted to stay annoyed a little longer, but the touch of his hand and his words melted every reserve I had. Maybe I didn't need the words. I mean, this was the guy who didn't want to be seen with me around his friends, and now he was making no effort to hide our relationship from his siblings, not to mention he was holding my hand. Xander Keen—stone-faced, motorcycle riding, teen hooligan, and Wellfleet's resident bad boy—was holding my hand. Asking for more would be asking him not to be Xander.

"I wasn't going to tell Finn about this," I admitted after a minute.

"I was."

I pulled up short and turned to face him. I remembered my flash of embarrassment when he'd pulled me out of the cave and left the godlings gaping after us. Or in Eliot's case, giving us a knowing smile. I didn't know how to take all this, how to do it. I'd never even had one boyfriend before, let alone five.

"You're going to tell Finn? Are you crazy?" I asked, throwing my hands up.

"You told us you wanted us all," he said. "I know you're going to be with all of us eventually. If I wasn't cool with that, I wouldn't be here right now. And neither would anyone else."

"Finn's not here," I pointed out.

"Not because of you," Xander said.

"It's totally because of me."

"No," Xander said. "Finn's got issues like the rest of us. We all lost Mom."

"Yeah, but he didn't go into a mental hospital then."

Xander shrugged. "Maybe he should have. And even if part of what he's dealing with is what happened with you, that's not your fault. He's a big boy. He chose to have sex with you, just like you chose him."

"I chose you all," I said. This time, I reached for his hands, taking them both in mine and facing him.

"And we all know what that means," Xander said. "We're going to have to hide from enough people in our world. We don't hide things from each other."

"Okay," I said, squeezing his hands.

"In case you haven't noticed, the Keens stick together," he said, his fingers stiff inside mine. "We don't have secrets, and you're not going to be the one who makes us start."

"Okay," I said again. "I wasn't trying to come between you or make you keep secrets. I just... I didn't know how it would work."

"If you want us, you get all of us as a package deal," he said. "We come as one unit, not five separate boyfriends. You're the one who wanted it that way."

I nodded, relief sweeping over me. I had wanted them all, but I'd been afraid of how they might react. It would be hard enough to hide it from our parents. It would have been impossible to hide my relationship with each one of them from the others. If I didn't have to, if we were all in it together and they would help to cover for each of us, it might just work in the human world, too.

"Okay," I said. "We all protect each other, whether it's from giants or assholes who get too nosy." I had never felt like part of something more than in that moment. I really was a member of their family now. I was finally one of the notorious Keens.

I squeezed Xander's hand, pure happiness filling me as we continued to the cave.

When we stepped into the cave, the others were sitting around a pile of smoldering coals.

"Bro," Zeke said, jumping up and slapping Xander's back. "If I'd known all I had to do was grab her hand and say I was ready, I would have done it a long time ago. Thanks for showing me how it's done."

My face was so hot I thought my skin would peel like a sunburn. I liked not hiding, but I had a long way to go until I wasn't awkward about the others knowing what we'd been up to.

Zeke laughed and grabbed me in a bear hug. "I'm kidding, Gwen," he murmured into my hair.

"It's okay," I said, forcing an awkward laugh.

"But whenever *you're* ready, I totally am," he said.

When he released me, Peyton hooked her arm through mine and dragged me away while Xander settled at the fire with Zeke. "How was it?" she whispered.

"Um. It was good." I chewed at my lip, trying to bite back a smile. "Really good."

"You really should have gone in the opposite order," she said. "Starting with the one who knows most about what he's doing."

My eyes landed on Eliot, who was lounging by the fire watching us with the slightest hint of a smile. When our eyes met, my heart skipped a beat. God damn. If Xander didn't know what he was doing, I didn't know if I could handle someone who did.

Before I could answer, electricity crackled up my spine, as if I'd touched a hot wire. I stiffened, and Peyton's eyes widened. Everyone around the fire straightened or jumped up, too.

"What was that?" I asked, instantly on alert.

In answer, a figure stepped out of thin air into the faint glow of embers. For a second, no one moved.

"Finn," I whispered. His warm eyes found mine, and something inside me settled. I'd missed him, but I hadn't realized just how wrong everything had felt without him until he was back, and in an instant, everything was right again.

"Is that really you?" Peyton asked.

I didn't need his answer. Joaquin could disguise himself as a human, even my mom, but he couldn't disguise the magic of the god inside Finn. I had more trouble convincing myself this wasn't a beautiful dream. Forgetting our past awkwardness, I ran to him and threw my arms around him, my eyes brimming with tears. "You're back," I whispered, stroking my hand over his wavy hair, as if the familiar silky strands could convince me this was real.

"I'm back," he said, his gentle hand landing on the swell of my hip. He closed his eyes and pressed his lips to my forehead. "I won't leave again."

"You better not," Peyton said, punching his shoulder. "Now, come sit by the fire and tell us about the last month."

"I don't have much to tell," Finn said, shifting and shoving his hands in his pockets. "I'm sure you guys have all kinds of stories, though."

"We totally do," Zeke said, pulling Finn in for a quick hug and clapping him on the shoulder.

The elven twins took turns hugging and smacking Finn on the back. "Since it's our last night together, we're staying up until Bifrost appears."

Eliot put his hands on Finn's shoulders, searching his face as if he could find answers there. After a minute, he said, "It's good to have you back."

They embraced quickly, but Eliot kept watching Finn carefully, even as he resumed his seat by the fire. Smith and Finn greeted each other awkwardly before Smith took a seat beside Eliot.

Finn shuffled to the fire and then paused, staring at Xander, the only one who'd remained seated when Finn appeared.

"I did it," Finn said. He slipped something from his pocket. A bolt of instinctual terror wrenched through me when he flicked open the knife that had impaled me. Finn threw it into the bed of coals, where it stuck with the blade buried in embers and the handle sticking up, trembling from impact. For a moment, no one moved.

Then Xander stood and pulled Finn into his arms. It wasn't the kind of bro-hug guys did. It was a full embrace, with their chests pressed tightly together. They stood in silence while the rest of us waited.

"You are fucking brave," Xander said at last, and they stepped apart and regarded each other for a long moment before they took their places with the rest of us at the fire, as if that had solved everything between them. Maybe it had. They'd been brothers for a long time.

I knew as well as anyone how one moment, one action, could erase what was wrong between two people. I remembered my last minutes in the hallway at Cedar Crest with Finn, when we'd finally spoken again. I remembered the fear that I was leaving my mother in the same place as Joaquin with only the promise of a man who had left her there before. I remembered how scared I had been to leave Finn with him, and the calm strength in Finn's resolve to stay. He hadn't only stayed to work on himself. He'd stayed to kill Joaquin. A fierce, protective instinct rose inside me for my quiet, misunderstood Finn. He had caused the group so much struggle, so much strife, but in the end, he had redeemed himself. He was the hero of our story.

"Okay, who goes first?" Peyton asked, pulling me from my emotional turmoil. "We've only got a few hours until sunrise, and we've got a lot to tell."

"Go on, fill him in on our last month," Zeke said. "You know you want to tell it."

As she began to speak, a warm arm slid around me. Eliot smiled down at me and gave me a reassuring squeeze. Like always, he seemed to know exactly what I needed. Now, when I'd just hooked up with Xander, and I wasn't sure how to act around the others, he was here to show me that it was okay. Nothing had changed between the rest of us. I still loved each of them just as I had before, and they still felt the same about me.

I relaxed into him, laying my head on his chest. Listening to his heartbeat and the lull of Peyton's voice, I was filled with a contentment I'd never known. We were all going home together, though we would come back to see the elves. We were all one, but we were also separate.

The elves sat side by side, forming Thor between them, their identical faces watching Peyton with lazy smiles. Smith, the newest member of our god and the one I knew least, sat beside them. I didn't know what would become of him, but I knew we'd find him again when the time was right. For now, he was going back to his world to see if he would be accepted not as a dwarven craftsman but as a piece of a god.

And then there was us—not just parts of Heimdall, but the Keen family. Chatty, brave, beautiful Peyton, who rallied us when we were down and who had welcomed me with open arms from the start, told our story. Quiet, vulnerable, sensitive Finn listened with steadfast interest. Zeke, the strong, loyal, protective brother with a heart of gold and the panty-melting smile added details. Xander, who I thought might never let down his guard and stop brooding, had finally made me feel like I was truly one of the family. And Eliot, the mystery I might never solve, sat holding me like a treasure, his every movement attentive to me even as he listened to his sister.

For one more night, for a few more hours, we had each other, and everything was right. I could feel the human heartbeat of our group—the one making these nine people one god. I knew that no matter what happened, we'd find our way back together whenever one of us needed it, not just for a god-appointed mission, but for any one of our members. The feeling of complete happiness when we were together was too pure to deny. Apart, we were fragmented and flawed. Together, we were powerful and perfect.

The End.

From the Author

Thank you so much for reading. Gwen and her men have completed their mission, which means that this book wraps up the trilogy. However, I have a ton of stories planned for these worlds. I mean, there's nine of them! How can I stop at just three books?

Some of my upcoming stories will feature Gwen and her group on new missions, and some will be spin-offs with other characters from *Hosting Gods*. I've already written Astrid's story, *Caged,* which is a standalone story that fits into my larger supernatural world.

Like all my YA/NA fantasy, every series is connected to the others. If you've read my *Girl Among Wolves* trilogy, you probably noticed the little seeds being planted throughout Gwen's story and were waiting for Stella to show up. If you haven't read it, I recommend grabbing that now. Don't worry, if you're strictly RH, you can skip *Girl Among Wolves* and still have a satisfying reading experience! But you'll get more explanation and exploration of my supernatural world by reading that one, too.

Lena Mae Hill

Also By This Author

Girl Among Wolves Trilogy
Unlikely Magic
Beastly Beauty
Ghostly Snow

Young Witch Series
Twisted
Caged

Winslow Witch Chronicles
Magic of the Void
Sister of the Sea